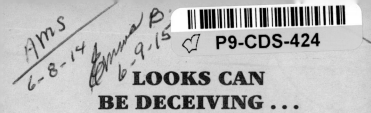

LOOKS CAN
BE DECEIVING . . .

Coatless, he was not so skinny after all. What she had assumed to be the flattering effect of good tailoring was in truth a very good set of shoulders. He rolled up the sleeves of his shirt to his elbows, revealing well-muscled forearms furred with dark red hair. The same auburn hair peeked out from the now open collar of his shirt.

Was this thoroughly masculine creature her misty-eyed, head-in-the-clouds poet? Eleanor stood mesmerized by the transformation. She thought back to that awkward business in the coach. If she'd had her wits about her she would have realized the body she was clasped so tightly against was no thin-boned weakling. She remembered what else she knew of that body, and her cheeks flared.

Eleanor could not help staring. He was not adorable. He was magnificent.

Other **AVON ROMANCES**

ALL MY DESIRE *by Margaret Moore*
CHEROKEE WARRIORS: THE LOVER *by Genell Dellin*
HER SCANDALOUS INTENTIONS *by Sari Robins*
HIGHLAND ROGUES: THE WARRIOR BRIDE
by Lois Greiman
HIS BRIDE *by Gayle Callen*
THE MACKENZIES: COLE *by Ana Leigh*
THE WARRIOR'S GAME *by Denise Hampton*

Coming Soon

INNOCENT PASSIONS *by Brenda Hiatt*
INTO TEMPTATION *by Kathryn Smith*

And Don't Miss These
ROMANTIC TREASURES
from Avon Books

CAPTURED INNOCENCE *by Susan Sizemore*
THE IRRESISTIBLE MACRAE: BOOK THREE OF
THE HIGHLAND LORDS *by Karen Ranney*
WHEN IT'S PERFECT *by Adele Ashworth*

CANDICE HERN

Once A Dreamer

AVON BOOKS

An Imprint of HarperCollinsPublishers

This is a work of fiction. Names, characters, places, and incidents are products of the author's imagination or are used fictitiously and are not to be construed as real. Any resemblance to actual events, locales, organizations, or persons, living or dead, is entirely coincidental.

AVON BOOKS
An Imprint of HarperCollins*Publishers*
10 East 53rd Street
New York, New York 10022-5299

Copyright © 2003 by Candice Hern
ISBN: 0-06-050562-1
www.avonromance.com

First Avon Books paperback printing: January 2003

Avon Trademark Reg. U.S. Pat. Off. and in Other Countries, Marca Registrada, Hecho en U.S.A.
HarperCollins ® is a registered trademark of HarperCollins Publishers Inc.

Printed in the U.S.A.

10 9 8 7 6 5 4 3 2 1

To Greg

*for literally supporting me throughout
this endeavor, and for many great story
ideas, including the notion that
the Busybody should be a man*

Prologue

London
May 1801

"**B**ut I love him!"

Eleanor Tennant wanted to shake her niece by the shoulders, but settled for a theatrical sigh of frustration. She was tired of this discussion, which had been repeated in one variation or another a dozen times in the last week. She reined in her impatience in one more attempt to provide mature and sensible guidance to the girl. "Belinda, my dear, you barely know the man. It is your first Season in town and Barkwith is the first man to flirt with you. Do not misunderstand his intentions."

"He is *not* flirting with me," Belinda said with an unladylike stamp of her dainty foot. "He loves me."

Eleanor groaned and reached for the teapot. "I suppose he has told you as much?"

"Over and over," Belinda said with a haughty lift of her chin. "A hundred times. A thousand."

It was worse than she suspected. Belinda had always been a headstrong, willful young girl. But of all things, this was the one situation Eleanor had hoped to avoid. Her niece was too innocent to understand the peril of encouraging the attentions of a man like Geoffrey Barkwith, a seductive charmer with a rakehell reputation and a penchant for gaming. He was a younger son with no fortune of his own, and was widely known to be under the hatches. A man like that could have no interest in a girl like Belinda. Though strikingly beautiful, Belinda had no particular fortune to tempt a man sorely in need of one. Her father, Eleanor's brother, was a naval captain who'd been away at sea for almost three years. The prize money he sent home now and then amounted to little more than was needed to support their household. Belinda was no heiress.

In fact, it had been Eleanor's fondest wish to establish her niece in a respectable marriage with a man of means. The girl's beauty and lively personality would outweigh her lack of fortune for the right man.

Eleanor took a long, restorative swallow of tea. "And what of Mr. Pendleton?" she asked. "He practically lives on our doorstep in hopes you will notice him. Don't you think you might give him a chance? And perhaps a few other gentlemen as well? The Season has only just begun."

"Oh, bosh. Mr. Pendleton is only encouraged by *you*, Aunt Ellie. I have given him no cause to expect anything from me. Besides, he's a dead bore."

Confound the ungrateful girl. Eleanor had worked hard to engineer an introduction to the Honorable Charles Pendleton, heir to a viscountcy and already in possession of a considerable fortune in his own right. On top of all that, he was sensible and grounded where Belinda was flighty and excitable. He was perfect, absolutely perfect. What a coup it would be for Eleanor to announce such a fine match to her brother.

"In all fairness, my dear, I do not believe you have given proper consideration to Mr. Pendleton," Eleanor said. "I think if you allowed yourself to get to know him better, you would see what a fine—"

"I don't want Mr. Pendleton. I'm in love with Geoffrey."

The obstinate child would be the death of her. How could Eleanor make her understand? She knew all about men like Geoffrey Barkwith. He could want only one thing from a beautiful girl with no fortune, and it was not marriage.

"Please try to be sensible for once, Belinda. You need a husband who can support you properly, who can guarantee you a life of security, and more. Mr. Pendleton is—"

"A dry old stick who happens to have deep

pockets. I don't care about his fortune, Aunt Ellie. Or about him. I want Geoffrey and none other." She sank down on the settee beside Eleanor and gazed at her with the smug, condescending look of the young who believe their elders are much too old to understand anything important. And though Eleanor was only twenty-nine, she was quite sure that Belinda thought her a stuffy, middle-aged nuisance.

"I know you want only what is best for me," Belinda said, "that you want to settle me in circumstances perhaps better than your own. I do understand that." Her voice had taken on a sweet, patronizing tone that made Eleanor's teeth ache. "But you must understand that the love Geoffrey and I share is founded on more than mere fancy. It is refined by delicacy, and exalted by a purity of heart and dignity of mind. He has poured vows of constancy and unalterable affection into the bosom of my heart, and my own affections are roused to the bliss of reciprocal delight. With such a love, a bare competence will be sufficient to subsist."

"Good heavens, where did you pick up such high-flown, mawkish, Byzantine language? What have you been reading? Oh, don't tell me. It's that dreadful magazine again, is it not?"

"It's not dreadful. *The Ladies' Fashionable Cabinet* is a fine publication with excellent articles." Her gaze fell to her lap, and she set about adjusting the arrangement of her skirts. "I took the liberty of writing a letter, anonymously, of course, to the—"

"Oh, no. Please do not tell me you have written to that beastly woman?"

"I sent a letter to the Busybody and set my case before her."

"Belinda! How could you?" Eleanor set down her teacup with such force, it was a wonder the saucer did not shatter into pieces. Dear Lord, give her the strength not to murder her brother's only child. "The Busybody! Never was a woman more aptly named. I cannot believe you pay the least heed to anything that interfering, sentimental old biddy has to say. And you actually wrote to her? Good God, my girl, I thought you had more sense. I suppose you are now to tell me she has published your letter for all the world to see."

"Yes, she has, and I think you ought to read her response, Aunt Ellie. She is a very wise woman, you know."

Belinda plucked the little magazine from behind a cushion where she'd hidden it, and offered it on her outstretched palm as though it were the Holy Grail. Eleanor grabbed it and began to riffle through the pages of essays, book reviews, fashion hints, and poetry until she found the dreaded article.

THE BUSYBODY

The letter which now claims my attention is from a young lady whose case is not, I believe, in any way singular, but instead represents a common misapprehension of those fond guardians of behavior who introduce young women into society. I brazenly intrude into this situation in hopes of encouraging other overzealous parents and guardians to allow some lenience in matters of such consequence to the happiness of their charges.

Madam,

I take the liberty of applying to you in a matter of the utmost importance, and solicit from your experience and good nature such advice as may serve to preserve me from a fate more wretched than can be described. My affections have recently become engaged by a wonderful gentleman. He is everything I could wish for in a companion for life—kind, loving, handsome, charming, considerate, honorable, and true. He is nothing short of perfect, and is in full possession of my heart. I am the most fortunate of women to know that he feels an affection for me as deep as mine for him. My happiness would be complete in knowing that I might become his wife.

Unfortunately, the aunt who acts as my guardian in the absence of my father cannot see the excellent qualities of this fine gentleman. Instead, she is blinded by old rumor and innuendo and sadly influenced by his lack of fortune. He is not destitute by any means, and his modest income is sufficient to support us both. My affectionate aunt, however, encourages me to accept the ad-

dresses of a man of superior wealth and rank. I am naturally desirous of conforming in all things to the wishes of my dear aunt, who on all occasions has so studiously sought my welfare and the promotion of my best interests. However, I cannot feel anything but repugnance at the notion of marrying a man for whom I feel no affection, most particularly when another is the object of them all. Please advise me as to whether I ought to be bound to my aunt's wishes and sacrifice all future happiness, or ought I to be allowed to accept the suit of the gentleman who holds my heart?

Miss Dora Doleful

It is my firm belief that the woman who unites her destiny with that of a man for whom she feels little more than indifference cannot expect to find any degree of comfort in the married state. Where mutual affection and esteem are lacking, felicity can never dwell. Worse still, if a wife's affections have been bestowed upon another than her husband, she is fostering a situation wrought with dangerous potential. Such a circumstance is unkind and unfair to both parties. Many well-meaning guardians are so determined that their charges marry well that it is sometimes allowed that they are not also married happily. Wealth may provide the means for material pleasure, but cannot bring consolation for the wounds of a broken heart. Moreover, the

deprivation of wealth does not presume the depri-
vation of happiness. If Miss Doleful's love for the
gentleman who holds her heart is a love founded on
more than mere fancy, is refined by delicacy, and is
exalted by purity of heart and dignity of mind, a
bare competence will be sufficient to subsist. It is
hoped that her esteemed aunt will modify her
thinking to favor a true attachment over the allure
of wealth and position, and encourage Miss Dole-
ful to follow her heart's desire.

Eleanor looked up from the page to find Belinda beaming with triumph.

"You see?" Belinda said. "She agrees with me about Geoffrey. She says I should follow my heart."

Eleanor's teeth were clenched so tight she could barely speak. "And I suppose you intend to take her advice?"

"Of course."

"Of course." And Eleanor intended to hunt down the Busybody and wring her interfering neck.

Chapter 1

A lady should never voluntarily resign her life to a gentleman, however generous, amiable, and honorable he may be, if it is not within her power to regard him with any sentiment more tender than gratitude and esteem.

The Busybody

"**M**rs. Eleanor Tennant to see Lady Westover."

The dour butler studied Eleanor's card, then said, "I am sorry, but her ladyship is not at home."

Eleanor, already beyond irritation over how long it had taken to track down the wretched woman, was not about to be so easily dismissed. The impudent fellow had not even gone through the motions of pretending to see if his employer would receive her. One look at her card and he'd made the decision on his own.

Officious prig. But he knew not with whom he dealt.

Eleanor pushed him aside and stepped into the entry hall. "Then I shall wait."

The butler, caught off guard by her temerity, lost no time in blocking her way. "Madam," he said in a voice dripping with icy disdain, "I am afraid her ladyship is away from home. I will, of course, see that she receives your card upon her return."

Undaunted, Eleanor stood her ground and directed a steely glare at the man. She was not about to be put off because her ladyship was not receiving today. This was no social call. "It is most important that I speak with Lady Westover. Today. Now. Please show me where I may await her, then inform her at once that I am here. You may assure her that I am not leaving until I have spoken with her."

The butler appeared near apoplexy, but somehow managed to maintain his dignity as he led Eleanor into a small salon off the entry. "Please wait here," he said, and left the room with more speed than she would have credited a man of his age.

Figuring the wait could be a long one if Lady Westover was not yet dressed, Eleanor settled into a comfortable-looking wing chair and took stock of her surroundings. It still surprised her to have discovered the Busybody—that loathsome dispenser of irresponsible advice—in one of the finest homes in Mayfair. The beautiful town house on Portman Square was a far cry from the modest home on Charlotte Street where Eleanor lived with her niece.

This room, though, was small and not particularly elegant. No doubt it was used only for those visitors not important enough for the grander rooms suggested by the majestic staircase rising beyond the arched columns of the imposing entry hall. It irritated Eleanor to be placed in such a pokey little room as though she were a common tradesman, but she could not fault the butler for doing his duty. It was not an uncomfortable room. In fact, it was only slightly smaller than their own drawing room on Charlotte Street. She suspected the main drawing room here was larger than the entire house on Charlotte Street, but she was unlikely ever to see it. So she inspected what she was allowed to see and tried to imagine the mistress of the house.

And she rehearsed in her mind what precisely she would say to her when she walked in. Or perhaps she should get straight to the point and simply whack the idiot woman over the head with her parasol.

When Eleanor had enlisted the aid of her cousin Constance in tracking down the Busybody, they had both been shocked to find the trail leading straight to Lady Albinia Westover. They had first approached the publishing house where *The Ladies' Fashionable Cabinet* was printed, but no one would provide them with so much as a hint as to the identity of the Busybody. The printer himself claimed not to know, but Eleanor had not for a moment believed him and had haunted his premises for days before deciding he was never going to divulge the information she needed.

Constance had come up with the idea of sending a packet in a very distinctive wrapper to the Busybody in care of the printer. They would then watch the building to see if anyone came to claim the package, which is exactly what happened. But the Busybody was no fool and went to some lengths to protect her identity. They followed the courier who left the building with Eleanor's package, only to find him handing it off to another man. Hidden behind the draperies of Constance's elegant carriage, the two women watched one hand-off after another, following a zigzag route that took them from one end of the city to the other, through St. James's and the West End, through Westminster and finally to Mayfair. When the last courier, had descended the steps to the servants' entrance to the house on Portman Square, it was Eleanor's cousin who'd recognized the house and knew its owner.

Constance, who had married well and was part of a much more elevated social circle than any Eleanor could claim, had met Lady Westover on occasion, but was not well acquainted with her. She was married to Sir Harold Westover, an outspoken Tory member of Parliament notorious for his long-winded anti-reform harangues and sponsorship of various conservative bills. Constance admitted to finding Lady Westover somewhat featherbrained, though dutifully supportive of her husband and his causes. The notion of her secret identity as the romantic Busybody had sent Constance into paroxysms of laughter as they sat in her carriage across the square.

Eleanor would like to have brought her cousin along for this difficult interview, since she at least had the claim of acquaintance. But Constance could not be trusted to take the matter seriously. It would not serve Eleanor's purpose to have her cousin burst into giggles at the first sight of Lady Westover.

So Eleanor had come prepared to do battle on her own.

While she waited, she looked about her and took note of the expensive though somewhat old-fashioned furnishings. She wondered if the public rooms were more up-to-date than this one. There was not a sphinx or gilded crocodile head in sight, though Constance had described Lady Westover as a woman uncommonly susceptible to the vagaries of fashion. What sort of woman would walk through the door? Eleanor could not reconcile in her mind the image of the fashionable, insipid, dutiful wife of a conservative politician with the flowery prose and starry-eyed Romanticism of the Busybody.

She hoped, however, that the contradiction would work in her favor. Most likely the politician's wife would not want her embarrassing secret identity revealed, especially to her stiff-necked husband. Eleanor was more than willing to dabble in a bit of blackmail to get what she wanted. In fact, she was shamelessly anxious to do so.

She would cajole, coerce, even threaten if necessary, in order to force the woman to face Eleanor's niece, Belinda, and retract her ill-considered advice. The Busybody would be made to face the potential dangers of her capricious counsel.

Eleanor wanted Lady Westover to squirm.

She was smiling smugly at the image conjured up by that thought when the salon door opened.

It was not the Busybody.

A man stood in the doorway, his head cocked at a quizzical angle as he gazed at her. Too well dressed to be a servant, he was about her own age, tall, a bit on the thin side, with a shock of reddish hair and bright blue eyes. The intense, but unreadable, expression in those eyes disconcerted her.

He stepped into the room. "I am Simon Westover. I understand you wish to speak with my mother."

The odd smile slid from the woman's face and she rose from her chair. Simon was glad she no longer smiled. She was much too pretty when she smiled, and he always became flustered around pretty women.

She looked him directly in the eye. Hers were green, he noticed, and fired with some sort of emotion: anger, defiance, determination—he could not be sure. "Yes," she said, "I wish to speak to Lady Westover, if you please. It is most important."

"I am sorry"—he looked at the card Felton had given him—"Mrs. Tennant. My mother is visiting friends in Richmond and will be away from home for several more days. But, if you will allow it, I would be honored to pass along any message you might have for her."

"Oh, confound it!" Mrs. Tennant pounded the air

with a balled fist, then began to pace the room, muttering to herself. Simon watched in fascination—muslin skirts swishing about her trim ankles—as she seemed to forget his presence altogether. She was seriously vexed about something. What on earth had his mother done to incense her so? He caught only a few words of her mumbled monologue. "Tiresome . . . too late . . . ought to have known . . . odious busybody."

"What?" Her last words sent a chill skittering down his spine. Surely he had not heard correctly. "Did you . . . did you say . . ."

She stopped pacing and turned to look at him. Her eyes narrowed, and then slowly widened as though struck by some revelation. Her mouth twitched into a sort of smirk. "I said," and each word was clearly enunciated with precise deliberation, "the devil take that odious Busybody."

"Oh, dear God." Simon thought he might become ill. He wanted nothing so much as to sink into a chair, but Mrs. Tennant stood and so he could not sit. Instead, he somehow managed to move toward the fireplace, where he leaned heavily against the mantel, his back to Mrs. Tennant.

Was he leaping to conclusions? It was a common enough term. She need not have been referring to *The Ladies' Fashionable Cabinet* advice column. But no. The look on her face had told him the truth.

"You know," he said.

"Yes, I do. That is why I am here. I have a bone to pick with the Busybody."

Oh, God. She might as well have planted him a facer with that confirmation. Simon twisted his throbbing head to look over his shoulder at her. He wished to hell she would be seated instead of standing there with that defiant tilt to her chin and green fire blazing from her eyes.

"How . . . how did you find out?" His voice came out thin and strangled, no doubt revealing to her every bit of the misery and apprehension he felt in that moment.

She gave a mirthless chuckle. "I am sure you would like to know. I confess it was not easy. But anger fueled my determination. I was not about to give up until I had found the Busybody. And I have found her, have I not?"

He hid his face from her. "Yes."

"And I do not suppose you or your mother would like the truth to be published."

"No. No, of course not." Hell and damnation. What was he to do? She must not be allowed to ruin everything. He had to stop her. But how? What did she want?

"Does your father know?"

Simon's head jerked up. "Good God, no." He made an effort to compose himself, to disguise the panic that had begun to grip the back of his throat. "Mrs. Tennant, please, I beg you, have a seat and tell me what it is you want."

Thankfully, she did as he asked, returning to the chair she'd occupied when he entered the room. She took an inordinate amount of time to settle herself and arrange her skirts before Simon allowed himself to sink onto the settee facing her. If anxiety had not wrapped itself around his chest like a leather strap, Simon would have appreciated the picture she made: green velvet and white muslin and flushed cheeks against the red brocade of the large wing chair. He had always been susceptible to a pretty face. Now was not the time, however, to give in to his libido. She was not there for him to admire. She came with the news he thought never to hear.

The Busybody had been unmasked.

She skewered him with her unflinching gaze, green eyes glittering with triumph. She had him and she knew it. "Now, Mrs. Tennant," he said, amazed at the even tone he managed, "I assume you want something in return for keeping the identity of the Busybody secret. What is it you want?"

"Retribution."

What the devil? He raised his brows in question.

"I want the Busybody to retract some rather bad advice before it is too late."

Not money. Not political favors. All she wanted was a retraction? Could it be that easy? "I'm afraid I do not understand you. Perhaps you had better explain."

"A letter was published in *The Ladies' Fashionable Cabinet* a short time ago from a young girl asking if she should be allowed to encourage the addresses of a man of whom her aunt disapproved."

"Ah, yes. Miss Dora Doleful, I believe."

"Quite so."

"And may I assume that you are the doting aunt?"

"I am indeed."

"As I recollect, Miss Doleful wrote with a heart overflowing with love, and elated that her tender affections were returned. Is that not what we all seek, Mrs. Tennant? To experience the full degree of happiness found in a reciprocal affection?

"When sympathetic souls unite
Each moment teems with new delight."

She glared at him as though he'd sprouted wings. Perhaps it was an inopportune moment to recite poetry. "I am sorry, Mrs. Tennant, that the advice given your niece was not to your liking."

"Not to my liking?" Her jaw tightened with anger. "It was more than not to my liking, Mr. Westover. It was thoughtless, inappropriate, imprudent, and quite possibly dangerous."

"Dangerous?"

"The Busybody's advice gave my seventeen-year-old niece permission to accept the advances of a man whose intentions do not include marriage. I consider that dangerous, don't you?"

"Good God."

"She even mentioned in her letter—here, let me read it so that I may not be accused of misrepresentation." She pulled a copy of *The Ladies' Fashionable Cabinet* from her reticule and turned to a page marked with a turned-down corner. "She writes: 'She'—that would be me—'is blinded by old rumor and innuendo and sadly influenced by his lack of fortune.' The advice printed here completely ignores the so-called rumor and innuendo and concentrates on the lack of fortune. Although I have, quite naturally, been in hopes that Belinda would marry well—she has no fortune to speak of—I am much more concerned that she has fallen under the spell of a scoundrel who only means to ruin her. Don't you agree that it might have been wise to address, even briefly, the concern of rumor and innuendo?"

"I am so sorry, Mrs. Tennant. But I don't see how anyone could have known—"

"Anyone with an ounce of sense," she said, and slapped the magazine hard against the arm of the chair, "would have advised that, at the very least, unsavory rumors should be investigated and laid to rest before the girl is allowed to 'follow her heart's desire.' That ridiculous advice may well lead an impressionable young girl to her ruin."

Genuine chagrin caused heat to rise in his cheeks, and cursing all his red-haired fair-skinned ancestors, Simon turned away in a vain effort to hide his blushes. He had never considered the Busybody's advice in this light. Mrs. Tennant's concerns might not be entirely unreasonable. "I hope you are wrong, Mrs. Tennant, and that you are able to offer more sound advice to your niece. I assure you that the response to her letter was well meant. It was never intended to sanction the sort of ruin you fear."

"And yet the Busybody constantly offers that sort of moronic follow-your-heart advice. So many of her readers are young girls filled with romantic ideals, each of them panting to become the heroine of a tale of tender sentiment such as they read in the pages of *The Ladies' Fashionable Cabinet* and other magazines. Not to mention the novels of Mrs. Radcliffe and her like." She rose from her chair and Simon sensed that he was in for a lecture. He stood as well and returned to his place before the mantel, facing her this time.

He wished he could forget the enormity of her unmasking of the Busybody, and the potential harm she could wreak with that knowledge. He wished she were there on some other errand so he could just sit back and watch her. The lovely Mrs. Tennant was glorious in her outrage.

"All these girls," she continued, "are seeking the heroes of their dreams, and will never find them in the upstanding, suitable young men brought to their attention by parents or guardians who only want what's best for them. But instead of being sensible, they are encouraged by the likes of the Busybody to receive a good impression from the first man answering their ideas of a handsome, romantic hero.

"In the case of my niece, Belinda, that man is one whose reputation would strike fear in the heart of any conscientious guardian. He is a gamester, a profligate libertine, and very likely an adventurer. He is known to be in dun territory and in dire need of an heiress. Belinda is no heiress, Mr. Westover. Now, I ask you: what does a man such as I've described want with a beautiful young girl with no fortune?"

Though there was likely some validity to her fears, Simon suspected the woman was overreacting. Despite the horror stories mothers often used to instill the fear of impropriety in their daughters, most gentlemen of the *ton* did not go about debauching innocent girls. Those men with reputations as libertines generally kept to widows, willing matrons, and Cyprians. There was the odd blackguard, of course, but he was rare. It was all the fault of Richardson and his *Clarissa*. Mothers, and guardian aunts, saw the villain Lovelace in every man who dared to flirt with their charges.

"I hope with all my heart that you are wrong," Simon said. "I never dreamed of such an outcome when I responded to your niece's letter."

Mrs. Tennant sucked in a sharp breath. "What did you say?"

"I never meant any harm in my response. I was just—"

"Are you saying that *you* write the answers to those letters? Not your mother?"

"My mother?" What the—oh, dear God. She had *not* known. She hadn't known the truth after all. She'd thought his mother—his *mother*, of all people!—wrote for the magazine. God help him, what had he done? Why hadn't he sat quietly and listened without admitting anything?

"*You* are the Busybody?"

Simon stifled a groan. *Idiot*. If he had only been patient he could have assured her that his mother was not the Busybody, and left it at that, giving nothing away. How could he have been so stupid?

"Well? Are you the Busybody, Mr. Westover?"

There was nothing for it now. It would be ridiculous to deny it. But his mouth had gone dry, and he did not believe he could speak the words. He took a deep breath and nodded.

"You scoundrel!" She drew her arm back and slapped him hard across the face.

Chapter 2

A sad reckoning awaits those who allow ambition to direct their preference and avarice to rule their hearts.

The Busybody

He reeled back from the force of her blow, then gave her a look of stunned disbelief. Eleanor felt not even the tiniest twinge of regret—well, perhaps the tiniest, but no more—for the bright red hand-shaped mark on his cheek. How dare the Busybody be—

"A man! I simply cannot believe it. It was bad enough thinking one of my own sex was capable of penning such nonsense, but the very idea of a *man* spouting such naïve, romantic, sentimental drivel is beyond belief."

He rubbed his cheek and continued to look thoroughly confused. "You do not believe men can be romantic?"

She felt her own cheeks flush. That was not what she had meant at all. She knew full well how romantic men could be, filling a girl's head with sweet lies.

"You might get an argument or two from Mr. Coleridge, or Mr. Wordsworth. But perhaps you have not read the *Lyrical Ballads*," he said.

Eleanor raised her eyes to the ceiling in silent exasperation. She ought to have known he was speaking of the ideal of Romance and not the more earthly notions of flirtation and seduction. "I was not referring to Romantic poetry, though heaven knows it is sometimes horribly foolish. No, I am simply astounded to discover that a *man* is the purveyor of such frivolous opinion, and in such florid language, as that doled out by the Busybody."

He seemed to wince at the comment about florid language. Recollecting his high-flown sentiments of a few moments ago, it should come as no surprise that Mr. Westover could have written those horrid bits of head-in-the-clouds advice.

"Why do you so object to the notion of the Busybody being a man?"

The question surprised her. Could he really be so blind? Or so stupid? "Well, for one thing, you pass yourself off as female. Your readers certainly believe the Busybody to be a woman."

"That is not unusual, I assure you," he said. "Perhaps it will surprise you to learn that most of the content of women's magazines is written by men. We assume feminine pen names so that our readers will be more comfortable. Like you, others might not be very receptive to a man's opinion of current fashion or instructions in housewifery."

"But you are not simply making note of the latest designs from Paris, are you? You are offering advice to young girls—"

"And the occasional young man."

"—*primarily* young girls and women who want advice on matters of the heart."

He arched a quizzical brow. "And why can a man not have as valid an opinion on such important matters? We are equally involved, are we not?"

Though his manner was serious, his blue eyes twinkled, momentarily distracting her from her purpose. Now who was being foolish? She gave herself a mental shake and refused to be diverted. "Perhaps you are right. But let us put aside for the moment the fact that you assume a false identity and deliberately dupe your readers. Let us consider the advice on its own merit. It is irresponsible and capricious."

"I am sorry you feel that way. As a strong advocate of the free agency of the heart, I do not feel it is my place to offer judgments on the direction the heart takes. My advice to your niece was simply to follow her heart's desire, something I believe we should all be allowed to do. Within reason."

"Ah, but you never do say 'within reason,' do you?"

"I always give my readers the benefit of the doubt, Mrs. Tennant."

"You tempt fate with such confidence, Mr. Westover. Many of your readers—my niece, for example—take your word as gospel, without any qualification. With the Busybody, they hear what they want to hear. You do not challenge them to think, to examine, to reason. You give them validation to make unrealistic and unreasonable choices. You do not dispense wisdom. You offer a crutch to their exquisite sensibilities and encourage them in their romantic follies. That is precisely why I am so upset over this entire business."

His mouth turned down in a grimace, and Eleanor thought a few of her arrows might have struck home.

"Perhaps you underestimate your niece," he said. "If the gentleman in question is as unsuitable as you believe, and for the reasons you believe, then it is likely your niece will eventually come to that same conclusion on her own."

"Oh, I'm quite sure she will. But it will be too late. She will be ruined."

He gave her a pained look. But Eleanor suspected it was not because he regretted his advice, but because he did not believe her. He did not believe Barkwith was out to ruin Belinda. No doubt his foolish Romanticism did not allow for such reprehensible behavior. He believed in love. He was quite wrong, of course.

"Had you simply added the words 'within reason,'" she continued, "I would have had some room for persuasion with Belinda. As it stands, I have none. She has placed the Busybody upon a lofty, ornate pedestal and will listen to no one else."

"And so you want a retraction? You want me to publicly refute my advice?"

"I had wanted that, yes." A smile twitched at the corners of her mouth. "But it is more complicated now, is it not?"

"How so?"

"Because you are a man, of course."

"What difference does that make?" His voice rose in frustration.

"It makes you a fraud. I wonder what your readers would think to discover the Busybody is a man? I wonder what your father would think?"

He gave a short intake of breath. "Leave my father out of this."

"Oh, I do not think I can do that. Sir Harold Westover is rather outspoken in his politics, is he not? If I am not mistaken, he is a very vocal supporter of the judicial attacks on private separation deeds. In fact, is he not a sponsor of the recent parliamentary bill to abolish such deeds?" She silently thanked Constance for providing her with so much background on the Westovers. Before tracking down the Busybody, Eleanor had never even heard of Sir Harold and Lady Westover. "My goodness," she said, "I should hate to imagine what such a formidable public figure would do if he discovered his son masquerading as a female and passing out advice to the lovelorn. The mind boggles."

Color drained from Mr. Westover's face so that

the pale freckles she had not noticed on his cheeks now stood out like flecks of burnt umber. She had him! She had wanted the Busybody to squirm, and though he stood still as a statue, Eleanor was quite sure he was squirming inside.

"What do you want of me?" he asked.

"Afraid for Papa to learn the truth, eh? Rather intimidating, is he?" She must be wicked indeed to so thoroughly enjoy his uneasiness.

Color was returning to his face, and his blue eyes blazed with anger. She had to give the man credit. She would have expected someone of his sentimental temperament to suffer a nervous collapse in such a situation. He was uncomfortable, to be sure. In fact, she guessed he was furious with her and more than a little anxious. But he stood tall with a sort of stoic dignity in the face of surrender. "What do you want of me?" he repeated.

"I suggest a bargain of sorts. If you will do something for me, I will promise not to publicly reveal your secret identity."

"What do I have to do?"

"You *are* anxious to keep your little secret, are you not?" It was almost intoxicating to know she held his future in her hands, and she could not seem to help taunting him.

Yet his gaze did not waver. "I have my reasons," he said, "for not being publicly associated with the Busybody or *The Ladies' Fashionable Cabinet*. Please put an end to this game and tell me what I must do to ensure your silence."

He was right. It was self-indulgent to toy with the poor man any longer. "I want you to come to Charlotte Street with me and admit to Belinda that you are the Busybody, and that you made a mistake in the advice you gave her. She must be told that upon reconsideration you have decided you can no longer support her wish to destroy her life with the wrong man."

"But I—"

"If you do not agree to my request, I shall be forced to use whatever means necessary to ensure that Belinda and other impressionable young girls will think twice before seeking your advice. You may be sure that I shall waste no time in publicizing the true identity of the Busybody. Perhaps in a rival publication. *The Lady's Monthly Museum*, for example. Or better yet, *The Gentleman's Magazine*."

He closed his eyes and took a deep breath. Eleanor could see that he made an effort to hold his temper in check. When he opened his eyes again, his gaze was direct and startlingly intense. Eleanor guessed she was seeing that part of him inherited from his indomitable father. "Can you swear to me," he said in a voice bristling with taut control, "that only your niece will be told, and that she can be trusted to keep silent?"

"I can speak only for myself, and you have my promise. But if you agree to my terms, I will do everything in my power to ensure Belinda's silence. She is a good girl. Once she knows the truth,

I believe she can be trusted. So, do you agree? Will you come with me to meet Belinda?"

The distance to Charlotte Street was not great, but the traffic was thick this time of day and the going was slow. Simon took advantage of the delay to study the woman on the seat opposite. Mrs. Tennant was a very attractive woman, despite the rather smug set of her mouth at the moment. She was extraordinarily pleased with herself.

Her white muslin dress and green velvet spencer jacket, though neatly made, were not of the latest mode. Simon knew more about such things than most men, due to his association with a ladies' magazine. He cared little for fashion, however, and generally only took note that a woman's dress was becoming or not.

Mrs. Tennant looked decidedly becoming in her morning dress. She wore a straw bonnet with the brim turned up to reveal dark brown curls spilling forward over her brow and framing her cheeks. Her eyes reflected the green of her jacket, and he wondered if they shifted tones depending on what she wore. It was her mouth, however, that truly captivated him. The upper lip was fuller than the lower, and dipped down to a slight point. Succulent. Ripe for kissing.

Simon jerked his gaze away. This was not the time or the woman to be inspiring such fantasies. She held an important part of his life in her hands, and if he made the mistake of showing an inappropriate interest in her, she just might renege on her promise and trumpet his secret from the rooftops.

Besides, there was probably a Mr. Tennant.

It was time to turn his mind to more pertinent matters. "May I ask," he said, "how it was that you tracked the Busybody to Westover House?"

She flashed a sly smile. "What's the matter, Mr. Westover? Are you afraid others might unmask you as easily as I did?"

"The thought did cross my mind."

"Though I probably should not admit to it—I much prefer to see you squirm with apprehension—you may rest assured that it was no easy task. The publisher was silent as an oyster."

Thank God.

"It was my cousin, Mrs. Poole, who conceived the idea of sending a distinctive package to the Busybody and following its path."

"The packet tied in red and blue ribbons." He ought to have guessed something was afoot when he received that odd package with nothing in it but an old issue of the magazine. Damnation. He thought he had protected against just such discovery by a complicated series of couriers. She smiled, as though reading his thoughts.

"If I had not been so determined in my quest, Mr. Westover, I would have given up the chase after the second handoff. That was quite an elaborate ruse you set up. You must be quite desperate to conceal your association with the Busybody."

He was. But he had no wish for the tenacious

Mrs. Tennant to make it her business to discover *why* anonymity was so important to him.

"Tell me about your niece," he said, hoping to steer the conversation in another direction, "and about her unsuitable suitor. It might help to know something more of the situation if I am to convince her to ignore my earlier advice."

"Belinda is my brother's daughter. He is Captain Benjamin Chadwick of the Royal Navy and has been away at sea off and on for most of her life. I have acted as guardian to Belinda since her mother died five years ago. I've had to run a tight ship, as Benjamin would say. She can be a willful creature, and I have often regretted she did not have a strong father figure in her daily life."

"What of your husband?"

"I am a widow, Mr. Westover."

Simon tried to look solemn, but felt inappropriately gleeful at this news. He could now, in better conscience, continue in his admiration of her mouth. Perhaps when he returned home, he would attempt an ode to her upper lip.

"Belinda has always been a bit headstrong," she continued. "She is quite beautiful and is used to having things go her way. When her father agreed to sponsor a Season for her, and Mrs. Poole agreed to introduce her to a higher level of society, I knew her beauty would attract a great many admirers. And a lot of trouble.

"My cousin helped to bring Belinda to the attention of several eligible, and perfectly suitable, young men. But from the moment she set eyes on Geoffrey Barkwith she had no interest in anyone else. Do you know Barkwith?"

"The name is familiar," Simon said, "but I cannot recollect meeting him. Perhaps my mother knows him."

"I'm sure she would tell you he is a gazetted rake. Not only a libertine, but a gamester as well. He has a very unsavory reputation, and I have no doubt of his true intentions. I depend upon my brother's goodwill, Mr. Westover, and I cannot imagine he would take kindly to me allowing his daughter to fall into the clutches of a man such as Geoffrey Barkwith. Besides, I am very fond of Belinda." Her voice took on a more gentle tone. "I have no wish to see her hurt. I only want her happiness."

Her eyes shone brilliant with contained emotion. Simon knew in that moment he could trust her. If asked, he could not have explained why he knew this, but he did. She would keep her promise to him. She had no hidden motive that he must guard against. She was simply a protective hen guarding her chick. No, that was too mundane an image for Mrs. Tennant. She was no hen. A mother dragon, perhaps. An avenging fury. A warrior queen. Boadicea enraged by the violation of her daughters.

Perhaps he would address his pen to those images rather than the delectable upper lip.

The question at hand, however, was trust. He must, absolutely must, trust her to keep his secret. And Belinda as well. There was too much at stake. "Are you confident, Mrs. Tenant, that we can convince your niece to keep my identity as the Busybody secret?"

"I believe so. She will be very disappointed, of course, to discover the Busybody is not the wise old woman she believes her to be. But I cannot think she would feel the need to proclaim the news all over town. She is an intelligent girl. She will understand your desire to keep it secret."

Simon hoped she was right. He had begun to compose what he would say to the girl when the carriage rolled to a stop in front of a modest town house on Charlotte Street. He helped Mrs. Tennant down from the carriage, and almost before they'd taken two steps the front door opened. An older woman—the housekeeper?—stood in the doorway frantically wringing her hands.

Mrs. Tennant stopped in her tracks. "Mrs. Davies? What is it? Has something happened?"

"You best come right in, Miz Tennant," the woman said and cast a skeptical look in Simon's direction. "I'm sure I don't know what to do."

Clearly they had arrived in the midst of some domestic crisis. It could not be the best of times to play out his contrite little charade. "Perhaps I should go," he said. "I could come back another time."

"Oh, no you don't," Mrs. Tennant said. "We

have a bargain." She astonished him by placing her hand at his back and practically shoving him up the steps and through the door.

"What is it, Mrs. Davies?" she said when she had followed him inside. "What has happened?"

The housekeeper glanced again at Simon and seemed reluctant to say anything.

"This is Mr. Westover. You mustn't worry about him. Tell me what has happened." Mrs. Tennant's calm demeanor suggested that her housekeeper might have indulged in melodrama a time or two in the past.

"She's gone, Miz Tennant. Miss Belinda's gone."

Mrs. Tennant stood stiff and unmoving though her face went quite pale. It began to seem very crowded in the narrow entry hall, and Simon felt awkwardly *de trop*. He had a very bad feeling about this.

"What do you mean, *gone*?" Mrs. Tennant asked. "Has she gone out with friends? Or out with . . . with Mr. Barkwith?"

"I don't know where she's gone," the housekeeper said, "but when I went up to tidy her bedchamber, I could tell something weren't right. Drawers were open and looked like they been rummaged. I checked her wardrobe and lots of dresses are missing. And her new bonnet."

"Dear God." Mrs. Tennant reached a hand behind her to grip the edge of a hall table.

"And then I found this, addressed to you,

propped up on the inkwell on her writing desk."
Mrs. Davies held out a folded sheet of parchment
sealed with red wax. "It's from Miss Belinda. I recognize her writing."

Mrs. Tennant took the note and quickly broke
the seal, heedless of the circle of wax sent bouncing
along the hall floor. She scanned the note in an instant and looked up. Directly at Simon. There was
no mistaking the rage in those eyes.

A bolt of pure cowardice shot through him—
how mortifying!—and he had a sudden urge to
turn and run. But she pinned him to the spot with
her gaze.

"You!" she said. "It's all your fault. Read this."

Simon glared at the parchment in her outstretched hand as though it were something slimy
and noxious. He had no desire to touch it.

"Read it."

She thrust it toward him so that he was forced to
take it. He did not need to read it. He could predict
what it would say. But her fierce glare compelled
him to do as she asked. He read the note.

Dearest Aunt Ellie,

*I have taken the wise advice of the Busybody to fol-
low my heart's desire and have gone away with
Geoffrey. When we return, I will be Mrs. Barkwith. Please don't be too angry. Be happy for me. I
am ecstatic!*

Belinda

Simon stifled a groan and wondered if the day could get any worse. He did not look up. He could not bear to look at her.

"Do you see?" Mrs. Tennant said, her voice rising in anger. "Do you see what you've done?"

Simon steeled himself for another blow, but it did not come. He would have welcomed it. He might actually deserve it.

"Follow her heart, indeed," she said in a tone of utter disgust. "Well, I suppose that is what I'm going to have to do."

He looked up at that and met her furious gaze. "What are you going to do?"

"I'm going to follow her foolish heart, of course. I'm going after her. And you're coming with me."

Chapter 3

A young woman of true merit need not repine lack of social opportunity. She is unlikely to remain forever undiscovered, for in daylight or dark, a diamond yet sparkles.

The Busybody

Eleanor turned on her heel and headed up the stairs. She stepped into the drawing room and stood before the window, pretending to watch something on the street below. She heard Mr. Westover follow her, but kept her back to him. Her hands shook and she had no idea how long she could keep her tears at bay.

Oh, Belinda.

"Mrs. Tennant?"

She acknowledged his presence with a lift of her chin, but did not turn around. She would not break down in front of this troublemaking ninnyhammer.

"Mrs. Tennant, I am so very sorry about what has happened. I understand that you feel it necessary to follow your niece, and I will do anything in my power to help you find her. But I do not believe it would be wise for me to accompany you."

Eleanor sighed. He was surely the most contrary, troublesome man she'd ever met, but she did not have time or energy to fight with him now. All she could think of was poor Belinda, being seduced by Barkwith, facing abandonment and ruin, having her heart smashed to bits by that cad.

No. She could not, would not allow that to happen. Belinda was a foolish, featherbrained girl, to be sure; but Eleanor was inordinately fond of the child and hated to imagine the heartbreak in store for her. Eleanor must find the girl and bring her back home while her reputation, if not her virtue, was still intact.

But she did not have the resources to do it alone.

She took a deep breath and turned away from the window. "I do not care what you may or may not think is wise, Mr. Westover. In fact, you are the very last person whose opinion I would trust just now."

He had the good sense to blush, but not enough to keep quiet. "That's as may be, but at least let me help. You must allow me to provide whatever transportation you require, as well as all traveling expenses."

Good heavens, she had not even thought how she was to pay for such a journey. She would have to hire a carriage, horses, postboys, and, depending on how long it took to track them down, rooms at various inns. And meals. And tolls. And bribes, no doubt, to get information she needed. It would all be quite expensive, much more than she could ever afford. Perhaps she could prevail on her cousin Constance to help.

"It is the least I can do," Mr. Westover said.

Eleanor studied him from across the room. As she had already noted, he was beautifully dressed, his bottle-green coat perfectly tailored, precise to a pin. There was the Mayfair mansion, too. Mr. Westover no doubt had a small fortune at his disposal.

"Yes," she said, making an impulsive decision, "I believe you have the right of it. It is indeed the least you can do. I accept your offer of transportation."

"Good. Now, I assume there is no time to waste. Do you have any idea how long ago they might have left London?"

"She was here this morning when I left to pay a visit to my cousin, shortly before I came to Westover House. At least I . . . oh, dear. No, come to think of it, I did not see her. She did not come down for breakfast. I assumed she took a tray in her room." Eleanor looked beyond him to where Mrs. Davies stood hovering in the doorway, and raised her brows in question.

"Lord bless me, Miz Tennant, but I could swear her bed hadn't been slept in." The housekeeper blinked back tears. "And when I asked Tilly if she'd taken in her morning chocolate, she said Miss Belinda told her last night to let her sleep late this morning, and not to disturb her until she rang."

"Dear God, she must have left during the night," Eleanor said. "They could be halfway to Scotland by now."

"Not quite so far as that." Mr. Westover moved toward the door. "But they have a hell of a head start. I'll dash back home and round up one of my father's traveling coaches. Do you suppose they took the stage, or does Barkwith keep his own carriage?"

"I have no idea." Eleanor suddenly realized how little she did know, and a wave of sheer panic almost overwhelmed her. She grabbed hold of the nearest chair and sank into it. "I have no idea when she left, or what sort of carriage she's in, or what direction she took." She could not disguise the despair in her voice. "How on earth am I ever to track her down?"

She looked up at Mr. Westover in a plea for help. He looked just as flummoxed as she felt, and Eleanor realized this romantic fool, this twaddle-spouting, sentimental idiot, was not the stalwart champion she needed right now. If she was going to find Belinda before it was too late, she must rely on her own resources.

Yet surely this vexatious gentleman could be of *some* use.

"Could you possibly discover where Barkwith lives?" she asked. It would be easier for a man, even Mr. Westover, to locate Barkwith's clubs, his cronies, someone who could tell him where the blackguard lived. "Perhaps someone could give us a clue as to when and how he left Town."

"Yes, of course. I'll do that at once. Then I'll return with a carriage and whatever information I can find. Oh, and it would help if I had a description of your niece, in case she and Barkwith were seen."

Eleanor groaned. "Good Lord, I hope not. Belinda has a very distinctive beauty, the sort that makes a person look twice. If they are seen together, she will most assuredly be remembered." She took a deep breath and tried to find words to describe her niece's unique beauty. "Belinda has very dark hair, almost black but not quite, and it usually falls in soft curls about her face. Her eyes, on the other hand, are very pale-bluish green, a sort of aquamarine. Most noticeable, and most dramatic, are the long, black lashes framing the pale eyes, and the very dark, perfectly arched brows."

Eleanor recalled quite clearly the beautiful little portrait miniature she had had painted of Belinda earlier in the year. It had been a gift for her father's birthday. She wished she had it now at hand, so that words, ineffective words, would not be necessary.

"She is slightly below average in height," Eleanor continued, "and . . . and"—how to describe the ample bosom that had turned heads all Season—"her figure is well proportioned."

Mr. Westover's brows lifted, and the hint of a smile tugged at the corner of his mouth. "She does indeed sound remarkably beautiful. Clearly, she takes after her aunt."

The devil. Was this horrid man actually flirting with her? At any other time, she might—*might*—have found some pleasure in the notion. But this was no time for such foolishness. She decided to ignore him. "And you may find it helpful to know that Geoffrey Barkwith is dark-haired and dark-eyed, and about your height."

"I'm sure both descriptions will be helpful, especially if, as I suspect, they are not traveling under their own names. I will discover what I can and return with a carriage as quickly as possible."

"Thank you, Mr. Westover. I'll pack a bag so we can leave as soon as you return."

He had made to leave but halted at her words. "We?"

"Yes, we." He began to shake his head, but she did not have time for argument, and held up her hand to stop him. "Mr. Westover, do you imagine I could make any headway on this search, traveling as a woman alone? Questioning innkeepers and ostlers and postboys? No. It will be much easier if a man accompanies me."

"Surely someone else could go," he said. "A relative, perhaps? You would not wish to tarnish your own reputation by traveling with a bachelor of no relation to you."

"Bosh. It is Belinda's reputation I am concerned about, not my own. There is no one else, Mr. Westover. I rely upon you."

It was true, as much as it galled her to admit it.

"You are overset," he said, "and not thinking clearly."

She lifted her chin toward the tall, lean gentleman and peered at him through narrowed eyes.

"My mind is perfectly clear, I thank you. You *will* accompany me, Mr. Westover. I need a male escort, but I also need you to help persuade Belinda of the error of her ways. She is doing this, you may recall, because she has the Busybody's blessing. It will take the Busybody to convince her she is making a mistake."

"I will be happy to speak to the girl once you return with her. But I cannot advise you to go haring after her accompanied only by an unmarried man."

"And you must know in what high regard I hold any advice from you."

He rolled his eyes toward the ceiling. "You would do well to listen in this case. It would be imprudent at best to travel alone with me in a closed carriage without benefit of a chaperone."

Eleanor arched a brow. "Indeed? Are you so dangerous then, Mr. Westover?"

He colored up again—the man was exceedingly susceptible to blushes—but did not look away. "Not in the way you imply," he said, "but my presence could pose serious danger to your reputation."

"I am not a young maiden, sir. As a widow I can take certain liberties with propriety, particularly in an emergency. This is certainly an emergency, so please stop wasting time by arguing with me. And remember, if you will, that we had a bargain."

"This was not part of the bargain."

"It is now. If you do not agree to accompany me,

I promise you I will reveal the truth about the Busybody. You may depend upon it. Now please, please go find out where Barkwith lives, and any other information you can discover about his movements during the last day." She could not disguise the plaintive note in her voice, and feared she might burst into tears. Eleanor had no wish for this stranger to see her in such a state. "Please hurry," she said, her voice little more than a whisper.

He gave her a very intense look, then nodded his head and said, "As you wish. But in the meantime, I suggest you consider alternatives, or at least arrange for a maid or companion to come along. I'll return as quickly as I can."

He left in such a rush Eleanor could offer no further argument.

She collapsed against the back of the chair, almost crushing the bonnet she had forgotten she was still wearing. It reminded her that she had no time to give in to despair. She stood and untied the ribbons beneath her chin, then removed the bonnet and pressed a hand to her brow. Mrs. Davies said that Belinda had taken her new bonnet, the one she'd insisted on buying because the chocolate-brown ribbons were the exact shade of Geoffrey's eyes. The poor girl was deep in the throes of first love.

Eleanor wondered how Belinda would withstand the heartache that would surely result from this madcap escapade. Would she at least insist on maintaining her virtue until she was properly married? More likely she would give in to Barkwith at the first opportunity. And having got what he wanted, there would be no reason for Barkwith to marry her.

Oh, Belinda.

Her heart was breaking for the girl, but she would not resign to defeat just yet. The sooner Belinda was located and brought home, the easier it would be to mend her reputation, if not her heart. Eleanor took a deep, shuddery breath and headed upstairs to prepare for the journey.

Over two hours later, her small portmanteau packed and standing ready in the entry hall, Eleanor paced the perimeter of the drawing room. Where the devil was the wretched man? If not for the fact that she had no money to hire a post chaise on her own, she would not wait another moment for him. But they were losing precious time. What could possibly be taking so long?

She dashed to the window a few moments later when she heard the sounds of a carriage outside. She groaned in frustration to see that it was not Mr. Westover but her cousin Constance.

Damn and blast. How was she to face her elegant cousin with the news of Belinda's flight? A stab of mortification pierced her heart. What would Constance say, what would she think, to know how miserably Eleanor had failed as a guardian to her brother's only child?

The drawing room door opened and Constance swept in, a vision in lavender sarsnet. "Hello, my dear. I just thought I'd pop by and see what happened with Lady Westover. Was it—" She halted in mid-stride and stared at Eleanor. "Good Lord, what is it, Ellie? Something has happened."

"Oh, Constance." Eleanor's mouth trembled so she could barely speak. In the next instant, she was in her cousin's arms sobbing like a baby.

The big, luxurious traveling coach was with his mother in Richmond, but Simon was more than satisfied to have the newer, sleek, compact little chariot at his disposal. Though it comfortably accommodated only two inside, it would make better time.

Its snug interior was another reason not to agree to Mrs. Tennant's harebrained notion of dragging him along with her. He could not imagine a greater folly than spending long hours in a small carriage with such a vibrant creature. She might think it amusing to consider him dangerous—and she was probably right—but he had a certain partiality for women of strength and fortitude, especially when they happened to be beautiful as well. The tenacious, emerald-eyed widow was all of that, and very likely more.

Simon had never been able to resist a pretty face. He'd often been a fool where women were concerned, generally dancing to whatever tune they played. He couldn't help it. Women were enchanting creatures, and he was susceptible to their every lure.

Under no circumstances should he be allowed to accompany Mrs. Tennant on her pursuit of the runaway lovers.

He arranged for four of his own horses to begin the journey, with two Westover grooms to act as postboys. They would bring the team back to Town when new horses and postboys were hired at the first posting stop. He set them to readying the chariot while he set out to learn what he could about Geoffrey Barkwith.

It did not take long. By making discreet inquiries at his own club, he was able to discover that Barkwith was a member of Boodle's. Though not a member himself, Simon was able to convince the head porter that he had an urgent message for Barkwith and needed to speak with him at once. It took little more than a conspiratorial grin and a five-pound note for the man to abandon his scruples and provide Simon with Barkwith's direction. Simon thanked heaven Barkwith had not been a member of White's, where no bribe was big enough for any of the staff to betray the confidence of a member.

Barkwith's rooms were in a cramped house on Conduit Street. Unable, apparently, to afford the luxury of a gentleman's gentleman, he made do with the services of the housekeeper and the hall porter. A guinea to the latter bought Simon the information that the young gentleman had left the premises shortly before dawn, leaving word that he would be away for a short time. No information was known on his destination or mode of transportation. It would be up to Simon to discover that critical information, and he was not entirely certain how he was to do it.

The only thing he could think to do was check on all the main coaching inns for signs of the runaways. Assuming they went straight from Charlotte Street, Simon decided that Holborn, with its many large coaching inns, would be the most likely area to begin the search.

His first stop was the Bell and Crown, a busy inn from which several Royal Mail coaches and heavy stage coaches regularly departed. He sorted through passenger lists, talked with ticket sellers, ostlers, and postillions, but no one had seen a couple matching the description of Belinda and Barkwith.

Discouraged at how long it had taken to discover nothing, Simon moved on to the George and Blue Boar with little hope of success.

He had none there, nor at the Green Dragon.

There were four dozen or more coaching inns in London. If he was to check with each one, it could take days. And while he frittered away the hours, Mrs. Tennant was no doubt waiting anxiously for his return, impatient to be on the road. Dash it all, he was not good at being a hero. He wanted nothing more than to be a white knight in shining armor for this lady in distress, but the chance of that happening was fading with every minute that passed.

He needed help.

Ten minutes later, Simon was at the Bow Street Office, asking to speak with Sir Richard Ford, the chief magistrate. The court was busy, and Sir Richard was involved in a witness examination, and so Simon was led through a maze of narrow corridors and made to wait in a small, ill-ventilated office.

Thankfully, his wait was no more than a quarter hour. Sir Richard entered, introduced himself, and took a seat behind the large, cluttered desk in the center of the room. "I assume you have a crime to report?"

"Not a crime, precisely," Simon said. "At least, I hope not. Merely a bit of unpleasantness that I'm hoping one of your Runners can help me sort out." He proceeded to tell what he knew of the supposed elopement of Geoffrey Barkwith and Belinda Chadwick.

"And what is your relation to those involved?" Sir Richard asked.

Simon cleared his throat nervously and hoped to heaven he would not be forced to explain about the Busybody. "I am a friend of the family," he said. "I have been asked by the girl's aunt to help find her niece and bring her home before her reputation is irreparably ruined."

"I see. And so the aunt—Mrs. Tennant?—means to catch up with them before they reach Scotland. She wishes to put a stop to an over-the-anvil wedding?"

"She does not believe there will be any wedding."

"Ah." Sir Richard's piercing gaze was unnerving, but Simon met him square in the eye. "You understand, Mr. Westover, that Bow Street resources are limited. The Runners are committed to the business of inquiry, toward the pursuit and arrest of criminals. We cannot become involved in every minor domestic crisis brought before us."

"I understand," Simon said. "But I also know that they are sometimes allowed to take on private inquiry work for anyone willing to pay. I am willing and able to pay, Sir Richard."

The magistrate studied Simon for a long, awkward moment before replying. "I only have eight Runners available for outside service. I can spare one of them at the moment. It will cost you a guinea per day, plus fourteen shillings to cover expenses. Agreed?"

"Agreed."

Sir Richard shouted for his clerk, and sent the young man to locate someone called Hackett and bring him to the office. "The man I recommend to you is a constable in the newly formed Horse Patrol. He is a seasoned inquiry officer and an excellent horseman. If anyone can track down your runaway couple, it is Hackett."

As his name was mentioned, the man himself entered the office. He was a rotund, yet somehow compact man in late middle age with salt-and-pepper hair and matching bushy eyebrows. He wore the distinctive uniform of the Horse Patrol: blue double-breasted coat with large yellow metal buttons, scarlet waistcoat, blue trousers, black boots with steel spurs, a black leather hat, and white gloves.

He removed the tall leather hat and acknowledged his superior with a sweeping bow. "Sir Richard."

"Hackett, this gentleman is Mr. Westover. He has need of your services in a matter of private inquiry."

Simon had risen from his chair, and the Runner turned toward him and swept another bow. "Obidiah Hackett, at your service, guv'ner."

"Perhaps you should explain the situation once again," Sir Richard said, "for the benefit of Hackett."

And so Simon repeated his story. "I have determined," he said, "that it will take more than one of us to inquire at every coaching inn. That is why I've come to Bow Street for help."

"Beggin' your pardon, guv'ner, but you'll be needin' more than a few interrogations of ticket sellers, I reckon," Hackett said. "Once we ascertain their point o' departure, we shall be obliged to follow their trail from inn to inn. Even if you was absopositively certain they're headin' to Gretna—and you ain't—it is never wise to speculate on the precise itinerary of the fugitive. And I'd wager my fee they went by post. That mischievilacious sort don't want a passel o' nosy passengers sitting alongside 'em." The brindled brows rose and fell, punctuating his colorful speech with constant movement. "And considerin' the matutinal commencement of their journey, it'll take hard ridin' to effect an interception. You say the aunt'll be followin' in a carriage, ready to take the girl home?"

"That's right."

"Well, that poses a problesomatical complication, don't it? If I'm ridin' ahead, someone else has got to relay messages back to the aunt. A synchronized operation of such extraordinal precision takes two men, guv'ner. Two men at least, or there's no guarantee of success."

Simon looked to the magistrate. "Can you spare a second man?"

Sir Richard sighed. "Who did you have in mind, Hackett?"

"Mumby, sir. Between the two of us, I believe we can quickly resolve the situation."

"All right." The magistrate looked at Simon. "Hackett and Mumby for *two* guineas a day and fourteen shillings *each* for expenses."

"Agreed," Simon said, and wondered if this had been the plan all along.

"But let them do the work, Mr. Westover. They are both experienced investigators. I know you wanted to help, but—forgive me—you would just get in the way."

"I understand," Simon said. Nothing would please him more than to step aside and let the Runners do the job. "I will leave everything to Mr. Hackett and Mr. Mumby. Now, if—"

"Beggin' your pardon once again, guv'ner," Hackett said, "but I feel obligitated to acquaint you with a small detail Sir Richard has yet to mention. The reward."

"Reward?"

"Aye, Mr. Westover. In a criminal case, you see, the Runner what brings in the perpetuator shares in the statutory reward. In a private case . . . well, the same sort of compensation is expected if the inquiry reaches a satisfactual conclusion. You take my meaning, guv'ner?"

"Yes, of course." It was an effort not to smile at such twisted eloquence, even if it was extortion.

"And with two men on the job," Hackett continued, "the reward would naturally have to accommodate an equitacious remuneration for each."

Simon gave up the fight and flashed a smile. "I'm sure Sir Richard and I will come to an arrangement agreeable to all involved."

Hackett returned the smile, his eyes crinkling up into mere slits beneath the bushy brows. "It's a true gentleman you are, Mr. Westover."

Simon reached inside his coat, pulled out a small leather purse, and shook out a few coins. "In the meantime, take this for today's expenses." He then pulled a calling card from his a waistcoat pocket, took a quill from Sir Richard's desk, dipped it in the well, and scribbled a note on the back of the card. "Here is the direction of Mrs. Tennant, the runaway girl's aunt. Let her know the instant you discover any news of the elopement."

"Right you are, guv'ner. We'll have the young lady restored to the bosom o' her fambly in no time."

"I hope so, Mr. Hackett. I truly hope so."

Chapter 4

No match is recommended where a critical nature emphasizes petty faults and disallows the full engagement of the heart.

The Busybody

"Of *course* you must accompany Mrs. Tennant on this journey." Constance Poole's steely glare skewered Mr. Westover to the spot. "There is no question about it. She cannot travel unescorted, and she certainly should not be forced to deal with a pair of Bow Street Runners on her own."

Mr. Westover slanted a plaintive glance in Eleanor's direction. She almost felt sorry for the man, but she needed his assistance. It appeared Constance was going to use her most autocratic manner—the one that brooked no challenge—to see that she got it.

After a good, long cry, Eleanor had confessed the entire situation to Constance, who agreed that the erstwhile lovers must be pursued. She also promised to put the full force of her own social standing behind all efforts to hush up the affair and restore Belinda to a respectable position in society.

Eleanor was exceedingly grateful to have Constance's unwavering support, and knew that if Belinda came out of this foolish adventure with her reputation intact, it would be due in large part to the formidable Mrs. Poole. Even so, Eleanor could not disguise her exasperation with her cousin over the subject of the Busybody. Constance had laughed until tears were streaming down her face. She was flabbergasted, and deliciously entertained, to learn that Mr. Simon Westover, and not his mother, was the Busybody. She found it so hilarious, in fact, that Eleanor had almost lost all patience with her.

One had to wonder what all those high sticklers of the *ton* would think to see the oh-so-proper Mrs. Poole chortling and snorting and guffawing in a most unladylike manner.

Worst of all, it had been very clear that Constance did not see the man's perfidy in this business with Belinda. More amused than distressed, she did not seem to understand the seriousness of Belinda's situation.

Until Mr. Westover had returned with a beautiful traveling chariot and the services of two Bow Street Runners. The news of Geoffrey Barkwith's predawn departure had had a sobering effect on Constance. For Eleanor, the news only added fuel to her anger. She was not sure whose neck she most wanted to wring: Belinda's, Barkwith's, or the Busybody's.

"Having been asked for your help in this sorry

business," Constance said, "I can hardly credit your reluctance to join my estimable cousin in her crucial quest to save poor Belinda's virtue."

"My reluctance," he said, "is due to fear of potential harm to Mrs. Tennant's reputation if she were to be seen traveling alone with me in a closed carriage. Surely someone else could accompany her. Perhaps you—"

"Impossible."

Eleanor stepped in to the fray. "My cousin is in a delicate condition and cannot travel any great distance."

As she expected, Mr. Westover's face flushed scarlet. Constance covered her mouth to keep from smiling.

"I beg your pardon, Mrs. Poole," he said. "Someone else, then? Anyone else." The poor man looked positively stricken. "It simply cannot be seen as proper for me to go along."

Constance waved her hand in a casual dismissal. "You are too nice in your sensibilities, sir. My cousin is a respectable widow. No one will dare question her actions."

"Yes, but—"

"Besides, all concern at the moment must be for Belinda. Her reputation is much more fragile than Mrs. Tennant's."

"Yes, but—"

"Under the circumstances, Mr. Westover, I do not believe you have a choice. There is, after all, that little matter of the Busybody."

His head snapped toward Eleanor and his eyes blazed in sudden anger. A tiny knot of guilt momentarily seized her stomach. She had given her word, and lost very little time in breaking it. "Forgive me, Mr. Westover, but it was necessary to reveal your secret to Mrs. Poole. She believed your mother to be the Busybody. She knew I had gone to confront her at Westover House and—"

"And I coerced the information from her," Constance said. "You must not blame my cousin. It was all my doing, but I assure you that your secret is safe with me. It will be, that is, so long as you agree to accompany Eleanor."

She had him there, and he knew it. Another bit of blackmail. The look in his eyes suggested fear that he might be paying for his folly for a long, long time. Though the set of his jaw hinted at restrained anger, resignation marked the slight loosening of his rigid stance.

He would go with her.

"Besides," Constance went on, "I will feel much more confident of my cousin's safety if you are with her."

The twinkle in her cousin's eye sent a chill down Eleanor's spine. In that instant, it became uncomfortably clear that Constance had other reasons for wanting Mr. Westover to accompany her. Dear heaven, what was she thinking? Surely she did not believe that being thrown into close quarters together would foster some sort of romance between them? Did she truly believe that forced proximity would cause Mr. Westover to fall in love with her? She could not possibly think that Eleanor would ever be interested in such a man.

What an idiotic notion. What a foolish, lame-brained, nonsensical idea.

Constance flashed a sheepish smile, and Eleanor knew without question that her cousin had lost her mind.

"I bow to your judgment, ladies," Mr. Westover said. "I will ask one of the grooms to return to Westover House and have my man pack a valise for me. I would do so myself, but I prefer to be on hand if the Runners arrive with news. If you will excuse me." He made a slight bow and left the room. The echo of his brisk tread on the stairs sounded suspiciously like a man running for his life.

As soon as he was gone, Constance collapsed in laughter. "Oh, Ellie! He is adorable! Did you see how he blushed?"

"He is *not* adorable."

"Oh, but he *is*. I cannot believe this is the horrid man you described. I expected a frail wisp of a man with his head in the clouds and inkstains on his fingers. How is it you never mentioned what a tall, handsome fellow he is?"

"I never mentioned it because it isn't so."

"Ellie."

"All right. He is rather tall."

Constance grinned from ear to ear, smug as the cat that swallowed the canary, and her brown eyes sparkled with merriment. "He is tall and slender and beautifully dressed, with a face that might have been fashioned by a classical sculptor. Don't be a fool, my dear girl, just because the man has a charming tendency to blush. He is an extremely attractive gentleman—*extremely* attractive—who will be in your pocket for the next few days at least. You would do well not to waste such a prime opportunity."

"I knew it!" Eleanor pounded the arm of the settee hard enough to raise a cloud of dust. "I knew you had lost your mind. This pregnancy is having a strange effect on you, Constance. You've lost touch with reality. You must have done, or you would never even begin to think what I know you are thinking."

Constance giggled like a naughty schoolgirl. "You have no idea what I'm thinking."

"Yes, I do. You've got some sort of dim-witted idea of a romance. Lord, you're as bad as he is."

"What?" Constance leaned forward, curiosity crackling like electricity in her eyes. "Ellie, has Mr. Westover expressed a romantic interest?"

Eleanor groaned. "Don't be ridiculous. I only meant that you're as much a starry-eyed romantic as he is. Neither of you appreciates the seriousness of the situation. Instead, he's spinning dreams of love for Belinda and you're imagining some sort of romance for me. Crackbrained, that's what you are, the both of you. Blast it all, Constance, what I need right now is clear-thinking, level-headed common sense directed at the problem at hand. It serves no purpose to twirl off into these irrelevant, useless, and thoroughly annoying fantasies."

"Don't be so sure it is all fantasy, my dear. I saw how the man looked at you. Heavens, he could hardly keep his eyes off you. He is *interested*, Ellie. It would do you no harm to show a bit of interest yourself."

Eleanor clicked her tongue in exasperation.

"Honestly, Constance, can you really imagine I'd be attracted to a romantic fool who just may have helped lead my niece down the garden path? I'm furious with the man, for heaven's sake, not smitten by him. Besides, I have always preferred dark-haired men, and his hair is practically red."

Constance only just managed to stifle a crack of laughter as Mr. Westover walked in. He was not alone.

"Good news," he said. "I have just intercepted our two gentlemen from Bow Street, on their way to report a remarkably swift success."

Eleanor rose to greet the Runners, but was distracted by sounds of choking. She turned to find Constance looking near apoplexy as she tried not to laugh. Every aspect of this sorry business seemed a great source of amusement to her odious cousin.

She could hardly blame Constance this time, however. The men standing just inside the doorway, though dressed in nearly identical uniforms, were as different as it was possible to be. One was short, round, and bandy-legged, with bushy hair and eyebrows. The other was well over six feet tall, thin as a rail, and spindly-legged, with pale, limp hair hanging over his collar.

Eleanor could not help thinking that with the somewhat bowed legs of the one and the skinny knocked-knees of the other, they appeared to spell out *ox* as they stood together. It was no wonder Constance had buried her face in a chair cushion, her shoulders shaking with suppressed laughter.

But they were here on serious business, and she hoped they would believe Constance to be overcome with emotion.

Mr. Westover lifted an arm in her direction. "Gentlemen, this is Mrs. Tennant. It is her niece, Miss Belinda Chadwick, who has gone missing."

The round one stepped forward and swept a creditable bow. "Obidiah Hackett at your service, ma'am. And this here is Francis Mumby."

"Good afternoon, gentlemen. You have news of my niece?"

"That we do," Hackett said. "Mumby here has a most superior and prodigitous brain, you see. Unique among the brotherhood of Bow Street. He approaches an inquiry real cerebralistical, like. In this case, with an expedicity beyond all expectations, he located the inn what hired out a post chaise and four to Mr. Barkwith shortly afore dawn this mornin'. And ascertained, with equal perspicasticalness, that a young lady matchin' the description of your niece was in his company."

Somewhere in all that eccentric verbosity—more fuel for Constance's traitorous mirth—was news that brought Eleanor a sigh of relief. "Thank God," she said. "At least we have somewhere to begin. What else did you learn? Do you know which direction they took?"

"Mumby here says they was headed north on the Islington road."

"All right, then," Eleanor said. "Let us be off. There is no more time to waste."

It was decided that the two Runners would leave immediately to ride ahead toward Islington and begin the leapfrog relay that would track the runaways and send word back to Mr. Westover.

A message would be left at the Dolphin in Islington, giving instructions for the next stop. Eleanor saw Mr. Westover slip a money pouch to Hackett, and was reminded how much she would owe him when this was over. She would simply have to remember all the trouble he'd caused with imprudent advice to an impressionable young girl. Weighed in the balance, she figured he might still be found wanting.

His back ached and his legs felt cramped, but Simon kept himself squashed up close against the door of the carriage. Of course, he was being ridiculous. It would not kill him, or her, if he happened to brush his thigh against hers. But if he did so, he was afraid he might be tempted to keep his leg pressed against hers, to feel the warmth of her flesh through the fabric of her pelisse—and have his face slapped for his impertinence.

Dash it all, how was he to endure the long hours, even days, sitting next to this glorious creature, so passionately driven to rescue her young charge? With the fire of determination and urgency lighting her green eyes and tinting her soft cheeks. And the occasional hint of anxiety when she absently chewed her lower lip, causing the full upper lip to grow more deliciously plump.

It was more than flesh and blood could bear.

He began to consider once again the idea of an ode to her upper lip.

Sweetmeat tempting, ripe and lush
Pink tinted with a rosy blush
And kissed by dust of groveland fairies
To taste as sweet as summer berries

Or should that be cherries? Or plums? Or perhaps pomegranates? No, nothing rhymed with pomegranate. He would have to give the object more study, though he was quite certain that *perfect* and *soft* and *delectable* would figure in the verse.

Mrs. Tennant had been chewing her lip more often since picking up the Runners' messages in Islington, then Highgate, and then Whetstone. The two unlikely-looking detectives were certainly earning their pay, and making good time on horseback. But the fugitives were still at least twelve hours ahead of them. If they were lucky, Simon figured they might catch up with them in time for the wedding breakfast.

"Oh, dear. Do you think it's going to rain?"

Mrs. Tennant's voice pulled Simon from his reverie. He looked out the window and up at the gray sky. "Yes, it does look as if it will rain. But not quite yet, I should think. Certainly not before we have stopped for the night."

"Oh, but we can't stop anytime soon. Assuming there is a message at Chipping Barnet, we can continue for several more hours yet. We are so far behind them, we must go on for as long as we can."

"Yes, I am afraid they are at least a half day ahead of us." Simon watched her teeth sink into her lower lip once again. Dragging his attention from her mouth, he concentrated instead on her obvious concern. "I fear, Mrs. Tennant, that you must be prepared for us to be too late."

She turned to look at him through narrowed eyes. "Oh, I am quite certain we will be too late, Mr. Westover. Once they stop for the night, I have no doubt it will be too late for Belinda."

"Oh. Well, then . . ." A telltale warmth spread across his cheeks. "If you believe that to be true, then surely you must support their marriage."

"There will be no marriage."

"You plan to stop it?"

"There will be no marriage to stop." She released

a sigh of sheer frustration. "Are you so naïve? Barkwith will not marry her after tonight. My only hope is to get her back home as quickly as possible and try to hush up the affair. All I want, all I can hope for, is to avoid her complete social ruin."

"They are heading north," he said. "Surely their destination is Scotland."

"Unlikely."

He suppressed a smile at her stubborn resolve. "Mrs. Tennant, I do believe you are a cynic."

"A realist, Mr. Westover."

"You might have a little more faith in your niece. Her letter led me to believe she was very much in love."

"So she thinks."

"And that Barkwith returned her affection."

"Again, so she thinks. But he will break her heart, poor thing."

"How can you be so sure? How do you know he is not in fact madly in love with her and has every intention of marrying her?"

"Because Geoffrey Barkwith is a scoundrel, a cad, a womanizer." Her words were laced with anger and frustration. "He is a notorious libertine who has used his charm and good looks to win his way into more bedrooms than you could count."

"That may be true. But he is also quite young, I believe. He may have been simply sowing wild oats until the right young lady came along—your niece—and captured his heart."

"Bosh. Tell me, were you quite so wild in sowing your own oats, Mr. Westover?"

Dammit, but she seemed determined to make him blush. Or perhaps she would simply believe he had a permanently florid complexion. "Not every man spends his youth chasing the same folly," he said. "If Barkwith is as handsome and charming as you say, he might have had more than a bit of feminine encouragement. Besides, even if he were a rake of the first order, that does not mean he could not have fallen in love with your niece."

She gave a contemptuous little snort. "Next, you'll be lecturing me on how reformed rakes make the best husbands."

He smiled, for that was precisely what he'd been about to say. "Stranger things have happened."

Mrs. Tennant sighed and sank back against the velvet squab. "I don't know why I waste my breath arguing with such an incorrigible romantic. You're hopeless."

"Because I believe in love?"

"Yes."

"And you do not?"

"No, I do not."

Her words shocked him. He'd spent most of his life in the pursuit of love and romance. He could not imagine such disdain for the most important aspect of one's existence. Could she really be so cynical?

No, he did not believe her. She was simply too stubborn to give an inch. "And so you and Mr. Tennant—"

"It was an arranged marriage. Not a love match, I assure you."

She had crossed her arms tightly over her chest and turned her face toward the window. Simon was not sure if she was hurt or angry, or both.

"I'm sorry," he said.

"You need not be. It is the way of the world. The real world, not the make-believe romantic fantasy world you seem to live in."

He ought to let it go, but the sentimentalist in him felt compelled to press on. "And there has never been anyone else? Someone you cared about? Someone you gave your heart to?"

The slightest stiffening of her shoulders warned him that he'd touched a nerve. "You go too far, Mr. Westover. I have no intention of discussing my personal life with you."

There was no need for her to do so. It was clear to Simon that she had indeed cared for someone, once upon a time. But an arranged marriage got in the way, and she'd forgotten what it was like to be in love.

Poor woman. Poor beautiful, obstinate woman.

"Forgive me," he said. "I had no right to ask. I was simply trying to help you understand that what you perceive as a tragedy for Belinda may in fact be a love story with a happy ending in store. You could be mistaken about Barkwith, you know."

"Nonsense. I know exactly what he is up to."

"All right. Let us suppose for the moment that

you are correct. What happens if and when we catch up with them? What do you propose we do?"

"Rescue Belinda, of course."

"And what if she does not want rescuing?"

She turned her fierce, determined gaze upon him, and she was once again Boadicea incarnate. "Then we shall have to kidnap her. Bind and gag her, if necessary. Drag her away kicking and screaming. Anything to get her out of the clutches of that villain."

"Anything?"

"Anything."

Dear God, what had he got himself into?

Once he'd resigned himself to accompanying the lovely widow, Simon had decided he rather liked the idea of having her depend on him. He hoped he might have an opportunity to be her knight in shining armor after all, to be a hero in her eyes by finding her niece and bringing her home to safety.

It had never occurred to him that abduction and derring-do would enter into it.

He was a poet, and she wanted a swashbuckler.

What the devil was he to do?

Chapter 5

Neither absence nor distance nor hardship nor time can ever break those tender ties that bind two hearts in love.

The Busybody

"There is nothing for it, I'm afraid. We're going to have to stop for the night at St. Alban's."

Eleanor pressed her nose to the glass and watched the rain coming down hard outside. It pained her to admit it, but Mr. Westover was right. They would have to stop. Their progress had slowed as rain turned the road to mud. Throughout most of the journey they had been able to watch the actions of the postillions through the front window. But the window was now so splattered with mud it was difficult to see anything at all.

Even in such a well-built, beautifully appointed carriage the ride had become rough. For the last few miles, despite keeping a firm hold on the grip, she had been tossed hard against her long-legged companion more times than she could count. And the gleam in his blue eyes told her how much he enjoyed each encounter.

Men. Gentleman or plowman, they were all alike.

"How long until we reach St. Alban's?" she asked.

"It is less than five miles into town, I believe, though I'm not certain about the location of the Red Lion. In any case, it should not be long."

Eleanor sensed him watching her and it made her uneasy. Constance's words kept returning to taunt her. *He's interested*, she had said. Had she made a huge mistake in asking him to join her?

"I suspect you will be glad to stop for the night, will you not?" he said. "To be out of this carriage at last."

Was it so obvious what she had been thinking? "I confess the jostling about has become a bit tiresome," she said. "But in truth, I am not so happy to stop for the night. It only means more time lost in our pursuit."

"They will have stopped as well."

She spun around to face him. Damn the man for reminding her, for prompting her to envision what would surely take place between Belinda and Barkwith this night. "I know." Her voice sounded chilly and accusatory. "I know."

"I understand your concern, Mrs. Tennant, and I am sorry for it. For myself, I am going to keep good thoughts and assume all will turn out happily."

"Oh, you foolish man. Don't you dare start in again on true love and happy endings."

He chuckled softly. "I cannot help it. I believe in the power of love. I've always been an optimist about such things."

"And it shows with every piece of idealistic advice you dispense as the Busybody."

"Is that so wrong? To offer hope? To encourage young women to reach for happiness?"

"We have been over this ground before, sir. I need not repeat my views on your sometimes dangerously ill-conceived advice."

"True," he said. "But I do enjoy a good debate, and we have nothing else to do at the moment. I should like to hear more about your views on the Busybody's advice. Your enlightened critique could perhaps be of use to me in future articles."

At that moment, another lurch of the carriage brought them bumping up against each other once again. He flashed a wide smile, and for the first time Eleanor noticed the dimples.

Dimples, for heaven's sake. How had she missed them? She supposed he had been somewhat reserved throughout the day. Until now, when the perfectly matched set of indentations twinkled on either side of his mouth.

A smattering of freckles, a tendency to blush, and now dimples. She refused to listen to the insistent echo of her cousin's voice in her head. He was *not* adorable.

"You mock me, sir," she said. "You cannot convince me that you believe my opinions to be enlightened. We are as opposite as . . . as Mr. Hackett and Mr. Mumby."

His smile widened and the dimples deepened. "You are suggesting one of us is narrow-minded and the other broad-minded? Hmm. I wonder which of us is which?"

"You mock me again, sir."

"I am but making conversation to pass the time. Or attempting to do so. And making a poor job of it, apparently. Perhaps you would prefer that we sat in silence."

"No, I would not prefer it," she said and offered a faint smile. "It is just that I am feeling more than a bit prickly after the events of the day. But you are right, Mr. Westover. Conversation is preferable to a strained silence. Even if that conversation results in heated discussion."

"I shall do my best to curb my temper, ma'am."

The laughter in his eyes said he mocked her yet again, but Eleanor did not rise to his bait.

"Let us stick to less volatile topics, then," she said. "Tell me about your family. We can ignore for now the very formidable father who strikes fear in your heart and who, of course, must never learn about your Busybody activities. Unless you would care to explain why it is so important he not find out?"

"No, I would not."

"It does not signify. I can guess the reasons in

any case. We shall disregard the estimable Sir Harold for the moment. Do you have brothers and sisters?"

His eyes had narrowed at the mention of his father, but he smiled at the change of subject. "I have one younger brother, Malcolm."

"Is he like you?"

The dimples flashed again. "You mean is he a foolish romantic with his head in the clouds?"

"No, I meant is he"—she would *not* say adorable—"red-haired?"

"You think my hair red? Hmm. I always preferred to think of it as auburn. That sounds so much more exotic."

It was not exotic. It was practically red.

"But red sounds so schoolboyish, don't you think?" he said, as though reading her thoughts. "Yes, I can see that you do. Well, luckily for Malcolm, I got all the schoolboy hair in the family. But Malcolm got all the brawn. He is a great strapping fellow and sporting mad. I'm afraid I've never been much in the sporting line. Could never hope to measure up to Malcolm in that respect. I was always the skinny, bookish brother. A bit of a scribbler."

Bookish. What could be more useless during a time of crisis? Eleanor was willing to bet he even wore spectacles in private. And skinny? His height probably made him appear thinner than he was, though he was certainly not brawny. The big, strapping brother would probably have proved more useful when they caught up with the run-aways. He could have pummeled Barkwith into mush while she spirited Belinda away. Instead, she was stuck with the brother who'd kept his head buried in books, a romantic scribbler, a man of words when she needed a man of action.

But the wretched man's words were partially to blame for this whole beastly business. She must rely on his words to make everything right again. His words and her determination.

"How did you come to write for a ladies' magazine?" she asked.

He did not answer right away, and Eleanor thought he had not heard. She was just about to repeat the question when he finally spoke.

"I am acquainted with some of the others who write for *The Ladies' Fashionable Cabinet*. They were in need of someone to offer advice to readers on affairs of the heart, and I imagine they figured I—"

"Was the most qualified?"

"I suppose so."

"Why? Have you had an extraordinary amount of experience in affairs of the heart, Mr. Westover?"

He smiled. "Not extraordinary. Just the usual sort of thing, I should think. No, I was asked to write the column because my friends knew that I had modest literary aspirations and an affinity for . . . romance."

"You are a sentimentalist, sir."

He gave a noncommittal shrug.

"It is a wonder that with such strong inclinations

in that direction, you have never fallen in love and married. At least, I assume you have not."

"I am still seeking my heart's desire," he said, and wry amusement glimmered in his eyes. "I fear I have yet to meet the right woman. Not for want of seeking, I assure you. But I keep a great deal to myself. I don't go out much into society. My mother will drag me to an affair now and then, but I confess I have never particularly enjoyed *ton* events."

"Then I am more than ever astonished that you should take it upon yourself to offer advice to young girls when you have so little experience of society. No wonder that advice is so often misguided."

"I am not without experience of the world, Mrs. Tennant. In fact, I—"

"You view the world from the lofty heights of your ivory tower. If you lived more *in* the world, you would understand how unrealistic it is to so cavalierly advise young girls to follow their heart's desire. The romantic heroes of their fantasies either don't exist or are completely unsuitable."

"I write from the heart, Mrs. Tennant, with fond hopes that every young woman, and young man, will set high expectations and strive to achieve them. My responses are based on what I think will bring the most happiness."

"I wonder how many of those girls who followed your advice found happiness?" she said. "Or how many ended up alone and brokenhearted, or bound forever to a sham hero who makes her life a misery, or ruined forever by some cad. Like Belinda."

The carriage hit a deep rut, and the two of them were bounced clear off the bench. Eleanor was almost certain Mr. Westover had knocked his head against the ceiling, but he ignored the discomfort and continued as though they sat relaxed and at ease in his Mayfair drawing room.

"I choose to trust in a more felicitous future for the majority of my correspondents," he said. "I have more faith in love. And dreams. Do you never dream, Mrs. Tennant?"

"Yes, of course I do, but I dream with my eyes open. I know exactly what it is like to live in the real world. For women especially, it is often a bitter reality." The carriage took another bounce and she was thrown hard against his side. She pulled herself away but not before intercepting an intense look in those bright blue eyes. She ignored the odd stirring in her breast set off by that look, and continued the conversation as though no awkward interruption had occurred.

"Your encouragement of romantic ideals in a young woman," Eleanor continued, "does nothing to prepare her for life in the world. It is irresponsible at best, dangerous at worst, to dole out sentiments that offer false hopes of everlasting love and devotion."

"I am afraid I cannot be so cynical on the subject of love. I rejoice in those tender emotions that refine and exalt the human character."

He smiled as she raised her eyes to the ceiling in silent exasperation.

"Nothing is more important in life than love," he said. "And nothing more joyful than two hearts bound in mutual affection."

"But one must be mindful of the future. Those tender emotions of the moment do not last, and that temporary burst of mutual affection most often dissolves into indifference or contempt."

His brows lifted in surprise. "You do not believe love can last?"

"Not your ideal of love, which is based on an illusion of passion and desire. But passion fades."

"And so you would forbid your niece even a short-lived joy? You feel compelled to nip the blossom of love in its full blooming, like a killing frost, simply because you do not believe it will endure?"

Good heavens, when he got wound up he sounded just like the Busybody—overwrought, florid, and oh-so-grandiloquent. "I'll wager you write poetry, too," she muttered under her breath.

"I . . . um . . . I do dabble a bit in verse now and then."

"Yes, of course you do." And she would also wager it was perfectly dreadful stuff.

"I am afraid I do not understand what my attempts at poetry have to do with your opposition to your niece falling in love."

"I am not opposed to Belinda falling in love. With a girl like her it is bound to happen. If it had been almost anyone else, I would not have objected. There was a very nice young man, Mr. Pendleton, who was mad for Belinda. He would have been a perfect match for her. But he did not answer her dreams of a romantic hero. She found him tedious and uninteresting. Now that I think on it, he had reddish hair, too."

Mr. Westover winced. It had been a low blow, but no less than he deserved.

"No, as I have told you and told you over again, what I most object to is the offhand manner in which you sent Belinda running straight into Barkwith's arms without the least concern that he might be objectionable. I do not trust him. If his intentions were honorable, I could accept his lack of fortune. But I know his type. He is not honorable. He will not marry Belinda. Not unless someone holds a gun to his head."

"And when we find them, will you be holding that gun?"

She gazed out at the rain, sheeting down the window like a waterfall, and considered the question. "I don't know. I daresay it will have to wait until we discover if it is necessary." Eleanor sighed with a sudden rush of renewed concern. "Poor Belinda. Poor, foolish girl."

"They ain't been difficult to track." Obidiah Hackett removed his dingy white gloves and dropped them into his upturned leather hat. "Miss Chadwick has very distinctual looks what all the ostlers and postboys recollect in fine detail. Pretty little thing, I gather. But they still got a prodigitous lead. Can't go on in this rain tonight, though. I'll ride out at daybreak and catch up with Mumby." He rummaged in his saddlebag and pulled out a thumb-worn copy of *Cary's Itinerary*. Running his finger down a page, he said, "I'll leave word for you at the Black Bull in Redburn. In the meantime, you can find me in the taproom where I plan to nurse a pint or two and work the chill out o' me bones. If you'll be excusin' me, guv'ner. Ma'am." He nodded toward Mrs. Tennant, then hoisted the saddlebag over his shoulder and made his way toward the public rooms.

Simon noted the concern in her eyes. "Well, at least we haven't lost their trail," he said.

"Yes, I thank heaven for that. I only wish the rain had not forced us to stop so soon."

"We might as well make the best of it. I understand the food here is quite good. I suggest we shake off the dust of the road and settle down to a pleasant dinner. Will half an hour do?"

She agreed, for which Simon was grateful. He had thought she might ask for a meal to be sent to her room. Instead, he was to be given an opportunity to make a better impression on her than he had done so far. He hated that he had got off to such a bad start with her, that she thought so poorly of him. A leisurely dinner in a private parlor would be just the thing to turn the tide in his favor. A bit of flattery, a bit of flirtation—Simon knew a thing or two about wooing a lady.

After arranging for hot water and soap to be sent up to both of their rooms, he made his way to his own bedchamber, situated along the same corridor as hers. It had been a while since he'd made do without Jennings, his valet. But since Mrs. Tennant claimed to have no maid to accompany her, it seemed overindulgent to bring Jennings. Besides, it would do Simon good to manage on his own for a while. Perhaps Mrs. Tennant had a point about his isolated ivory-tower existence. A few days on the road fending for himself would help to clear away some of the cobwebs. The lovely traveling companion was simply an added bonus.

Half an hour later, clean-shaven and sporting fresh linen beneath a dark blue coat and figured silk waistcoat, he knocked on Mrs. Tennant's door. She had changed into a dinner dress of striped Indian muslin tied round the waist with a long sash of embroidered Indian silk—slightly out-of-date but quite pretty. The square neckline, which might have provided an enticing display of bosom, was sadly too high and edged with an unfortunate amount of lace, and he was allowed only a teasing hint of what lay beneath. Her hair, dark as Turkish coffee and with no bonnet to hide its glory, was gathered full in the back in a Grecian style—another bit of feminine lore he recognized from the *Cabinet*—with soft curls framing her face. Those tantalizing curls were still a bit damp, and the faint smell of soap clung to her.

His gaze, as ever, flicked down to her mouth.

The irresistible upper lip pursed slightly, accentuating the enchanting little point that overhung the lower lip.

Though moist and plump to tantalize
A winsome hallmark draws the eyes:
The tiny cusp that dips below
The sweetly curving Cupid's Bow.

"Mr. Westover?"

Devil take it, had she been speaking to him? Simon dragged his thoughts away from the ode and its object. "I beg your pardon?"

"I asked where we might find the private parlor." She was looking at him in such an odd way, he wondered how long he'd been lost in contemplation of her mouth.

"Oh." He gave himself a mental shake. Damn. She already thought him a fool. If he was not more careful, she would think him demented as well. "Oh, I am sorry. I am afraid there were no available private parlors. But there is a formal dining room that appears perfectly respectable."

"I am certain it will do nicely. Let us—"

"I feel obliged to remind you, ma'am, that it is a public place and I still have concerns about your reputation. Misconceptions may be drawn about—"

"Bosh. If we are going to chase my idiotic niece halfway across the country, I am certain there will be more than one occasion when we are seen together in public. If I am not concerned about it, neither should you be, Mr. Westover."

"As you wish," he said, but still hoped to heaven they did not run smack into her stiff-rumped Great Aunt Straitlace. Or some gossipy grande dame of the *ton* on her way into Town. Would the obstinate Mrs. Tennant remain so sanguine if confronted with such a situation? "The inn is quite full," he said, "so the dining room may be somewhat crowded."

"Then let us make haste," she said, and led the way down the long corridor, displaying for his hungry eyes an expanse of ivory flesh exposed by the low back of the dress, almost making up for the too-high bodice.

One ode at a time, he cautioned himself. He would address the gorgeous neck and back later, after the upper lip. And the emerald eyes. And the dark glory of her hair. And the fiery temper. And the mule-headed stubbornness.

Lord, but she was a banquet. A poet's feast. Memories of Mrs. Tennant would keep his pen busy for months.

The Red Lion was a large and luxurious inn. Neither the Mail nor the stagecoaches stopped there; instead it catered to private post travelers, and so was not as rough and rowdy as other inns. Since they did not have to accommodate the quick group meals required of the Mail and coach stops, dinner was leisurely and pleasant.

Tonight, though, it was crowded, and Simon

procured the last available table in the dining room. He ordered their meal and poured the wine when it was brought. Vowing to avoid all topics that might renew discussion of the Busybody, and anything else designed to diminish him in her eyes, he steered the conversation toward more innocuous subjects. He asked about Belinda's father, Captain Chadwick, which led to a discussion of the war, the new Lord of the Admiralty, and renewed rumors of an invasion by Napoleon. Simon was thoroughly enjoying the conversation and the company when the landlord approached their table.

"I do beg your pardon, sir, madam, but I wonder if I might impose upon your good natures?"

"Yes?"

"We are quite full up, as you see. And yet a woman traveling with two young ladies has just arrived, and we have no place to accommodate them for dinner. I wonder, sir, if you might be willing to share your table with them? She is a gentlewoman, I assure you, and the two young ladies are extremely well mannered."

Damn. Here was the very sort of situation he had hoped to avoid. If others were to join their party, what might they think of a beautiful young widow alone in the company of a man of no relation to her? Simon knew exactly what they would think.

He turned toward the entrance where three women stood. One was plump and middle-aged, the other two were quite young and rather wide-eyed with curiosity. He looked to Mrs. Tennant to see how she felt about the matter. She smiled and nodded her head. She was either very stubborn or very naïve. But the landlord had seen her obvious sign of assent, so there was nothing for it. "Yes, of course," Simon said. "We would be happy to share our table. Please send the ladies over."

"Thank you, sir, madam. I am most grateful. I did not wish to turn the ladies away."

Before Simon knew what was happening, three chairs were added to their table, one separating him and Mrs. Tennant, dashing his hopes of at least sitting beside her. He stood as the ladies made their way across the room. The woman was short and round with fat ruddy cheeks and small dark eyes, and wore a fichu so bouffant it gave her the look of a ship's prow. The younger girls followed in her wake, like white-muslined frigates behind a ship of the line. Introductions were made all around. The older woman was Mrs. Fitzhugh of Lutterworth, wife of a local squire. The girls were her daughter, Miss Sally Fitzhugh, and her niece, Miss Delia Banks. They both appeared to be about seventeen or eighteen, each one, in her own way, as plain as a sparrow.

"It is most kind of you," Mrs. Fitzhugh said, "to allow perfect strangers to join you, Mr. Westover and Mrs. . . . Mrs. Tennant, was it?"

Simon almost groaned aloud. It was just as he

had anticipated. Mrs. Fitzhugh was fidgeting nervously with her elaborate demi turban and darting glances about the room as though in search of a more suitable arrangement. Well, dammit, he could not just sit there and be a party to the ruin of the lovely widow's name.

"Mrs. Tennant and I are cousins," he said, and ignored the green eyes he could feel glaring at him from across the table. "We are traveling north together on a family mission. A bit of a crisis, actually."

"Oh?" She looked from Simon to Mrs. Tennant and back. "Nothing too serious, I hope?"

"We trust not," Mrs. Tennant said, and gave him a chilly smile. "In any case, we are happy to have you ladies join us. I can't tell you how pleased I am to have someone else to talk to. We have been cooped up together in that wretched little carriage all afternoon. I am sure my cousin will agree that we are both quite tired of the other's company, are we not, *Simon*?"

Oh, the little she-devil! "Quite so . . . *Eleanor*. Dreadfully tired." He leaned toward Mrs. Fitzhugh and said in a voice of mock vexation, "You know how odious one's relations can be."

"Especially one's tiresome male relations," Eleanor said.

Eleanor. He was going to keep the name. He would not give it back to her and resort to Mrs. Tennant. From now on, she was Eleanor. It suited her—strong and beautiful. Eleanor of the emerald eyes. Eleanor, the avenging angel. Eleanor, of the beautiful, sharp-tongued mouth.

"I know precisely what you mean," Mrs. Fitzhugh said, and accepted a glass of wine from the waiter. "I've never got on well with my male cousins, and my brothers and I quarrel like cats and dogs. But I have always enjoyed the company of my female cousins, and especially my dear sister Ann, Delia's mother, may God rest her soul. And these two girls"—she nodded at her charges, plumes aflutter—"are as close as two inkle weavers. They *will* do everything together."

The woman was clearly satisfied that the proprieties were in order, and had settled in for a cozy chat. "Why, when it was time for my Sally to make her bows in London, she would have nothing of it unless her Delia could come along. And it's only right, after all. Delia's dear mama would have wanted it."

Eleanor smiled at the girls. "How lovely for you. There is nothing so exciting as one's first Season. I hope each of you has a grand time."

Delia, freckled and boasting an unfortunate chin, covered her mouth and giggled. Sally, all sharp angles and big brown eyes, was more self-assured. "Thank you, ma'am," she said. "We plan to have a wonderful time, see all the sights, and attend loads of fashionable events."

Her mother shot Eleanor a look that cast doubt on their activities being as fashionable as Sally might hope. Clearly, the Fitzhughs were not wealthy. The girls' simple muslin dresses had not been designed by or even copied from any of the *modistes du jour*. In fact, Simon would not be surprised to learn they had sewn the dresses themselves. The girls might as well have had the words "country mouse" tattooed on their foreheads.

"There are many exciting things to do in Town," Eleanor said, "and wonderful places to see. You must be sure to go to the Tower and Westminister Abbey, and see the paintings at the Royal Academy."

"Yes, ma'am," Sally said. "We certainly intend to see as much as we can."

"But we mostly want to go to parties and balls," Delia added in a shy voice.

"That's right," Sally said. "You see, we're going to London to meet the men of our dreams, and to come home with husbands."

Eleanor shot Simon a look that spelled danger, then returned her attention to the girls. "Husbands, eh? Well, I wish you good luck and a grand time. But do not be too discouraged if you do not get offers right away. It often takes more than one Season for a girl to attract a husband."

"I'm afraid one Season is all we can afford," Mrs. Fitzhugh said. "If they don't bring any gentlemen up to scratch by summer, I've told them they will have to look more closely about the neighborhood back home."

"Mother!" Sally said. "All the gentlemen back in

Lutterworth are dull as ditch water." She turned to Eleanor. "She is forever trying to foist some up-standing country clod upon us. But we do not want to settle for anyone so ordinary as that, and so we're going to London where there are ten times more gentlemen to be met—dashing, handsome gentlemen who are interested in something other than crop rotation and grain prices. Delia and I want to be swept off our feet by valiant young men who fall madly in love with us."

A moment of stunned silence followed this as-tonishing speech. Eleanor was the first to react. "In-deed?" She turned and met Simon's gaze squarely across the table. "And what do you think, cousin? Do you think these young ladies will find their ro-mantic heroes in Town?"

"I . . . um . . . I do not see how two such lovely ladies can fail to do so."

"Well, I do," Mrs. Fitzhugh said. "I keep hoping they will be more sensible. I love these two, but will be the first to admit that neither is a great beauty. London is sure to be filled with beautiful, rich, and fashionable young women who will garner all the male attention. I don't wish them to be disap-pointed, but I—"

"Mother! You haven't a romantic bone in your body. I don't know why you must always be so pessimistic. Thank heaven there are others who be-lieve differently. Just last week—"

"Yes, yes I know." Mrs. Fitzhugh held up a hand

in defeat. "The Busybody says everyone should seek their heart's desire."

"The Busybody?" Eleanor slanted a glance in Simon's direction.

He wondered if it would be possible to crawl under the table and slink out of the room on his hands and knees.

"Yes," Mrs Fitzhugh said, "that woman who dispenses advice in *The Ladies' Fashionable Cabinet*. The girls live by that woman's words."

"Is that so?" Eleanor said. "And what sort of words are those?"

"Don't you read the Busybody?" Delia's quiet, bashful voice almost squeaked in stunned disbelief. "My goodness, I thought *everyone* read the Busybody. She is *so* wonderful. And so wise."

"She is indeed," Sally said. "And we believe in what the Busybody says. We know we are not beautiful, but we have good hearts. And just last week she said—here, let me read it. I cut it out to keep in my reticule, as a sort of token of hope. She says, 'A young woman of virtue, sensibility, and a tender heart, even if she has neither beauty nor fortune, will ultimately attract the attentions of a worthy suitor. For a true gentleman will always recognize the intrinsic merit in a deserving young lady, and will never withhold his affections merely to satisfy society's ambitions.' You see? There *are* gentlemen out there for simple country girls like Delia and me. The Busybody says so."

"Indeed she does," Eleanor said, and her eyes regarded him with smug amusement over the rim of her wineglass.

"I only hope she is right," Mrs. Fitzhugh said.

"So do I," Simon muttered. "So do I."

Chapter 6

*If a young woman of weak character hopes to bind
her intended husband with any cords except those
of love, she will not be long in discovering her im-
prudence.*

The Busybody

An early start and sunny skies did little to lift
Eleanor's spirits the next morning. A new
day simply meant that Belinda had spent a night
with Barkwith, had thrown away her maidenhood
and very likely her reputation. A gloomy sense of
finality held Eleanor in its grip. There was no
longer any hope of saving the headstrong girl from
taking such a reckless step. All that was left was to
catch up with them, get Belinda away from that
horrid man, and do what they could to cover up
what had happened.

"What is it, Eleanor?"

It was her fault that Mr. Westover had appropri-
ated her Christian name. She had all but given it to
him during that ghastly meal with Mrs. Fitzhugh
and her girls, and he had made frequent use of it
ever since. In truth, she did not mind. The situation

kept them alone together for so many hours on the road, the familiar use of names seemed only natural. But there was something about the way *he* said her name, the way he seemed to savor each syllable, that was oddly unsettling.

She gave him a quizzical look.

He reached out and ran a gloved finger ever so lightly over the bridge of her nose. The delicate touch set off a soft tingling at the back of her neck.

"Your brow is all in knots," he said, "as though something especially troubling weighs on your mind. You are thinking of Belinda, I daresay."

He gazed at her with such genuine concern that she had to look away. Despite all that foolishness with the Busybody, he was a kind man who meant well. If it was true that Belinda had given in to Barkwith last night—and Eleanor had no cause to doubt it—then there was no longer any reason for Simon to continue the pursuit with her. It was too late for any words of the Busybody to help avert disaster. There was nothing much he could do now, except perhaps help to convince Belinda to come back home. He already admitted he was not in "the sporting line," so it was unlikely he would be willing, or able, to beat Barkwith into a bloody pulp, as he deserved. When it came right down to it, Eleanor could probably do the job well enough herself.

Yet she had no intention of releasing Simon from his promise. Though she hated to admit it, she had grown accustomed to his long-legged presence at her side. She was glad not to be alone on such a journey and had begun to find it somewhat comforting to have him next to her. She was even growing a bit fond of his red—all right, auburn—hair and dimples. And sparring with him about his idiotic sentimentalist philosophy kept her thoroughly entertained.

Besides, she needed him. He was paying for everything, after all. She couldn't do this without him.

No, she would not ask him to leave.

"Yes, Belinda is hard on my mind," she said. "I am hoping that Barkwith does not abandon her just yet."

"What? I thought you wanted her out of his clutches?"

"I do. But not until we find her, when I will do whatever it takes to get her away from him. As long as they travel together, however, they can contrive some sort of fiction to lend respectability to their relationship. No doubt Barkwith will pass her off as his wife. But once he abandons her, how on earth will she manage as a young girl on her own?"

"I wish you were not so determined that he will not marry her. He may surprise you."

"It would shock me to the core if he married her."

A smile tugged at the corners of his mouth, and Eleanor found herself watching for the dimples.

"I believe it would indeed shock you," he said. "If I may say so, Eleanor, you are hopelessly unromantic."

"Better that than the unsuspecting wide-eyed romanticism of Mrs. Fitzhugh's girls."

"Ah." He chuckled, and the dimples finally made their appearance. "I wondered when you would return to that troublesome topic. My goodness, how you did relish my discomfiture. I believe you thoroughly enjoyed the evening, did you not?"

"Immensely."

"I confess I have never been confronted face-to-face with any of my readers while they discussed the Busybody. It was . . . interesting."

That made her smile. She could not help it. The thought of a good argument with Simon somehow caused her black mood to fade a bit. Matching wits with him was more fun than she'd had in years. Sometimes she disagreed with him out of sheer playfulness. But not this time.

"Really, Simon, you cannot think those poor girls will find romance in Town. They will be ignored or scorned by every buck and beau up for the Season."

"You assume they will attend *haut ton* events. I think it unlikely, given their rather obvious circumstances. In a somewhat lower level of society, the gentlemen may not be so jaded or callous as their more affluent counterparts. It would not surprise me to learn the girls had each attracted the attentions of some perfectly suitable young men who appreciate their artless country charms."

"You really are an optimist, are you not?"

"I admit it. However, it is more than just optimism that Sally and Delia will find their hearts' desires, but also that they believe enough in themselves to go after it. That is the most important thing to me as I pen advice to young ladies. I want to give them the confidence to hope, to dream, to reach for the stars. Young people, especially young ladies, need self-assurance and strength of character to enter into society. Without a bit of mettle they will find it difficult to succeed. If they are taught to believe in their own worthiness, to believe they are deserving of high regard—and they *are*, for the most part—then that regard is more likely to come to them. A woman of confidence is much more liable to attract a gentleman's attention than one who does not believe she is worthy of his attention."

Eleanor was quite sincerely taken aback. She had been so angry about the wretched advice given to Belinda, it had not occurred to her that there might be *some* merit in the Busybody's philosophy. It was possible—merely *possible*—that the man had a point.

But she was not about to let him know it.

"I still think you do more harm than good," she said, "with your rose-colored idealism. What happens if those girls join the ranks of this Season's wallflowers and return to the country disappointed and dejected?"

Eleanor kept the debate alive for most of the morning as they followed the messages of the Runners from one posting inn to the next. The rains of the day before had made a mess of the roads, and the going was not as fast as the postillions would have liked. The team was made to slog through miles of muck and mire, and the beautiful carriage was so covered in mud, it looked as though it had been retrieved from a bog.

They met up with Mr. Mumby at Pagnell, where the bridge over the River Ouse had washed out and carriages were being ferried across. He was on horseback and leaned down to speak to them through the carriage window. Less voluble than his colleague, Francis Mumby was a man who got straight to the point.

"We're too far behind," he said. "Can't afford more obstacles like this. Unless they crack a wheel or land in a ditch and lose a day's travel, it's gonna be tough to catch 'em afore Gretna."

"But at least you haven't lost their trail," Simon said.

" 'T'ain't hard. It's what yer payin' us for." He led his horse onto the ferry ramp and called over his shoulder, "We'll leave word at the Peacock in Wellingboro."

As they waited for their turn at the ferry, Eleanor watched the Runner gallop away as soon as he reached the other bank. Despite the delays, she was grateful for the Runners' efforts. And for Simon's ability to pay them.

"I do not believe I have properly thanked you for hiring those two," she said. "They are certainly efficient."

"Indeed they are. I determined it would be best to have professionals lead the pursuit. It seemed the only sensible course of action. I do a few things well, but tracking runaways across the country is not one of them."

"I think you are doing a fine job of it," Eleanor said, and then wondered why she had felt the need to reassure him. She must be feeling guilty about all the money he was spending on her behalf.

"Following the footprints of Hackett and Mumby isn't much," he said. "Anyone could do that."

"But no one could keep me diverted half as well as you have done. Arguing with you makes me forget for a time the seriousness of Belinda's situation."

His blue eyes twinkled with roguish delight. "It is my pleasure to distract you, ma'am."

Blast it all, the man was flirting with her again. This time, and quite unexpectedly, she allowed herself a small degree of pleasure in it. She turned away quickly, hoping to hide her smile, and gave her attention to the postillions now leading their team onto the ferry.

It ought to have been a simple thing, to follow the trail of messages left by the Runners, for the runaways had kept to the main roads. But it had become almost as frustrating an experience for Simon as it must surely be for Eleanor, for they had run into one time-consuming obstacle after another.

They had lost considerable time at Pagnell waiting to be ferried across the river. Shortly afterward they had been delayed by what seemed an endless flock of sheep being herded across the road. When the shepherds had stopped to chat and allowed the sheep to roam about in all directions, Simon had been frustrated enough to shout out the window at them to hurry along, which, as he ought to have known, had the reverse effect.

At one of the posting inns they had had to wait for a fresh team—the only available horses were being reshod, and they were forced to await the smithy's pleasure. At the next stop there had been a shortage of postboys, and they had to make do with only one riding postillion instead of two. But he was efficient, even a little bit reckless, and got good speed out of the team.

Until the next obstacle. They came upon a collision between a fully loaded stagecoach and the first wagon of a small Gypsy caravan. It appeared no one had been injured, but the horses had become entangled and the elaborately painted Gypsy wagon had overturned, spilling a profusion of colorful debris across the road.

Simon's was not the only carriage forced to stop and wait for the vehicles to become disentangled and the road to be cleared enough for passing. Gypsy families and stagecoach passengers disembarked and milled about the road while the drivers shouted and cursed at one another. A couple of old women also flung loud abuse at the coach driver in their own language, gesturing wildly, while they supervised the recovery of the overturned wagon's contents.

Some of the Gypsies took advantage of the situation and brought out all manner of items from their wagons to offer for sale. They mingled among the coach passengers, and the various carriages held up by the accident, offering pastries, ale, ribbons, scarves, beads, jewelry, pottery, utensils, herbs, and anything else they were carrying that might be sold. A few women appeared to be reading palms. The sultry strains of a violin could be heard beneath all the commotion.

Simon let his window down, looked to Eleanor, and gave a shrug of resignation. "It looks like we're going to be stuck here for a while," he said. "We might as well get some air. The coach driver will have a schedule to meet, though, and will hopefully be able to move on very soon."

"If we weren't so pressed for time, I might enjoy it all," Eleanor said, and let down her own window. "It is almost like a spontaneous little fair, is it not? How fortunate to be in a chariot so we are able to watch the whole spectacle through the front window."

"Ribbons, sir? Pretty ribbons for the pretty lady?" A black-eyed Gypsy woman held out a handful of colorful ribbons just inside the carriage window on Simon's side. Her head was wrapped in several bright-colored scarves, and she wore a profusion of jewelry, including long, swinging earrings and an enormous brooch holding together a shawl. Gold bracelets reaching almost to her elbow jangled as she waved the ribbons about. "Ribbons? You buy my ribbons?"

Simon shook his head, but the woman persisted. "You buy your pretty lady some ribbons, yes? See how many colors. See how pretty."

The woman looked ready to stand there jingling and jangling for as long as it took for him to capitulate. Simon looked over at Eleanor and winked. "Yes, I do believe the pretty lady needs a ribbon, do you not Eleanor?"

Was it possible the self-assured Mrs. Tennant had turned bashful? She looked positively sheepish. "It is not necessary, Simon."

"Oh, but I think it is." The woman would probably never leave otherwise. "What color would you like?"

"I don't know."

"I'll pick then, shall I? Let me see. What color would be most suitable for Eleanor?" He fingered the ribbons when the woman thrust them farther into the carriage. "Hmm. Red, I think. I'll take a red one, please."

He held out a few small coins to the Gypsy woman in exchange for the ribbon. "*Nais tuke. Zhan le Devlesa tai sastimasa,*" she said and scurried along to the next carriage.

"Lord, I hope that wasn't some sort of Gypsy curse." He laid the ribbon in Eleanor's open hand. "Here you are, then. As the Gypsy said, a pretty ribbon for a pretty lady."

Good Lord, he could swear she was blushing.

"Thank you, Simon. That was very kind of you."

"Kindness had nothing to do with it," he said, and gave her another wink. He took the ribbon from her hand, wrapped it around her wrist, and tied it in a bow. Then he held her hand for a moment and admired his work. "There. It suits you very nicely, I think."

Keeping hold of her hand, he ran his fingers along the silky fabric of the ribbon, brushing against the bare skin just above her glove. He turned her hand over and continued his exploration of the underside of her wrist. The skin there was very white, so pale the blue veins beneath showed clear and dark. And it was very soft, too, like a child's. Even through his own gloves he could sense the softness.

To his delight, she did not pull her hand away, and Simon would swear he noted a tiny tremor dance up her arm. Was it possible this beautiful, self-assured, proud woman was susceptible to his modest flirtations? Was she simply unaccustomed to such attentions? Impossible. Would she allow it if he lifted that pale wrist to his lips, as he was longing to do?

"Why did you choose red?" she asked in a small voice.

Before he could convince himself it was not a proper thing to do, he dipped his head and kissed her hand. He allowed his lips barely to graze the soft skin on the underside of her wrist. She gave a tiny gasp, just a soft intake of breath, but it was enough to encourage his lips to linger a bit longer. He lifted his head, smiled, and said, "It reminded me of you."

"Red?" She laughed softly and retrieved her hand, and, thankfully, did not then use it to slap him for his impertinence. "I would have thought the poet in you might have chosen green. For my eyes. Accompanied by flowery sentiments on my emerald orbs."

He gazed into those green depths and knew he would indeed pay poetic tribute to them someday soon. But the ode to her upper lip had kept his pen busy last night.

Like crimson silk, this lip so fair
Is held a prize beyond compare.
How plump, how ripe this rare confection.
With potent hint of sweet connection.

"Green was too obvious a choice," he said, returning his concentration to the moment. "I decided on red to match your fiery spirit."

She laughed. "My fiery spirit? I am not sure if I should feel complimented or insulted."

"Complimented, to be sure. From the moment you slapped my face, or perhaps somewhat later," he added with a sly smile, "I have admired your ruthless determination to save your niece from ruin. In my mind—my Romantic poet's mind, you will say—you appear as a bold avenging angel, ready to combat anything to ensure her safety, strengthened with righteous anger, like Boadicea taking on the Roman army."

"Good heavens. As formidable as that?"

"As admirable as that."

She gave a little shrug. "Any mother would do the same. It's a powerful instinct, to protect one's young."

He realized in that moment how very little he knew of her. "Do you have children of your own?"

A shadow flickered across her eyes for an instant, but she recovered quickly and said, "I was not so fortunate."

"I am sorry," he said. It was obviously a painful, and very personal subject he ought not to have broached.

"But I have had the care of Belinda these last five years," she said. "She has been like a daughter to me."

"And like a good mother, you shall avenge her, I have no doubt. In fact"—Simon took her hand once again, just for the sheer pleasure of it, and fingered the bright ribbon at her wrist—"let this red band be a symbol of your quest. You must wear it as a sort of talisman until we find Belinda. Then I will remove it myself and retain it, with your permission, as a keepsake of this journey. *And* as a reminder to the Busybody to take more care in the advice handed out."

"A talisman it is, then." She tugged her hand gently out of his. "For both of us. And I shall hold the Busybody to that pledge."

The strains of the violin grew louder as the musician wandered close by. They each grew silent and allowed the melody to waft into the carriage and weave its spell. By turns melancholy and passionate, plaintive and sumptuous, the lush music held Simon captive as it seemed to seep right into his skin. He did not believe he had ever before heard music quite so sensuous. The moment would be perfect, if only he were still holding Eleanor's hand.

He looked to see if she was equally spellbound, and she appeared to be so. Her eyes had become heavy-lidded and her lips were parted slightly, as if the music held her in its hypnotic, seductive sway.

She looked thoroughly, deliciously irresistible. A sudden rush of pure desire swept over him. Simon wanted nothing more than to kiss her right then and there. No, that was not strictly true. He did indeed want more. He wanted to toss her back against the plush velvet squabs and make love to her.

He would do neither, of course. He was a gentleman, and had known her for only two days. They were on a serious mission, not a lark. Besides, she didn't think much of him. She would not relish being kissed by a man she did not respect, a man who was no more to her than an irksome, sentimental fool.

Yet the music moved him, stirred him. He felt a need to be connected to her somehow.

She had placed her hand on the squab beside her. Her fingers were curved and relaxed as she listened to the smoldering melody of the violin. Simon laid his hand next to hers, inching closer, until the kid leather of his glove touched the knitted silk of hers. She did not move, did not even seem to notice.

And so he grew bolder. He arched his little finger and ever so gently rested it atop hers. Still, she did not move or raise her voice to object. Simon closed his eyes and savored the tiny, innocent joining. It was sweet. It was warm.

It was just a beginning.

He lifted his other fingers to bring his full hand to rest over hers—

The carriage jerked into movement. Simon opened his eyes and snatched his hand away. Eleanor had been thrown back hard against the seat and shifted her position on the bench. Had she even noticed his hand—his finger—on hers?

Hell and damnation.

"The stage has moved off to the side of the road," Eleanor said, craning her neck to watch the action. "At last, we can pass. Thank heaven. We have lost so much time. But the music was lovely, was it not?"

It was indeed. Too lovely. It had made him stupid. Thank God he had been saved from making an even bigger fool of himself. For if she had allowed his hand to rest on hers—and he thought she would, after letting him place a fulsome kiss upon her wrist—he would have been tempted to press on, to kiss more than her hand.

The moment was gone, however, and they did not speak of it as they hurried along the road to Market Harboro. It was just as well. He would have spoiled the amity growing between them by pressing unwanted attentions on her. Eleanor had grown less strident with him, seemed to be more in charity with him. She still had little respect for him, because of the Busybody, and the notion galled him. She continued to think him a fatuous fribble because he wrote for a ladies' magazine. But he could not reveal the truth about *The Ladies' Fashionable Cabinet*. It was dangerous enough that she knew Simon to be the Busybody. He could not put others at risk.

So he would continue to suffer her scorn for being the Busybody, but there were other ways to win the good opinion of the very desirable Mrs. Tennant. He had made some progress already: she had let him kiss her bare wrist. It was a small step, but it was something.

The single postillion kept up an almost reckless speed to make up for lost time. The road was muddy from the rains, and the front window soon became streaked and dirty so that it was difficult to see.

The countryside of Northamptonshire did not

offer much in the way of scenery in any case. Even Simon, who was moved by natural beauty in all its forms, could find little to inspire him as they traversed the undistinguished landscape. Once graced with great forests, the land had been almost thoroughly cleared in the last few years to accommodate new enclosures that created a crisscross pattern of hedges, drains, and ditches. Tiny limestone hamlets scattered about interrupted the grid, and an extraordinary number of church spires were silhouetted black in the distance against the dark blue skies of approaching twilight.

They had just driven past one of those squat hamlets when the carriage took a hard bounce, dipped to the left, and jerked wildly. In the next instant, horses shrieking and mahogany creaking, the carriage took a dangerous tilt and came to a noisy, ungraceful, and very abrupt halt, landing half on its side in the thick mud.

Simon was thrown hard against the window. And Eleanor was thrown on top of him.

Chapter 7

The parent who marries off his daughter for monetary gain should be reminded that wealth alone cannot bestow that reciprocity of affection without which matrimony is at best a state of contention and misery, a dreadful prospect for the future of one's child.

The Busybody

She fell so hard against him the breath was knocked clean out of her with a whoosh.

"Eleanor! My God, are you all right?"

Stunned and a bit disoriented, she did a quick survey of her body and found nothing amiss, nothing broken, no great pain. Except that she couldn't seem to breathe properly. She tried to answer him, but found her mouth buried in the stiff, starchy-smelling fabric of his neckcloth. When she lifted her head and said, "Yes," she caught Simon's nose sharply with the brim of her bonnet.

"Ow!" He recoiled as best he could, flattened against the carriage door, which now stood almost, but not quite, horizontal. When he lifted a hand to his nose, his elbow whacked Eleanor on the chin.

"Argh!" Her hand reached instinctively for her abused chin, and her elbow crashed violently into Simon's with a loud thwack.

Trying to get his long arms out of her way, Simon knocked her bonnet askew, causing the ribbons tied beneath her chin to tighten along her jaw almost to the point of strangulation. Lord, he was choking her! She gave a constricted gasp, and Simon, visibly alarmed, fumbled about trying to loosen the bow. But in doing so he somehow managed to pull her sharply down so that their foreheads crashed together with a resounding crack.

They groaned in unison and lay silently face-to-face, each of them breathing heavily. Then, lifting her head, Eleanor looked down into Simon's perplexed face and choked on an uncontrollable gurgle of laughter. It bubbled up until she could no longer contain it, and she lowered her head to his shoulder and gave in to the absurdity of the moment. Simon's laughter joined her own, and his body beneath her rumbled with it so that she bounced up and down atop him. One of his arms was squashed beneath her. He snaked the other tightly around her waist, holding her close so she would not fall.

She lifted her head at last, blinking away the moisture from her eyes. "Don't move an inch," she managed between chuckles, "or one of us is likely to kill the other."

His eyes twinkled with mirth as she gazed, smiling, down at him. But all at once he stopped laughing and his expression darkened with something more intense. Eleanor sobered and met his gaze squarely. A heavy silence fell between them. Her face mere inches from his own, their eyes locked, their breath mingled. She suddenly became aware of the unbecoming and thoroughly improper nature of her position as she lay sprawled and ungainly on top of him.

Simon was the first to break the silence. "Are you truly all right, Eleanor?" Anxious blue eyes studied her face. "You are not injured? You are not hurt?"

"Aside from the whacking you gave me, I believe I am unharmed." Disconcerted by her sudden, unsettling awareness of him, she wanted to get away. She shifted her weight a bit, but Simon held firm.

"You're certain?" he asked.

"Yes, I am quite all right. Just shaken and flung about like a pair of hazard dice. And irritated at the prospect of yet another delay. Drat it, we seem to have nothing but bad luck. Maybe that *was* a curse the Gypsy woman spoke. Now if you will just let me go—"

"Oh, I do not think I should do that." Wry amusement, and something else, glinted again in his eyes. "I think I should do this instead."

He brought his arm up from her waist and snaked a hand beneath the bonnet to rest on the back of her neck. He pressed her head down to close the distance between them, and kissed her.

It was a gentle kiss, not urgent or hungry or particularly passionate. It was a simple meeting of lips. Even so, it sent shafts of heat darting through Eleanor's body and awakened a terrible yearning she thought she'd overcome years ago.

She pulled back, a bit frightened at her reaction, at how tempted she was to let him take the kiss to another level. But she could not allow that. It would be too dangerous. Besides, now was not the time or place for such foolishness.

"Let me go, please."

He did, and Eleanor wriggled herself slowly and rather clumsily into an upright position, straddling his waist. She looked down and found the merriment gone from his eyes and replaced by an intense and horribly disconcerting gaze. Even worse, she could not fail to recognize what her rough movements had inadvertently brought about. She froze at the realization of his arousal. Their gazes locked for another charged moment before she got hold of herself and crawled off him.

She refused to consider what had just happened and gave herself over to the business of getting out of the carriage. It was awkward in every possible way. She pushed open the door above her with some difficulty—the angle made it almost impossible to keep it from closing again. She had to hold it open with one hand and swing herself, very ungracefully, up and out, all the time giving the still prone Simon a view of much more than any man had a right to see. Once she had all arms and legs out of the door, she slid down to the road with a splat, landing in mud up to her ankles.

So much for her second best pair of half boots.

The horses were frightened and dancing about while the poor lone postboy darted between them trying to keep them calm and untangled as they heaved against their harnesses. They made their unhappiness clear in a barrage of whinnies and snorts. "Are you all right, ma'am?" he shouted to her over the cacophony of discontent.

"Yes, thank you. And you? The team?"

"They're just confused an' all. They'll be fine once we get this rig upright ag'in. What 'bout Mr. Westover? Is he injured?"

Eleanor was ashamed to realize she did not know. She had never bothered to ask. The carriage door had slammed shut after she'd got herself out and had remained shut. Wrenching her feet from the mud, she had to half crawl over the carriage to reach the door and open it again. Poking her head sheepishly inside, she found Simon exactly as she'd left him. He had not stirred an inch. Good God, was he hurt?

"Simon, are you injured? Dear heaven, why didn't you say something? Can you move at all?"

He stared at her for a moment with an unreadable expression in his eyes, then drew a deep breath and began to shift his weight. "Yes, I can move. I am quite unharmed." He had to twist his long legs into a contorted arrangement, but was then able to lift himself up and swing out of the door with rather astonishing catlike grace.

Eleanor, on the other hand, fell to her knees when she let go of the door. Simon, pristine but for his boots, reached out and pulled her to her feet. She looked down at her dripping skirts and pelisse and swore beneath her breath, cursing the heavens for more than mere mud.

She did not appreciate the niggling and entirely unwelcome little stirrings, low in her belly, brought about by this contrary, provoking, odious trouble-maker. Not only was it the wrong time and place for such nonsense, it was the wrong man. He was a foolish Romantic with his head in the clouds. He had a perfectly silly occupation and was afraid to stand up to his own father. He wrote horribly overblown prose, and probably worse poetry. Some might find his blue eyes, straight nose, and classic cheekbones handsome, but that did not sig-nify. Besides, there was that red hair. He might call it auburn, but it was red. Dark red. And Eleanor had never liked red hair.

He was not remotely adorable. She had no busi-ness feeling anything but contempt for the wretched man whose advice had sent Belinda into the arms of a scoundrel. Any other feelings must be stopped. Now. At once.

The object of her muddled thoughts was confer-ring with the postboy and helping to manage the horses. He then set about examining the carriage.

"The axles are sound," he reported, "and the wheels are unbroken. The damned thing is simply stuck. Once it is pulled out of the mud, it should be fine."

Not for the first time, Eleanor reflected on how unfortunate it was to be saddled with the skinny, bookish brother. The brawny, sportsman brother would have been more useful in the current situation. With only Simon at hand, however, she figured there was nothing for it but to lend her assistance. Her garments were already filthy, so a little more mud would certainly do no harm. She unbuttoned her pelisse, which was too close-fitting to allow free movement, and began to shrug out of it.

"What the devil are you doing?" Simon asked, his brows lifted in wary surprise.

Eleanor nodded her head toward the stuck back wheel. "I believe if the two of us work together, we may be able to work it free."

"Are you out of your mind?" He stared at her as though he thought she must be. "Do you realize how heavy this carriage is? It may appear light because it is so much smaller than a four-passenger coach, but it is deceptively sturdy, with an extremely solid undercarriage. And even if it were lightweight, do you think I'd allow you to attempt to lift it? Dash it all, Eleanor, you could injure yourself."

"Not if we worked together. You cannot—"

"I will not have you lifting this carriage, so you can stop arguing right now."

"Simon, if you refuse to allow me to assist you, then we'll have to wait for help. And who knows how long that could be? But you and I could—"

"Go help Meeks with the horses. He needs your help more than I do. I will need them to pull out as soon as I have this thing upright again."

"But I—"

"Dammit, Eleanor, do as I say. You're always harping on me to be sensible. Well, this time it is you who must be sensible. It is much more important that you help manage the team. Now, get out of my way. And as soon as I give the word, get those horses moving."

Eleanor stood gaping at him while he removed his jacket, waistcoat, and cravat, pulled the carriage door open—no easy task at that angle, as she knew—and tossed the garments inside. She was still gaping when he turned back around and stood facing her in white shirt, buff pantaloons, and top boots. He looked . . . different.

"What are you waiting for?" he said irritably. "Go!"

She could hardly believe it. He really thought he could do this alone. He would no doubt cause himself an injury, and then where would they be? She did as he asked, though, and went to help Meeks. The postboy mounted the left leader, and Eleanor held the harness of the right wheeler while she watched Simon.

Coatless, he was not so skinny after all. What she had assumed to be the flattering effect of good tailoring was in truth a very good set of shoulders. He rolled up the sleeves of his shirt to his elbows, revealing well-muscled forearms furred with dark red hair. The same auburn hair peeked out from the now open collar of his shirt.

Was this thoroughly masculine creature her misty-eyed, head-in-the-clouds poet? Eleanor stood mesmerized by the transformation. She thought back to that awkward business in the coach. If she'd had her wits about her she would have realized the body she was clasped so tightly against was no thin-boned weakling. She remembered what else she knew of that body, and her cheeks flared.

From her angle, she could not see all that he did, and after some testing and adjusting, he seemed to disappear altogether.

And then the carriage moved.

"When I call out," he shouted from somewhere behind it, "start pulling."

Creaking and groaning, the carriage shifted inch by slow inch to an upright position. Simon, grunting with effort, came into view at last, in a squat position as he pushed the vehicle from below. The muscles of his neck, thighs, and arms flexed taut with the massive weight of the vehicle, and his teeth were bared in a grimace. He was moving it! He was going to free the wheel.

Just when she thought he'd done it, he continued to push and the carriage began to tilt slightly in the opposite direction.

Good Lord, he was going to overturn it again.

But then he shouted, "Now!" and Meeks started the leaders moving. Eleanor had little to do but guide the wheeler straight, and the team began to pull hard. In only a few steps, the stuck wheel came free with a jolt, and the horses flew ahead, pulling the released carriage. Eleanor stepped quickly out of the way. Meeks slowed the team and led them to a drier stretch of road up ahead before bringing them to a halt.

Eleanor turned back to look at Simon. Covered in mud, he was bent over, hands on his knees, and taking in great gulps of air. His face was flushed, but for once it was not from embarrassment.

Eleanor could not help staring. He was not adorable. He was magnificent.

Simon straightened, and every muscle in his body screamed in disapproval. Lord, he was going to be sore tomorrow. But at least the damned carriage was still intact. He had better check it out, though, before going any farther.

Extricating his boots from the thick mud, he began to slog toward the carriage. Eleanor stood like a statue in the middle of the road, staring at him. He looked down to find he was covered in mud. His shirt clung to him like a second skin. Lord, what a fit Jennings would have to see him like this.

"I suppose I look a fright," he said, and chuckled at the thought of his valet's ire when he returned home with ruined clothes and dull boots. He looked back up and noticed Eleanor's skirts were thick with mud from the knee down, as were her sleeves from elbow to wrist. The Gypsy's bright red ribbon, though, must have been protected by the cuff of her pelisse, for it stood out like a beacon amidst the mud. She had a muddy streak across one cheek and a delightful smudge at the end of her nose. Her bonnet listed to one side, its ribbons limp. He grinned at the sight of her.

"I may look a fright, but if I may say so, Eleanor, you are not exactly spotless yourself. What a pair we make."

She did not speak, but only stared, her green eyes wide with . . . something. What the devil was the matter with her? Was she so shocked to see a man covered in mud? She did not strike him as the type of prudish woman who was horrified by the sight of a man in his shirtsleeves.

Recollecting their brief kiss, and how boldly she had pressed against him in the overturned carriage, he did not believe she was prudish at all. Though their kiss had been almost chaste, there was no doubt in his mind that she had been very much aware of his arousal. There had been that heated moment when their eyes had locked before she came to her senses and rolled off him. So heated that he had remained behind afterward to get control of himself. Even now, he had to fight against the memories of her lips against his, her soft, round breasts pressed against him, the almost unbearable carnality of her untangled legs straddling his tight groin. Then there had been the sight of those shapely legs as she crawled out of the carriage.

No, she was not prudish. Or helpless. If he had to guess, Simon would say that Eleanor was a very self-possessed woman who nevertheless was not entirely comfortable with her sexuality. She was a woman of passion insofar as her convictions were concerned, and probably in other areas of her life as well. But he would wager a monkey she did not often allow physical passion to overcome her. A pity, that. One day he would like to see what he could do about releasing that passion. Of course he would have to change her opinion of him some-how. She didn't much like him, and at the moment he looked about as appealing as a swamp rat.

But what the devil was she staring at? He looked down at himself again to see what held her atten-tion and saw nothing but mud. "What? What is it?"

"Hmm?"

"Why are you staring at me, Eleanor? Have I sprouted horns, or a barbed tail?"

"Oh." She shook her head as though to clear it. "I am sorry. It is just . . . You were . . . My goodness, but that was a spectacular feat."

Good God, was that a spark of admiration in her eye? The tiniest spark? Well, well, well. Simon straightened his stiff shoulders and puffed his chest out like a cock of the walk. "It was nothing," he said, lying, for he had in fact strained every muscle in his body. But to have this woman's admi-ration was worth almost anything.

They walked to the carriage where Meeks held the restless team. The postboy had done an excellent job, and Simon thanked him. He would slip the fellow an extra coin or two at the next post. Simon made a more thorough examination of the wheel and found one of the spokes to be cracked. "Blast. This will have to be mended. How far to Market Harboro, Meeks?"

" 'Bout four miles, sir."

Simon tested the wheel again. "If we keep a modest pace, I think it will hold until then. But we will have to have it repaired when we get there."

"I assume that means we get no farther today?" Eleanor asked in a resigned tone.

"I'm afraid so. We cannot risk it with this wheel. It could break and throw us in a ditch next time."

"That would not signify," she said. "I could hardly get any dirtier."

Simon laughed. "True, but you might crack your head next time. No, the thing must be repaired. Besides, I believe I would sell my soul for hot water and soap."

She gave a wistful sigh. "As would I."

"Then let us be off. Meeks, get us to the Swan in one piece and there will be an extra half crown for you."

"Right you are, sir."

They hauled themselves and their mud into the carriage and were soon moving along at a conservative pace, with Meeks carefully quartering the team, maneuvering in a zigzag pattern back and forth across the road to avoid any ruts and potholes.

Simon was miserably uncomfortable. The damnable mud was drying, and his shirt felt stiff in some places, sodden in others. And it smelled. He lifted the formerly white lawn from his chest and found that the mud had not seeped through to his skin. He would have it off, by God.

"Turn your head, Eleanor. I cannot bear this mud another moment." She snapped her head toward the window, and he smiled at her discomposure. He undid the linen buttons and carefully eased the garment over his head, leaving streaks of mud in its wake. Cautiously turning the ruined garment inside out, he used the relatively clean underside to wipe the mud off his chest and arms and face. Then he flung the filthy mess onto the floor and kicked it aside. He retrieved his coat, wriggled into it, and buttoned it as best he could while seated. It left a V of bare chest, but he supposed it was better than nothing.

"It is the best I can do for now," he said. "Not precisely indecent, but not a model of propriety, either. I apologize, Eleanor, but I daresay the carriage and our muddy garments will be evidence enough of our misadventure when we arrive at the Swan, and hopefully I will be forgiven a certain *déshabillé*."

Eleanor turned to face him and her gaze immediately dropped to his chest. She looked abruptly away. Damn. His state of undress obviously unsettled her and so he reached for the discarded neck-cloth, wrapped it once around his neck, and tucked the ends into the coat. There. Considerably less bare skin. Nothing to discomfit her now.

Or had it been something else entirely? There had been the kiss, after all, which he was fairly certain she had enjoyed before she pulled away. He also recalled that intriguing glimmer of admiration he was almost certain he'd seen earlier. He hoped he'd seen it. No, he *had* seen it. She had admired what he'd done.

His partially covered chest puffed up again with a ridiculous pride.

"I thought you said you were not in the sporting line."

She had barely spoken since entering the carriage, and her sudden unexpected words took him aback. "I was not aware hauling carriages out of the mud was a new Corinthian pastime."

"That is not what I meant."

"Then what?"

"You said your brother is the sportsman and you are the bookish one."

"Ah. You think because I do not spend my days sparring with Gentleman Jackson or crossing swords with Henry Angelo that I am a mollycoddled milksop?"

She did not answer right away, and his confidence deflated a bit. The damned stubborn woman was determined to think badly of him. "Yes, I suppose that is precisely what you think."

She turned to face him. Her green eyes, clear and steady, fixed on his. "No, you surprised me, that is all. You were the one who claimed to be the skinny, bookish brother, and I believed you. I didn't think you could do it."

That tiny spark of admiration flickered again in her eyes. He was sure of it.

"My father would not allow either of his sons to be weaklings," he said. "He forced us into every sort of strenuous physical activity from the time we could walk. But Malcolm has always enjoyed it more than I do. He pushes himself to excel in all manner of activities that hold absolutely no interest for me. I would never dream of dropping everything to travel a hundred miles or more just to see a mill. He's also much broader than I am. Next to Malcolm I am positively puny. And I am most definitely the bookish brother. I would be astonished to learn he reads anything more than *The Sporting Magazine*."

Eleanor smiled. "In any case, I am grateful you are not the scrawny, delicate brother you would have had me believe. But for you, we might still be sitting in the middle of the road waiting for help to arrive. Your efforts have saved us a great deal of time."

Simon could not hold back a smile. He had gained a modicum of respect from her. It pleased him more than he could ever have imagined. "Thank you," he said. "But recall that we are not gaining any time at all. Meeks is taking it easy, thank goodness. But regardless of how long it takes us to get there, we must stop for the night at Market Harboro and get the blasted wheel repaired."

"And wash off the mud."

"Lord, yes. The poor coach looks as bad as we do. I'll ask to have it washed down while the wheel is being fixed."

"With our luck, it will begin pouring rain any moment and you won't have to bother."

She offered a smile and looked so thoroughly enchanting, he had a powerful urge to touch her face and wipe away the mud from her cheek. But he did not want to tamper with the meager progress he'd made today. Yes, she'd let him kiss her, but it had been more sweet than passionate. He would not rush his fences. He wanted that tiny germ of admiration he'd seen to grow and prosper. Nothing would please him more than to shake off the mantle of the Busybody and appear to her as a man. An ordinary man who also happened to be a hopeless Romantic, who adored women, and who was coming to adore this one beyond all reason.

Chapter 8

The gentleman who abandons the suit of a fine young woman from such unworthy motives as lack of fortune or rank does not deserve happiness and is unlikely ever to obtain it.

The Busybody

They arrived in Market Harboro not a moment too soon. If Eleanor had been forced to sit in her muddy clothes for another minute, she thought she might have started screaming. Or perhaps removing the offending garments, as Simon had done. He still looked as grimy and mucky as she did, but at least he'd been able to make himself a bit more comfortable.

The sight of his bare chest had made her anything but comfortable. Thank heaven he had partially covered it with his neckcloth. Even so, it was another reason to be glad this leg of the journey was coming to an end. Neither of them mentioned the kiss. Eleanor preferred to pretend it had never happened. Simon probably thought it too insignificant to mention.

It was late, and the town was relatively quiet,

with only a handful of markets still doing business. One of them was situated beneath a lovely old timber-frame structure raised above the street on oak legs. Just beyond it was a church with an impressive spire overlooking the town. Eleanor remembered both distinctive buildings from another time she had come through the town, many years before. It was not a time she cared to dwell upon.

"Ah. This must be the Swan."

She looked to the other side of the High Street and saw that he must be right. Overhanging a handsome bow-fronted building was a fabulously intricate wrought-iron grill with a painted swan in the center. The postboy steered the team through an arched entrance just beneath the large sign, and Eleanor expelled a breath in a long sigh.

Simon smiled. "I feel just the same," he said. "I am sick to death of all this dirt."

When the carriage came to a halt, Simon leaped out and took a quick look at the back wheel. He then came to the other side and helped Eleanor down. "Not a moment too soon," he said. "That wheel is about to go. Let me arrange for our rooms, and then I will see about getting it repaired."

The innkeeper, a barrel-chested, cheerful man who introduced himself as Mr. Pettigrove, was extremely solicitous and sympathetic about their accident. He also had a message from Hackett, which he promptly turned over to Simon.

"Still on the trail," Simon reported after scanning the note and handing it to Eleanor. "That is good news, anyway. Derby is the next stop where they were seen. We're to find more instructions there at the King's Head." He turned to address the innkeeper. "I hope you can accommodate my cousin and me. Two bedchambers and a private parlor?"

Eleanor did not object to being cousins for another night. She was too tired to protest in any case. Thankfully, the rooms were available. Or perhaps Simon had ensured their availability by slipping the innkeeper a few coins. She sincerely hoped Simon was as rich as she assumed him to be, for she was certainly costing him a great deal of money. How was she ever to repay him for such generosity? With a few kisses? Or would he expect more?

The innkeeper's wife showed Eleanor to her bedchamber while Simon went to see about the wheel. Plump and round as a Christmas pudding, with gray corkscrew curls peeking out from an enormous mobcap, Mrs. Pettigrove made sure a fire was lit and the shutters drawn. She fussed and fretted over the sorry state of Eleanor's clothes, chattering without pause the whole time.

"All this horrid mud! It's a right shame, it is, the state of the roads these days. Well, it's no use complainin', I expect. Can't stop the rain, can we? Here, let me help you out of these things, dearie. Oh, will you just look at this nice pelisse. But don't you worry. We'll dry it by the big fire in the kitchen and that mud'll brush right off, you'll see. Oh, but this muslin dress tut, tut . . . it'll have to be washed out.

And will you look at that? The mud soaked clear through to your chemise. You'd best give me that, too. Turn around, dearie, and I'll unlace your corset."

The woman continued to chatter nonstop as she helped Eleanor out of her clothes and into her wrapper. She also took the dress Eleanor was to wear for dinner and draped it by the fire to let out the wrinkles.

"I'll just take the rest of these things downstairs and we'll get 'em all cleaned up for you," the land-lady went on. "You'll have 'em back afore breakfast or my name ain't Pettigrove. A little mud never ru-ined nothin'. Oh, and just look at those boots. You be sure to put them out tonight and our boy'll take care of 'em. You might as well give me them stockin's, too, dearie. I'll have 'em washed out with the dress. Now you just sit right and tight and I'll have some nice hot water and soap sent up and then you'll feel much better, eh?"

When she had gone, Eleanor sank down onto the feather bed, exhausted by the events of the day as well as the woman's incessant chatter. She fell back against the billowing mattress and savored luxurious solitude. There was much to think about, all of it upsetting in one way or another.

She forced other matters aside and gave consid-eration to Belinda. Though her niece's plight had always been uppermost in her mind, Eleanor had allowed other concerns to occupy her thoughts today, and she felt guilty for it. Belinda's safety was the only thing that mattered. She must never forget that.

She and Barkwith were still on the road and apparently together. Where was he taking her? The Midlands area was prime hunt country. Lots of men kept hunting boxes in the Shires. Had Barkwith borrowed the use of one from a friend, one that sat empty now, out of season? Wherever it was, Eleanor had faith in Hackett and Mumby. They would find the place. If only Belinda could be trusted to stay there and not go flying off on her own when she discovered the truth.

Barkwith, though, would be unlikely to spoil his game so soon. He would keep Belinda in a daze of physical passion for a bit longer. And the poor girl would be so in love, she wouldn't realize what was happening.

Ah, Belinda.

And what about Benjamin? Would her brother toss Eleanor out on her ear when he found out what a careless guardian she'd been? What would she do then? Return to her parents' home? No. Not that. She would never go there again. Perhaps Constance would help her find a position as companion to a respectable older woman.

A chambermaid arrived with hot water, soap, and towels, and Eleanor set about washing off the dirt and mud of the road. She would have loved to soak in a deep tub filled with hot, scented water, but she supposed such a luxury was too much to ask at a coaching inn, and would have to wait until she returned home.

She wondered when that would be. How much longer before they caught up with the runaways? Her thoughts drifted again to all that lay ahead for Belinda, the crashing depths of despair after such heights of joy and passion. Her heart ached for the girl, even at the same time she wanted to throttle her.

Eleanor poured the hot water into the ceramic basin and removed her wrapper. She dipped a coarse cloth into the water and began to wash. Lord, but it felt good to be clean again. While she scrubbed away the day's grime, her mind drifted to the events of the afternoon. The ribbon at her wrist, which she was inexplicably loath to remove, reminded her of the Gypsy woman, and she wondered again if her words had been a curse. Given all that had happened, all the delays in this journey, it was a definite possibility.

And then there was Simon.

She *would* think of him while she stood naked in the middle of the room. Damn the man and his lean, muscled body and his bare chest.

Eleanor's new opinion of Simon both confused and disturbed her. It had been so much easier to feel contempt for a man she did not respect, whose opinions she scorned, and who was not at all attractive to her. His romantic idealism, which she despised, had colored her perception of him as a man, so that she had considered him weak in every way.

It was disconcerting to admit she had been wrong on several counts. She still could feel little but disdain for his role as the Busybody, though she was coming to accept that his underlying philosophy might be built on more than romantic pipe dreams. His convictions, wrong though they be, were as strongly held as hers.

Strange, but it had taken a display of physical strength for her to recognize other strengths in him. Or was she only trying to convince herself she was not that shallow, not that easily impressed, and that it was not merely his physical attributes she found attractive?

Yes, absurd as it seemed, she did indeed find him attractive. She wondered if she had thought so all along but suppressed the idea because of his role in Belinda's flight. Constance had certainly found him attractive. Actually, she'd found him adorable, and she probably hadn't even seen the dimples.

Eleanor finished washing and stood close to the fire while she dried herself off. She shook out the dress Mrs. Pettigrove had draped over the chair. It was the same one she'd worn last night. Would Simon notice? Did she care if he did?

It had been a long time since Eleanor had allowed herself to be interested in a man. She did not *want* to be interested. It was too dangerous.

For now, though, there was Belinda to worry about. Until she was found and her situation resolved, Eleanor could not afford to be distracted by anything else.

Sometime later, clean and dressed, she joined Simon in the private parlor he had hired for their supper. It was a small, cozy room with old wood paneling, comfortable furniture, and a fire blazing before an elaborate iron fireback that recalled the inn sign. Simon stood when she entered. He spoke over his shoulder as he walked to a sideboard and poured a glass of wine. "You will have to make do with only myself tonight," he said. "No mothers and daughters to entertain us."

"What a pity. You might have further honed your advice-giving skills." She accepted the glass he offered and noted his smile when he saw the red ribbon still tied around her wrist. She had told him she would not remove it. It was to act as a reminder of her mission to find Belinda, nothing more, and she saw no reason it should make him smile. She sat in the chair he pulled out for her at the round pedestal table in the center of the room, and glanced over her shoulder when he seemed to linger a bit longer than necessary. What was he staring at? Simon picked up his wineglass and went to stand near the fire, and Eleanor took the opportunity to study him while he updated her on the carriage wheel.

Having once admitted to herself that he was good-looking, she wondered how she had ever thought otherwise. He was beautifully dressed, as always, in pristine linen, a bottle green coat, and striped silk waistcoat, and she now knew the clothes that looked so well on him owed much to the body beneath. His face was equally well shaped, with the clean lines and planes of Greek sculpture, set with eyes the color of a summer sky. Though she'd always preferred dark hair on a man, she was beginning to think auburn hair was really rather attractive. Even though it *was* a dark red, at least Simon's hair wasn't carroty orange. It was more like burnished copper. It was also thick and slightly wavy, and made one wonder what it would feel like to run one's fingers through it.

Heavens, what was wrong with her? Run her fingers through his hair? How perfectly ridiculous.

"I hope you aren't too disappointed, Eleanor."

And now perfectly embarrassing as well. She had no idea what he was talking about. "I beg your pardon?"

He smiled, showing even, white teeth. And dimples. "Have you heard anything I've said?"

"I'm sorry, Simon. I was woolgathering." She certainly was, but the last thing she wanted was for him to know he had been the object of her thoughts. It would not do to have him getting the wrong impression. She was much more comfortable when they argued. "Tell me again why I am going to be disappointed?"

"I was saying that the wheelwright will not have the spoke repaired until after ten tomorrow morning. If you were hoping for an early start, I'm afraid it's simply not possible."

"Oh, blast! Another wretched delay. I wonder if we shall ever find Belinda."

"Perhaps they've had equally bad luck on the muddy roads and are not so far ahead as you might think."

"Far enough. Two nights together already."

Simon pulled up a chair and sat across the table from her, bringing with him the wine decanter. Her glass was still almost full, but he refilled his own and took a sip before speaking.

"I know how distressing this must be for you," he said.

"It is worse than distressing, I assure you, to realize that Belinda has more than likely thrown her life away for that man. Do not assume you know how I feel."

"I'm sorry, Eleanor. For everything, truly. I know you do not wish to hear this, again, but they *are* still heading north. They have so far kept to the primary coach route that will take them straight through Carlisle to Gretna. They may be—"

"No, they are not going to Gretna. I have told you so, over and over."

"Is there something you are *not* telling me? Something that makes you so certain of Barkwith's plans?"

There was a great deal she was not telling him. "I know his type, that is all. He may have taken her to a hunting box somewhere right here in the Shires."

"Just for the sake of argument—"

"Which you are forever instigating on this topic."

"—let's say they do go to Scotland and marry. Just pretend for a moment that it happens. What would you do?"

"Do? There isn't much I *could* do in such an unlikely situation, is there?"

"Would you accept it?"

"Yes, of course. I would prefer it above any other outcome, in fact. It is the only solution that allows Belinda to retain some level of respectability. Though heaven only knows what sort of life she would have with that man."

"She loves him, you have said."

"As if that mattered."

"People who love one another often find contentment together for the rest of their lives. Love can transcend the years, you know."

"Bosh. Another one of your romantic fantasies."

"I'm sorry you do not believe in the longevity of marital happiness. It is a life's goal for many."

"An unachievable goal. Passion is short-lived. Once that fire is out, there is little to keep a marriage warm."

"What a sad pronoucement. I suspect your own unfortunate experience, an arranged match apparently without love, has colored your attitude. Have you never known a happy marriage? Your parents, perhaps?"

"My parents had nothing but contempt for each

other. Once my mother had done her duty and presented a son, she felt free to engage in a string of love affairs matched in numbers only by those of my father. I am told I was the result of a moment of madness never again repeated."

"Good Lord, no wonder you are cynical. But surely you have known other happy marriages? What about your cousin, Mrs. Poole?"

"Constance is a dewy-eyed romantic. Rather like you, in fact. Against all odds, she is still madly in love with Mr. Poole after eight years and four children. Her period of marital bliss has lasted somewhat longer than most, I admit. But she will find the love faded and the passion spent in due time."

"Not necessarily," he said. "I have known many marriages that retain love, and even passion, for decades. My mother, for example, still lights up whenever my father enters a room. They adore each other. I would not be surprised if your cousin is still dewy-eyed and content in twenty or thirty years. It can happen, Eleanor."

She wanted to object, but at that moment the door opened to admit two waiters and Mrs. Pettigrove.

"Here you are, dearies," the landlady said. "Straight from the kitchen, all nice and hot."

She took away the wine decanter and flung a white tablecloth over the table. One of the waiters put down his burden on the sideboard and quickly set out the plates and utensils for their meal.

"It's good food you'll get here at the Swan.

Nothin' fancy, but good, hearty country cookin'. Sticks to your ribs and all. Which is a good thing for you, sir, if you don't mind my sayin'. You could use a bit of plumpin' up. Look like you been pulled through a keyhole and back again, all stretched out, like. Here's a nice leg of mutton, fresh, and a joint of ham. Sam, put it down just there. And Ned here has a nice little roast game hen. Here's a dish of potatoes, a plate of spring peas, and a bit of stewed cucumber. Just the thing, eh? I'll send one of the boys up in a while with the cheese and one of my gooseberry tarts. Is there anything else you'll be wantin', sir?"

"Not at the moment," Simon said. "It all looks delicious. And I look forward to that gooseberry tart."

"Well, I ain't one to boast, but folks do seem to love my tarts. I been makin' 'em ever since I first come to the Swan thirty-four years ago."

"Thirty-four years? That's quite a long time."

Eleanor willed Simon not to start a conversation with the woman, who would no doubt chatter on and on for hours. He had no idea what he was getting into.

"I came to the Swan when I married Mr. Petti-grove," she said. "Been workin' here ever since. I used to—"

"You've been married to Mr. Pettigrove for thirty-four years?" His eyes flickered briefly in Eleanor's direction.

"That I have, sir. We been—"

"Happy years, may I ask?"

Eleanor groaned. She knew exactly what he was up to. Would he never give up?

The landlady was actually silenced by the question. It seemed to catch her quite off guard. "Happy years?" She shrugged. "Mostly. There was some rough times early on, but since the inn passed to Mr. P from his Pa, we been quite comfortable. We got—"

"But what about you and Mr. Pettigrove? Aside from struggling to make ends meet, has your marriage been a happy one? Are you still . . . fond of one another?"

The woman's plump face split into a grin. "Here now, are you flirtin' with me, Mr. Westover? Tryin' to find out if I'd be up for a bit of the dillydally?" Her hand reached up to fluff the lace at the edge of her cap, and she thrust her ample bosom forward. "Cheeky devil, ain't you? Well, you best not let Mr. P catch you shakin' my tree, cuz he won't have none of that."

Simon's blue eyes twinkled. "The jealous type, is he?"

She laughed, and her plump body shook with it. "I should say so! The man's an animal, I'm tellin' you. A tiger."

The sweet-faced, soft-spoken innkeeper, a tiger? Eleanor bit back a smile.

"He don't like other men showin' an interest, so to speak. Makes him mad as fire." She fluttered her eyelashes like a pert ingenue. "Of course, I never encourage such a thing, do I? So if you've a mind in that direction, sir, I'm tellin' you it won't do. Mr. P will have your hide. Besides"—she lowered her voice to a conspiratorial whisper—"it ain't right to sweet talk me in front of the lady."

"He's still in love with you, then? Mr. Pettigrove?"

"Well, I never! Persistent devil, ain't you? But I always say you big, tall, redheaded men are nothin' but trouble." She winked at Eleanor and gave Simon what she must have thought a provocative smile. "Yes, if you must know, Mr. P still fancies me, after all these years. We married in a fever, we was so crazy in love we couldn't wait. Couldn't keep our hands off each other. And I'm here to tell you that man still can't keep his hands off me."

She covered her mouth and giggled like a naughty child. Eleanor was hard pressed not to do the same.

"I shouldn't be sayin' such things," the landlady continued, "but 'tis true. He can be as contrary and stubborn as a mule sometimes, but I wouldn't trade my Mr. P for any man on earth. Not even for a handsome young devil like you. So just you mind yourself around him, Mr. Westover, and don't let him know you had a fancy for me."

With that she turned and left the parlor, broad hips swinging, chuckling merrily to herself. Simon looked at Eleanor, grinned, and raised his brows in question. "Well? What do you say to that?"

"I say you had better not let the innkeeper catch you flirting with his wife."

Simon threw back his head in a roar of laughter.

Despite a late start the next morning, they made good time to Derby. It was an old town, with well-paved and spacious streets and many fine houses and public buildings, including a handsome guildhall.

They stopped at the King's Head near the market square, where the Runners had left word that Barkwith, traveling with "his wife," had been seen in Ashbourne. They ordered cakes and a pot of tea before going on, and Eleanor's mouth was set in a grim line as she poured.

"At least there is a pretense of respectability," Simon said. "It is what you had hoped, is it not?"

"Yes, of course. Better that she should be treated as his wife than his . . . his mistress. It is just very sobering to know now with absolute certainty that they have become . . . intimate." The expression in her eyes told how distasteful the notion was to her. "She is so very young."

He touched her hand briefly where the ends of the red ribbon hung from her wrist. He was pleased that she had continued to wear it. "If she is traveling as Mrs. Barkwith," he said, "at least Miss Chadwick will not be associated with this journey."

"Perhaps. But she has those distinctive looks that everyone remembers. I can only hope no one who knows us in London hears of the beautiful young brunette with the aquamarine eyes traveling with that rogue. They will know at once who it is. Oh, damn the man! Why did he have to spirit her away like this? Why couldn't he have courted her properly, like any normal gentleman?"

"Would you have approved his suit?"

"No. Of course not."

"Then surely that is why he chose flight instead."

She gave a sound like a growl, and he was not certain if she was angry over Barkwith, or angry with Simon for believing this whole business to be an elopement and not something more sinister. "Oh, why could Belinda not have fallen madly in love with someone like Charles Pendleton?"

"He was perhaps not as dashing as Barkwith?"

She gave a weak smile. "Not in the least."

"Well, you can hardly blame her, then. We dashing, handsome, charming fellows are forever having women fall in love with us. Those other dull chaps don't stand a chance."

Her smile widened. "We agree at last. You dashing fellows make it difficult for an impressionable young woman to make a sensible decision. They see you as knights in shining armor, and the ordinary Mr. Pendletons of the world as crushing bores."

Did she think *him* a knight in shining armor? No, of course not. What a stupid idea. She was only following upon his silly joke. But to actually *be* her white knight . . . now, that would be something.

They finished their tea quickly and returned to

the carriage. With clear roads and fast, efficient
changes of horses and postillions along the way,
they made good time to Ashbourne. But the news
that met them at the Golden Lion was dishearten-
ing.

The Runners had lost the trail.

Hackett's message told them to wait at the inn
while he and Mumby checked the various routes.
Ashbourne was a way point at the meeting of at
least six major coaching roads. The fugitives could
have taken any one of them.

Simon shared Eleanor's frustration. "Damn. I
would have expected them to take the road to
Leek, but Hackett says they did not. I suppose
there is nothing for it but to wait for word. I'll get
us a parlor where we can be comfortable. And I'll
order something for us to eat."

He made all the arrangements while Eleanor remained cross and silent at his side. He bustled her
into the hired parlor and led her into a chair by the
fire. She removed her bonnet and fluffed her hair.
The fire was cozy but a tad too warm, and it put a
charming touch of pink in her cheeks. He was not
surprised when she rose to take off her pelisse. The
dark green kerseymere fastened at the waist with a
fetching little gold buckle, and once she had it un-
buckled, Simon helped her out of the garment. The
printed muslin dress beneath was simple and unfortunately modest, with its high neck and long
sleeves. No tempting expanses of bare skin.

She sat again for a brief moment, then sprang up

once more like a puppet on a string and began to pace the small room.

"Curse it," she said, "this is maddening. How can we just sit here and wait? Surely we should be out searching the roads, too. *Someone* must have seen them."

"It is exasperating, I agree, but if we leave, then the Runners will have to waste time searching for us when they have news. I'm afraid it is best if we wait."

The arrival of food and drink gave them something to occupy the time. Simon attempted bits of inconsequential conversation while he sliced the cold ham, but Eleanor was unresponsive, all wrapped up in her anger and impatience.

"It cannot be too long a wait," he said between bites of cucumber salad. "Between the two of them, Hackett and Mumby should be able to search all roads going north fairly quickly."

"If they went north."

She was determined to keep to her idiotic notion of Barkwith not marrying Belinda. All signs, despite this minor setback, pointed to Gretna as their destination. Why couldn't Eleanor accept that her niece was involved in a runaway marriage? Why was she being so stubborn?

"I think we should assume they are still headed north until we hear otherwise," he said. "It is the only logical direction."

"There are many large estates in Derbyshire. Barkwith runs with a very upper-crust crowd. One of them could have an estate here where Barkwith has taken Belinda."

Simon had been cutting into a cold pigeon pie, but her words caused him to stop and look up. "Eleanor, be reasonable. A man is unlikely to take his mistress to a grand country estate. It just is not done."

"Sometimes it is." Her voice had grown quiet, and she gazed into the distance, lost in her thoughts. Gradually, the fire returned to her eyes. "Confound it," she said at last, "I believe once we do find them I will be sorely tempted to do murder. I'm going to kill that man."

Obviously, she was not going to change her opinion about Barkwith's plans, and Simon did not want to aggravate her any further. He recalled the progress of the day before, when she had clearly admired him, and did not want to counteract that good by continuing to challenge her stubbornness. "We shall just have to wait and see. In the meantime, would you like some ham?"

Simon had been hungry and made a good meal of it, but Eleanor ate little. He wasn't sure if he should shake some sense into her or take her in his arms and let her cry. Of course, he knew which of those options he'd prefer, but he didn't think she'd cry. She was too stubborn, too angry, too proud.

Most men he knew were attracted to soft, sweet, fragile women who made them feel strong and protective. Simon had never sought that sort of reassurance. He preferred strong-willed women with minds of their own. Eleanor, splendid and beautiful in her righteous outrage, appealed to him more than any other woman he could remember.

And there was that delectable upper lip.

After they'd eaten there was still no word from the Runners, and Eleanor's agitation was palpable. She was pacing again. Simon had retreated to a window and perched himself on its broad ledge, hoping to find something outside that might offer distraction. However, there was nothing much within sight to comment on beyond the rows of almshouses and a church with a handsome spire. He was absently reading an old carved inscription on the window ledge when he became aware of more writing. Curious, he bent over to investigate.

"Well, I'm dashed," he said. "Would you look at this, Eleanor? The window is a veritable chapbook of verses." He gestured for her to join him. "See all these carvings? It looks like years and years' worth of visitors leaving their mark. Ha! I remember as boys Malcolm and I used to compete to find the oldest message carved in an old church or whatever place we were touring. Usually some poor fellow's tomb desecrated by centuries of visitors leaving their mark."

"I used to look for these, too," Eleanor said, a smile lighting her eyes for the first time since they'd arrived at Ashbourne. "I have always loved these little messages from the past. I remember go-

ing to the Tower as a child and having to be
dragged away from reading all the carved inscrip-
tions in one of them. I can't recall which tower."

"Beauchamp Tower."

"Yes, that's it. I remember I had read a history
book in school that mentioned how Guildford
Dudley had carved the name of his young wife,
Lady Jane Grey, into the stone wall of the tower
while he was imprisoned, awaiting execution. I
searched and searched until I found the tiny, single
word: Jane. Somehow, it was much more compelling than some of the truly elaborate carvings of
prisoners who were held for months and years.
Poor Guildford was not there long enough for anything more than that simple tribute."

"Why, Eleanor," Simon said, smiling broadly,
"what a terribly romantic story. How unlike you."

"Horrid man."

Simon took her elbow and tugged her closer.
"Look here:

*What better lass to think on
Than Selena Dobbs of Lincoln?*

"F.H. 1754. A poet after my own heart. I'll wager
the other window has as many messages. Let's see
who can find the oldest."

She gave him a smile as if to acknowledge and
approve his attempt to distract her. When she
leaned over to inspect the window on the other
side of the room, she said, "Good heavens, there

are hundreds of them. Not so many verses, though. Just short messages and initials, the usual thing. 'I love Dolly Walker–J.B. 1733.' And here's 'Sweet Jane Dorrit' with a carved heart, dated 1714."

"Aha. I can top that. 'E.G. loves P.T 1706.'"

"They are not *all* messages of love, you know. 'Peter Holdern was here—1701.'"

"Ah, but 'Annie S—my own true love—1698.'"

"You're incorrigible, Simon. Ever the romantic. Oh, here's an interesting one. 'We march with Prince Charlie—1745.' A poignant bit of history. I wonder who it was and if he survived Culloden?"

"But I still have you beat with 1698."

"Wait. I have one: 'Noe heart more true than mine to you—A.W. 1636.'"

"No. Really? 1636? And such a charming sentiment. Can I top that? Let's see. No. No, I can't find an earlier date, but how's this one for pure sentiment:

F.B. holds the key to my heart
From her side I never will part.

"J.M. 1762. You see, Eleanor? I am not the only one who dreams of lifelong love and happiness."

"And I wish you luck in finding it."

"Shall I carve something?" he asked.

"You have a soppy verse at hand, no doubt."

"I trust there's not enough time to carve one of my odes." Besides, the ode to her upper lip was a work in progress, not quite ready for immortality on a window ledge. "I thought something short and simple."

"Ah. Then perhaps, 'The Busybody—Impractical advice freely given.' "

He laughed. "No, even simpler. Just a name."

" 'Simon—1801.' A trifle uninspired, but straightforward."

"No, I would not carve 'Simon.' "

She gave him a quizzical look. "What, then?"

" 'Eleanor.' A simple tribute."

Simon met her gaze boldly across the room, and a charged silence crackled in the air between them. Her green eyes darkened with an expression he would swear was longing, a look that caught at his gut and almost stopped his heart. He took a step toward her . . .

The parlor door swung open with an earsplitting creak and Obidiah Hackett made a noisy and breathless entrance. *Damn.* Eleanor turned away from Simon and stood in the middle of the room with a hand clasped to her breast. Her eyes grew wide in anticipation.

Hackett removed his hat and wiped his brow. "We found 'em."

Eleanor gave a tiny gasp. "You found Belinda?"

"Beggin' your pardon, ma'am," Hackett said. "A misfortunate choice of words. I meant we found their trail again. They took the Buxton road and were last seen at the Three Crowns. I'll bet my brass buttons they returned to the main coach road at Stockport. Howsomever, I must leave now if I am to ascertain that information tonight. Mumby's already on his way. It's gettin' close to dark, so I recommend you remain for the night at the Three Crowns in Buxton. One of us'll ride back with a report." He swept a brief bow. "Ma'am. Guv'ner."

Simon followed him into the corridor and slipped him a few coins. "Please hurry," he said.

Hackett nodded, pocketed the money, and turned to leave, but then stopped. "By the by, guv'ner," he said, "all the inns at Buxton looked prodigitous busy. You might have to slap down a few extra guineas to find a room."

When Simon stepped back into the parlor, Eleanor had already put on her pelisse and was in the process of tying the ribbons of her bonnet. The lighthearted manner that so animated her face mere minutes ago, as well as that brief glimpse of something else, had disappeared, and she was all business once again.

"Let's go," she said.

Chapter 9

True affection may not always answer to a logical scrutiny. A thousand reasonable definitions and explanations will not help one to understand a whit more of it.

The Busybody

It was late when Buxton came into view. They had traveled through bleak forbidding hills and moorland heath, past desolate plateaus and dramatic limestone cliffs to reach the new spa town. It was like gliding into a natural bowl within the peaks; the sparkling, modern town was surrounded on three sides by an amphitheater of wild green hills.

"How lovely," Eleanor said. "Oh, look. There's a grand crescent." The magnificent, sweeping semicircular building with its bright new stone gleamed softly in the waning twilight. "It's almost like a miniature Bath."

"That's what the Duke of Devonshire hoped to achieve," Simon said, "when he poured so much of his money into building up Buxton. There are natural warm springs here, you know. The Romans are

152

said to have had wells here, though none survive. They named the place Aquae Arnemetiae—Spa of the Goddess in the Grove. St. Anne's well has for centuries been thought to be a holy place, its waters to have healing properties. Cromwell had the well locked up in hopes of destroying belief in its power."

"Good heavens, how do you know so much about it?" Eleanor allowed a note of mockery to color her voice. "Did you memorize a guidebook to impress me?"

"I know the area well. I have a small house here in the Peak." He smiled then, almost disarming her with the twinkle in that cornflower gaze. "But I am pleased to have impressed you."

She would not be disarmed again. "I thought you lived in your formidable father's house in London."

"I stay there when I happen to be in London. But I actually spend much of my time up here in Derbyshire. I have good friends with a home nearby, and we spend a lot of time together in leisurely conversation, writing, or tramping about."

"Communing with nature, I daresay."

His smile broadened. "Yes, as a matter of fact. I find the country much more inspiring, more *romantic*, than the city.

*"Once again
Do I behold these steep and lofty cliffs,
That on a wild secluded scene impress*

*Thoughts of more deep seclusion; and connect
The landscape with the quiet of the sky."*

Eleanor's brows lifted in surprise. This was not quite what she would have expected from the overwrought pen of the Busybody. "Yours?"

"Wordsworth."

Ah. It figured.

"But like him, I love the area with its wild moorland scenery and its bracing air. Some of the towns and villages are quite charming. Buxton"—he nodded his head in the direction of the town as they made their way toward its center—"though quite old, is newly developed. So far, however, it has not quite achieved Devonshire's expectations or gained the level of popularity he had hoped."

"Really? It looks fairly popular at the moment."

The postillions had slowed their pace due to an extraordinary amount of traffic in the supposedly sleepy little spa town. The High Street as well as all other roads and byways within sight were crowded with all manner of vehicles: large traveling carriages with caped coachmen at the reins and pairs of liveried footmen standing at the back; postillion-mounted teams pulling private escutcheoned chaises and hired yellow bounders; sleek two-wheeled curricles with their owners at the ribbons and young tigers seated behind; and an assortment of more humble country gigs and dog carts. Men on horseback wove between the vehicles and pedestrians strolled about.

It reminded Eleanor of Hyde Park on a late afternoon, though not quite as fashionable. Many of the gentlemen looked to be nattily attired dandies, but she saw no women sporting the latest bonnets, preening and posing in an open barouche or landau. Even so, it was not the sort of crowd one expected to find in the middle of Derbyshire's Peak district.

"Hackett mentioned that the town was crowded," Simon said, "but he didn't say why. I wonder what is going on? The town doesn't appear to be decked out for a fair, and it's not much of a market town."

"We might not be able to find rooms for the night with all this crowd. Perhaps we should just wait for another report from Hackett or Mumby and move on."

"I agree," he said, "but we can't be certain when one of them will return. It might not be until quite late, or even early tomorrow morning. I'm afraid we'll be at the Three Crowns for some time."

They soon reached the large coaching inn to find its yard jammed with carriages. The postillions somehow managed to find a clear spot and led the team to it. Simon jumped down and came to help Eleanor out. "I'd better see about a fresh team first," he said. "With the inn so busy, I want to make sure we have horses in the morning. You can wait here if you like."

"No, I'll just go inside and see about the possibility of rooms. Maybe there's an innkeeper susceptible to a bit of flirtation."

Simon grinned, showing the dimples. "No man could resist those flashing green eyes. I have no doubt that when I return I shall find you have secured the best rooms in town."

"And if I don't, I shall ask for the innkeeper's wife, and allow you to work your wiles upon her. You do have a way with them, as I recall."

Eleanor walked away with Simon's laughter in her wake. No matter how sarcastic or disparaging her words, Simon never seemed to take offense. He had an almost unbearably cheerful nature. It probably came from having dimples. It would be so easy to succumb to such a man, but she was determined not to do so. She would admit to finding him attractive, but that was as far as she was willing to go. She would not, under any circumstances, allow herself to be charmed, wooed, or seduced by Simon Westover. She knew exactly where such foolishness might lead; she had been down that path once before and had no intention of going there again.

The first door she came to seemed to be the public room. The sounds from inside indicated a boisterous, even rowdy clientele. Blast. She had little hope of finding available rooms with such a crowd. But neither did she relish a night on a hard bench in a noisy taproom.

She squared her shoulders, and her confidence, and pushed open the door.

"Well, well, well. What have we here? Look

what a pretty little thing the wind blew in, fellows. Come here, sweetheart. Give us a kiss."

Eleanor was a frustrating enigma to Simon. She had been cross as sticks ever since leaving Ashbourne. She never missed an opportunity to disparage his idealism and poke jibes at the Busybody. Even her joking and bantering was likely a prelude to a rousing but good-natured argument over dinner. He never minded their debates. She was an intelligent woman, and conversation with her could be exhilarating. He just wished she weren't so damned cynical. And afraid.

It seemed that each time they had experienced a pleasant moment together, even a chaste moment of mutual attraction, she withdrew afterward into this other more contrary, combative mood. He suspected she had the need to feel in control of every situation, and the possibilities of physical attraction threatened to break down that control.

Poor Eleanor. He wondered what had happened to make her so afraid to feel, so afraid to allow herself a little passion. Who had hurt her? Mr. Tennant? Whatever it was and whoever it was, the harm was deep and solidly rooted. She would not let go of it, no matter how hard she might want to. Instead, she used mockery and censure as a sort of armor.

There had been moments—when their eyes met in an intense, brief melding, when they had kissed—

when Simon was certain she felt the same charge of physical awareness he did. And there had been that blatantly sexual moment between them at the time of the carriage accident, after their chaste kiss. Each incident, though, had lasted barely an instant, and no more, before Eleanor had pulled away.

Simon decided his own private quest on this journey would be to gain her trust so that he might teach her how to stop being afraid.

He wandered over to the stables and made arrangements to have four fresh horses and two postillions available in the morning. The inn was popular and accommodated a large stable. The current busy state simply meant more work and more postboys to put up for the night, but no shortage of teams. Just to be safe, he dropped a few extra coins in the head ostler's outstretched hand.

"Right you are, sir. We'll have a team o' four and two boys ready to leave whenever you say. Might be sooner'n you think, though. Don't expect old Shorthose got a free cubbyhole or press this night. Three to a bed already, most like."

"What's all the activity, anyway?" Simon asked.

"The mill, o' course."

"Good Lord. There's to be a mill?"

"You mean you ain't here for it?" The ostler shook his head and clicked his tongue. "Silly time to come to Buxton if you ain't here for the mill. Every Lad of the Fancy from Birmingham to York has come to see Crawley and Duggan go at it tomorrow."

For the first time, Simon took closer note of the crowds of people milling about the inn yard and the streets. With the exception of a couple of old bawds, there was not a single woman in sight. The town was crowded with men. Lots of men.

Good God! Eleanor had just gone alone into the public room of an inn teeming with men who'd come to see a fight. High-spirited Corinthians out for a lark. Men who had no doubt already hoisted a few too many in honor of tomorrow's match. Rowdy sportsmen who would not expect to see a respectable lady walk into their midst.

Simon took off at a run. He flung open the door to the noisy public room, and his heart plummeted to his boots.

Eleanor!

Kicking and clawing, she was in the clutches of a beefy drunken lout. He had pulled her onto his lap, and though she fought to get away, he held her fast. One of the man's large hands covered her breast, and he was trying to kiss her.

Rage cut through Simon like a sharp knife and took full possession of him. In two long strides he was standing next to the lecherous oaf. He grabbed the man's wrist and removed the impudent hand from Eleanor's breast. He kept hold of the wrist in a viselike grip while he hauled back and rammed a solid fist straight into the great lummox's face.

The drunken fool tilted backward like a felled tree and hit the floor with a resounding thud.

* * *

Eleanor had never been more glad to see anyone in all her life. Simon put his hands on her shoulders, and his anxious eyes searched her up and down, making sure she was unharmed. "My God, Eleanor. Are you—"

"Simon, look out!"

He spun around, straight into the fist of one of her assaulter's cronies. Simon rolled back on his heels with a grunt, but did not fall.

The assailant glared at Simon, his fists held at the ready. "That's what you get, you impertinent, rufous-headed varlet, for moving in once a man's staked his claim. Yon fellow's my friend, you see, and we don't take kindly to strangers cutting the ground from under a chap."

Simon took a nonchalant step forward and smashed the man's jaw with a powerful right. "And that's what *you* get for insulting a lady."

And suddenly all hell broke loose as the entire taproom erupted in a mad frenzy of fisticuffs, shouting, and flying furniture. The man Simon had hit roared in outrage and lunged at him, delivering blow upon blow. Eleanor dropped to her knees to avoid a wayward fist and crawled behind an overturned table for safety. She was near the door and could have easily escaped, but some imp of mischief made her want to stay and watch.

Poor Simon. There were at least three men attacking him at once, and though he valiantly defended himself, he was badly outnumbered. Eleanor felt around on the damp floor and found a pewter tankard. She took aim at one of the men battering Simon, threw, and the heavy vessel struck the man just above the ear. Enraged but uncertain of the source of the blow, the fellow began swinging madly in all directions. He connected with the nose of a nearby man, who retaliated, and the two of them began to pound each other in earnest.

Just when she thought she'd have to launch a second missile to distract another of Simon's assailants, a very large gentleman shoved his way through the crowd. When he reached Simon, he took hold of one of the men attacking him, lifted him as though he weighed nothing, and threw the man over his back as casually as if he were tossing table scraps to a dog. Two other gentlemen, somewhat smaller, appeared to be companions to the large fellow, and the three of them, along with Simon, began to stage a mighty defense.

At least now the numbers were more even.

The noise was deafening: a cacophony of shouting, laughing, cheering; the crashing of furniture; the shattering of crockery and glass; the thwack of fist meeting flesh and bone; the grunts and howls of pain and fury; the rumble of walls quaking and windows rattling; the reverberating thud of fallen bodies; the high-spirited, tumultuous, and perfectly idiotic excitement of men having fun.

Amid the melee, Simon kept looking anxiously about the room, no doubt seeking out Eleanor. She signaled from behind the table to let him know she was all right. He caught her eye, looked relieved, and took a punch to the gut for his trouble.

He ducked the next few blows and began to make his way backward toward Eleanor's table sanctuary, swinging out defensive and very accurate fists to all would-be attackers. The large ally kept close by Simon, engaging in a series of one-on-one clashes with any who threatened him or Simon or either of his two colleagues.

By now, though, there were no particular sides to the battle—just general brawling for the sheer pleasure of it. No one seemed to focus anymore on Simon as the thrower of the first punch. In fact, no one seemed to notice, or care, that he was swinging less often and was making his deliberate way toward the door.

He had almost reached Eleanor, who was by now thoroughly sick of the whole business and wanted to leave, when a man leaped out of nowhere and clipped him with a left to the ear. In an instant, they were raining blows upon each other, and Eleanor was forgotten.

Disgusted, she rose from her safe haven, picked up an overturned stool, and brought it crashing down on the head of Simon's opponent. The man collapsed like a house of cards.

Simon laughed merrily, grabbed her hand, and tugged her through the rowdy crowd of spectators that had gathered. When they reached the door he pulled her outside to the inn yard.

They stood wordless and staring, each survey-ing the other for damage. Simon was a wreck. His coat was ripped at the shoulder, his neckcloth was loose, several buttons were missing on his waist-coat, and blood stained his collar. Somewhere in-side, he'd lost his hat. There was a cut bleeding over one eye, and a bruise was already darkening along his jaw. But his blue eyes blazed bright with some kind of fire.

"You are hurt," she said.

"Take your bonnet off," he said in a brusque tone.

"Why?"

"Just do it."

She did so; then, assuming it must have been ruined, she examined it for damage and found none. She instinctively reached up to adjust her flattened hair, then looked up and raised her brows in question.

"Put it down on the bench behind you," he said.

She met his gaze squarely, but for once was not compelled to challenge him. Something in his tone urged her to do as he asked. She turned and laid the bonnet on the bench.

All at once he swung her around, drew her into his arms, and crushed his mouth against hers in a kiss that was almost primal in its urgency. This was nothing like the sweet, almost innocent meeting of lips they had shared yesterday. This was raw and unrestrained, dark and greedy.

It was the most purely carnal moment Eleanor had experienced in over a decade.

She did not even consider fighting him, even though he held her so tightly she thought her ribs might crack. Instead, she kissed him back with almost equal passion, unable at first, and unwilling, to let her better judgment take control. He opened his mouth wide over hers, and she opened her own to let him inside.

It felt good. Too good. She ought not allow it. She ought not allow herself this giddy moment of pure sensual pleasure. She ought not give in to the indescribable comfort of his arms. But it had been a somewhat frightening experience to be manhandled by that drunken oaf, and she figured she was allowed this brief indulgence.

He broke the kiss, almost as suddenly as he'd begun it, and cradled her head against his shoulder. Both of them were breathing hard. Neither spoke for what seemed minutes. They just silently held on to each other. Then she began to feel a trembling in his chest and realized he was laughing.

"Eleanor. Eleanor." He muttered her name over and over, his lips against her hair, the laughter still rippling through him. Finally, still holding her close, he said, "Forgive me, Eleanor, but I could not stop myself. The heat of battle, I suppose. When I walked in to find that lout mauling you, I went a little mad. I wanted to kill him for daring to touch you, and now look what I've done. Did he hurt you?"

"No, he just infuriated me. You were marvelous, Simon."

"So were you, my dear. I hardly think you needed me at all. Clubbing that last fellow with a chair was spectacular. And I am almost certain the flying tankard that struck one of my attackers came from your direction, did it not?"

"You were unfairly outnumbered."

He laughed again and hugged her more tightly, then loosened his arms a bit so he could look down at her. "Most women would have fallen into a swoon if they had been treated so roughly by a drunken brute. But as I now recall, you were fighting him pretty hard. I always knew you were Boadicea incarnate."

"Not so strong as all that," she said. "I could not have fought him alone. He was much stronger than me. And no one else came to my aid. I'm sure they all must have thought I was some sort of lightskirt."

"I am so sorry for that, my dear. I learned from the ostler that the crowds are here for a mill. That's why there are no women—no respectable women—to be seen. I should never have allowed you to walk in there alone."

"A mill? Well, that explains a lot." She could not believe she was having this reasonably normal conversation with a man who'd just kissed her like a Viking raider. But perhaps he was right. It was just a matter of blood still heated from the fight. It had not meant anything.

"If only I'd paid more attention to the sort of crowd that had gathered in the town," Simon said, "I'd never have sent you into that taproom."

"It is not your fault. I entered that room of my own volition. But I cannot tell you how relieved I was to see you walk in the door."

He reached up and cupped her cheek. "Were you?"

Oh, God, he was going to kiss her again. Not in a mindless moment of heat this time, but with deliberate intent. She did not believe she could bear it.

He studied her mouth with that intense blue gaze and gently stroked her upper lip with his thumb.

"How plump, how ripe this rare confection
With potent hint of sweet connection."

He dipped his head slowly, slowly—
"Simon, old chap, what the devil—oh! Sorry."

He groaned and pulled away, releasing her from his embrace. Eleanor found that she wanted to groan, too, but with relief. It would have been a huge mistake to allow another kiss, though she would probably not have been able to resist. *Foolish woman.* And someone he knew had almost been a witness to such folly.

She tried to hide the embarrassment heating her cheeks by turning her attention to adjusting her skirts and replacing her bonnet. Simon, however, took her by the elbow to face his friend, the large gentleman who had come to his assistance inside. He was in a similar state to Simon: hatless, clothes askew, a bruise or two on his face, blood staining his shirtfront, the exhilaration of the fight lighting his blue eyes.

"Mrs. Tennant," Simon said, "may I introduce my brother, Malcolm Westover."

Surprised, Eleanor extended her hand to the young man. "I am pleased to make your acquaintance, Mr. Westover."

He took her hand, bent over it, and in a very suggestive tone said, "The pleasure, Mrs. Tennant, is all mine, I assure you." The blue eyes, so similar to Simon's, never left hers.

She retrieved her hand before he could plant a fulsome kiss upon it. "My goodness, Simon, you were certainly right about him."

Malcolm grinned. No dimples, she noticed. "And what sort of Banbury tale has my brother been spreading about me, ma'am?"

"Only that you are the larger brother, and you certainly are that."

The young man gave a bark of laughter. "I am indeed, though, as Simon always likes to remind me, he has an inch or so on me in height. And a whole lot more in his upper works." Turning his attention to his brother, he said, "But I say, old man, you could have knocked me over with a feather when you marched in and planted that chap a facer. Nothing less than a stunning right, I tell you. Absolutely stunning."

Eleanor could have sworn that Simon, the bookish brother, actually preened.

But she, too, thought his performance rather wonderful, defending her honor so thoroughly. She caught his eye and sent a silent signal of thanks, and admiration. He acknowledged her with a smile, dimples and all, and a slight blush colored his bruised face.

"I still cannot believe it," Malcolm said. "If anyone had told me my skinny, ginger-hackled, intellectual brother would throw a punch in public, I'd have said he was daft."

"It was necessary," Simon said.

"Yes, I saw how that brandy-faced sot was pawing Mrs. Tennant," Malcolm said, "but I had no idea she was yours. I'd have darkened his daylights myself if I'd known."

"Malcolm, Mrs. Tennant is not—"

"And that's another thing. I never knew you to parade one of your highfliers in public. Since when did—hey!"

Simon had grabbed his brother tightly by the collar and stood nose-to-nose with him. "Unless you want the same treatment as that lout who dared to touch her," he said through clenched teeth, "you will apologize to Mrs. Tennant this instant. She is *not* my mistress. She is no one's mistress. She is a lady, a lady who has already endured a public mauling this night. I will not allow her to suffer further insult from my own brother."

"Egad, Simon, I had no idea. Let me go."

"You will apologize first."

Malcolm cast his eyes in Eleanor's direction. Simon's grip would not allow him to turn his head. "I am most dreadfully sorry, ma'am. It was my mistake. I meant you no disrespect, I assure you."

Simon let go, and Malcolm rocked back on his heels. He rubbed his throat and said again, "I am sorry, Mrs. Tennant. I never did have any brains."

He looked so thoroughly mortified that Eleanor had to bite back a smile. "Apology accepted, Mr. Westover. It was an honest mistake."

The young man blew out a relieved breath through puffed cheeks. "Thank you, ma'am." Then he turned to his brother. "By Jove, old chap, you are full of surprises tonight. Not the least of which is finding you here to begin with. Never thought you cared much for the ring."

"We are not here for the mill," Simon said. "Mrs. Tennant is a friend whose niece has gone missing. We are searching for her."

"In Buxton?"

"We're not sure where she is just yet."

Malcolm's broad face broke into a grin. "Oho, I see what's up. The girl's bolted with some enterprising fellow, I'll wager. On the road to Gretna, eh?"

"Shut up, Malcolm. It's none of your affair."

"No, no. I'm sure it is not." He turned to Eleanor with a sheepish look in his eye. "But if I can be of any help, ma'am, you must let me know. It is the least I can do after . . . well, it is the least I can do."

"Thank you, Mr. Westover, but your brother has engaged the services of two Bow Street Runners. I prefer not to involve anyone else, if you don't mind."

"Yes, of course. But the offer stands nevertheless."

"Thank you, sir."

"I am curious, though," Malcolm said, "how my scholarly brother came to be involved in your niece's . . . er . . . predicament."

"You could say that he was partially to blame," Eleanor said, "with some of his nonsensical Busybody advice."

"His *what*?"

Simon grabbed Eleanor's arm and began to drag her away. "We really must inquire about rooms for the night," he said. "You will have to excuse us, Malcolm."

So his father was not the only family member who knew nothing about the Busybody. Simon clearly had no desire for his brother to be enlightened on the subject.

"No need to inquire," Malcolm said, still eying his brother skeptically. "There ain't a room to be had for miles."

"Damnation," Simon said, then muttered an apology to Eleanor for his language. "One of the Runners is to meet us here, or at least send a message giving us our next stop. And I will not take

Mrs. Tennant back into the taproom. What the devil are we going to do?"

Malcolm looked over his shoulder briefly, then said, "Got an idea in my head. Wait here a moment."

He went to join two men standing near the doorway. Eleanor recognized them as the two men who'd fought beside him in the taproom. They both appeared disheveled, bright-eyed, and slightly giddy. Or slightly drunk. Malcolm clapped each of them on the shoulder and spoke quietly to them, nodding his head in her direction.

"I'm sorry I mentioned the Busybody," she said to Simon while his brother conferred with his friends. "He doesn't know, does he?"

"No. Besides some of the others at the magazine, no one else knows. Except you."

"Why do you continue to write it if you are so ashamed of doing so?"

"I am not ashamed—"

"Mrs. Tennant, allow me to introduce my friends." Malcolm had walked up flanked by the two gentlemen. "This woolly-haired fellow is Daffy Arbuthnot."

The young man, whose hair was so blond and so curly he looked like a lamb in man's costume, stepped forward and sketched a bow. "Your obedient, ma'am." He stood back, straightened his neckcloth, and brushed off his coat. "Must forgive the frightful state of my togs. Bit of a tussle inside, don't you know. 'Course you know. Smack in the thick of, wasn't you? By the by, dashed fine show, Westover. Cracking good right."

Simon nodded acknowledgment with a sheepish grin.

"And this here black-eyed rogue," Malcolm said, "is Sackville Gates."

He, too, presented a fine leg as he acknowledged Eleanor. But where Mr. Arbuthnot was bright and gregarious, Mr. Gates was dark and reticent. He cleared his throat and said, "A pleasure, ma'am," then gave over his attention to brushing a bit of dirt from his cuff.

"The thing of it is," Malcolm said, "the three of us nabbed a room early on. Well, bound to, weren't we, when we toddled up from Town with everyone in our dust. Anyway, happy to give it up to Mrs. Tennant and take our chances in the taproom, or the stables. Afraid you'll have to do the same, Simon."

Eleanor offered a smile to each of the young men, none of whom, upon closer scrutiny, was entirely sober. "Thank you very much, gentlemen. That is most generous of you. I believe I will accept your kind offer."

"Well done, my lad," Simon said. "Now, I don't suppose there is a private parlor available where we might dine in peace?"

"Unlikely," Malcolm said.

"Yes, there is," Daffy Arbuthnot interjected. "Don't you remember, Westover? Got a cunning little parlor adjoining the bedchamber."

"By Jove, I think you're right, Daffy," Malcolm said. "Forgot, that's all. Never could keep two ideas in my brainpan at the same time."

"Stands to reason," Mr. Arbuthnot said. "Comes from getting your head busted up one too many times. But there is indeed a parlor of a sort. Gates and I had thought to make up a bowl of punch later on, and perhaps get up a private game or two. Take advantage of the wagering spirit in the air, don't you know." He turned his woolly head toward Eleanor. "Consider it at your disposal, ma'am. It could easily accommodate a meal for two." Malcolm gave him a sharp elbow in the ribs. "Or just for yourself, Mrs. Tennant. You could dine alone, away from the raff and rabble in the public dining room."

Eleanor smiled at his discomposure. He no doubt made the same assumption about her and Simon as Malcolm had. She was beyond caring about the proprieties, though, and had few concerns for her reputation. Even though it was only their third night on the road, it felt as if she and Simon had been together for weeks, and she had grown accustomed to traveling and dining alone with him.

But she would rather not be alone with him tonight. Not after that kiss. It might lead down a path she was unwilling to trod.

"I would not dream of monopolizing such a luxury for myself alone," she said. "I would be happy to share the parlor and supper with all of you."

"No, no, that would not do."

"We could not possibly."

"It would not be right."

"Not at all the thing."

"Do not concern yourself with us."

"We'll take our meal in the dining room."

"Or the taproom."

The three men continued to protest until Simon held up a hand for silence. "I, for one, have no desire to dine among those rowdies inside." He nodded toward the taproom door, where the sounds of brawling had subsided, but the raucous noise of scores of drunken men continued. "If Mrs. Tennant will allow it, I would be pleased to have dinner in her parlor. But only if one or all of you join us."

He darted a look in Eleanor's direction that told her he intended to look out for her reputation, despite his desire to be alone with her. Thank heaven he was a gentleman.

"Malcolm?" he prompted.

Simon's brother looked to Eleanor, who nodded encouragement. It might be interesting to learn from his brother a little more about the man who was the Busybody.

"All right," Malcolm said. "I will join you. I confess I am anxious to hear more about this . . . this quest of yours. But these two are already half seas over. Don't recommend allowing 'em to share your table, ma'am."

"Quite right," Sackville Gates said. "Not fit company for a lady." Relief was written large on his youthful face, as he grabbed the ready excuse for not joining them. The young man was quite uncomfortably shy. "You will know where to find us, Westover. Come along, Arbuthnot." He took his curly-haired friend by the arm and the two of them quickly disappeared inside the taproom.

"Well, that's settled," Simon said. "Now, Malcolm, I think we should allow Mrs. Tennant some privacy and time to freshen up. Give her the key to your room, and you and I will see about ordering dinner."

Malcolm handed the key to his brother, who took Eleanor's hand, placed the key in her palm, then curled her fingers around it. He did not let go of her hand. She recalled that more intimate embrace of a few moments before, and knew from the smoldering look in his eyes that he, too, was thinking of it.

"Thank you again, Simon, for coming to my rescue."

"It was my pleasure, madam."

She reached up with her free hand to touch the small cut above his eye. "Not so pleasurable, I think. I'm sorry you were hurt."

"Any service I can render you is indeed a pleasure," he said, his voice a little husky.

Eleanor remembered Malcolm's presence, tugged her hand away, and dropped the key in her pocket. "Yes, I daresay all you men find some sort of absurd pleasure in pummeling one another to pieces. It is not, however, so enjoyable for me. But at least now I have confidence, Simon, that when we meet up with him, I can ask you to pound Barkwith into mush. Now *that* would be a pleasure."

Chapter 10

The husband who truly loves and respects his wife will not deny her rights to free expression. It is by a mixture of concord and discord that music and matrimony are most agreeably composed.

The Busybody

"Barkwith?" Malcolm said when Eleanor had gone. "Geoffrey Barkwith?"

"Yes," Simon said.

His brother's eyes grew round with astonishment. "Mrs. Tennant's niece has run away with Geoffrey Barkwith?"

"Yes."

"The devil you say!" Malcolm shook his head and gave a whistle of disbelief. "Lord, what a pickle."

"Do you know the man?"

He shrugged. "Slightly. Buck of the first head, that one. Bit of a roving eye, but devilish good-looking and very popular with the ladies. Been linked to a string of 'em over the past couple of years."

"So I've heard."

"A bit quieter this Season, though. Seems to have had his eye fixed on a new young diamond," Malcolm said. "Beautiful dark-haired girl with the most incredible eyes." He sucked in a sharp breath. "Good God. Is that the niece? Miss Chadwick?"

"The very one."

Malcolm's jaw dropped and his eyes looked ready to pop right out of his head. "Egad. Barkwith and Miss Chadwick have eloped? What a dustup!"

This did not bode well. His brother's reaction was probably typical of what Eleanor might expect if the story got out. Simon recognized, with considerable chagrin, the spark of interest in Malcolm's eye, relishing the notion that he had a prime piece of fresh gossip. "Now, Malcolm, you must keep this to yourself. Mrs. Tennant is upset enough. She is trying to keep the whole business quiet."

"I should think so." He continued to shake his head in disbelief.

"You are not to repeat what I've told you, Malcolm."

"Yes, yes. My lips are sealed."

But his brain was obviously still at work, cogitating on the news. It would be a supreme effort for Malcolm to keep such a juicy tidbit to himself. And Simon did not trust his restraint when he was in his cups. His brother always talked too much when he drank.

"I mean it, Malcolm. If you so much as breathe one word of this, you will have me to deal with. Do

I make myself clear?" He did not often use his big-brother tone with Malcolm, but this was important. If his brother caused him to lose Eleanor's trust, there was more at stake than his own infatuation. He and Eleanor had a bargain, after all, and if he did anything to jeopardize it, she might feel free to publicize his role as the Busybody. Despite more personal considerations, he really must not forget the importance of keeping that bit of information a secret.

"Well, brother?" he said. "Do I make myself clear?"

"Yes, of course." Malcolm dug at the ground with his boot heel and ran a hand through the chestnut hair that had fallen over his forehead. The promise to keep such news a secret would be a tremendous effort, and he was clearly unhappy about it. "No need to get on your high ropes over it," he said in an almost comically petulant tone. "Said my lips were sealed."

"Just make sure they stay that way."

"Yes, yes, all right. But at least satisfy my curiosity. You're off to try and stop the marriage, I gather?"

"To tell you the truth," Simon said, "I think we will be too late. We're too far behind them. Tell me about this Barkwith fellow. Eleanor—Mrs. Tennant, that is—seems to believe he is an adventurer with no honorable intentions. What is your opinion?"

"Well, as I said, I only know him casually. Frightfully handsome devil. Women are always throwing themselves in his path. But I never heard anything really unsavory about him. A bit under the hatches now and then, but who ain't? A younger son, you know."

Simon smiled. "Is that a hint, Malcolm? Are you in dun territory again?"

"Not yet. Besides, I've laid a fat wager on Crawley, who is certain to win tomorrow's bout, so I'll be flush again in no time."

"Or shirtless. You'll come to me before you get yourself into trouble, won't you?"

"Not to worry, old man. Crawley's a sure thing," he said, snapping his fingers.

"I hope you're right," Simon said. "I trust you know a thing or two about these matters."

"I do indeed." He grinned broadly. "Enough to know that you did the Westovers proud tonight with that punishing right of yours. Capital science, brother. Beautifully done."

Simon was ridiculously proud of himself, to be praised for something in which he had never excelled and by a brother whose expertise was to be trusted. He wondered if Malcolm would feel as cocky if Simon praised a poem he'd written? He was unlikely to find out, for the day Malcolm penned a verse would be the day hell froze over.

"Let's go see about dinner," he said. "Then come with me to the carriage yard. I will need to send Mrs. Tennant's portmanteau up to her."

Malcolm nodded his agreement, and they walked together toward the inn entrance. "Now, you could use a little more work on your left," Malcolm said, and proceeded to expound on the art and science of pugilism, stopping for an occasional demonstration.

They found the innkeeper, who agreed to send up hot water and soap to Eleanor, for a price, and to have the young gentlemen's bags removed from the room, for a price. He was less pleased about serving a private dinner upstairs, but more accommodating after receiving an extra guinea for his trouble.

"That fellow will empty your purse for you," Malcolm said. "Knows there ain't another room to be had in the whole town. Sure to overcharge you. Probably dun you just for talkin' to him."

Simon agreed. This would no doubt be one of their more expensive stops on the journey north. But he'd come prepared. There was a hidden compartment in the carriage where he kept a strongbox. He would clear it out if necessary.

The two brothers walked to the crowded yard to find Simon's chariot. The carriages were lined up shoulder to shoulder and three deep so that it was no easy task. The mill had brought a veritable mob to the small spa town.

"Odd sort of place for a mill," Simon mused.

"Ain't it, though? Dashed inconvenient. Can't figure what brought it way up here."

"Devonshire, I daresay. The waters aren't drawing the numbers he had hoped, so perhaps he's trying to attract a different crowd."

"Well, it worked. Never saw such a full yard. Oh, I say. Here it is."

Once they had retrieved Eleanor's portmanteau and had it sent up to her, they took a seat on a bench outside the taproom. Simon refused to go inside, even though there were no more sounds of brawling. He would rather like to retrieve his hat, though.

"What's the matter, old boy?" Malcolm said when Simon made clear his resolve to remain outside. "Afraid someone will recognize you as the instigator of the last fight and start another?"

"The notion did cross my mind, and I have no desire to take that chance. I'm exhausted as it is, Malcolm. I'm not used to this sort of thing, you know."

Malcolm chuckled wickedly. "A little exercise never hurt you."

"On the contrary, it hurt me a great deal. I'm black and blue all over. And I was already stiff and sore from lifting the damned carriage out of the mud yesterday."

Malcolm regarded him thoughtfully. "Egad, Simon, you been as busy as the devil in a high wind, ain't you? All this effort in the cause of the beautiful Miss Chadwick? Or is it on behalf of her equally beautiful aunt? Is there a Mr. Tennant, by the way?"

"No, she is a widow."

"I'm glad to hear it, after witnessing that cozy little moment between the two of you. I never knew you to dally with married women."

It had been more than a cozy little moment. Before Malcolm had inserted his large self into the picture, it had been damned near perfect. After the brawl in the taproom, Simon's blood had been up and he could not have kept his hands off Eleanor for all the money in the world. He had wanted her with a passion that had made it difficult to remember he was a gentleman.

She must have felt the same primitive need, for she had not only permitted his kiss but had practically melted against him, and had kissed him back with equal fervor. It pleased Simon that she had allowed herself to give in to raw, emotional instinct for a moment, to relinquish a bit of that infernal control, however briefly. She would have allowed more if his interfering brother hadn't chosen that precise moment to announce his unwanted presence.

"For the second time in a single night," Malcolm said, "you practically knocked me off my pins. I never in all my life thought to see you paw a woman in public."

"You can forget about that, too, if you please. It was private."

"It certainly was." He smiled and pounded his brother on the back. "Nice work, old man. She's a real dazzler."

"Take care, brother. Mrs. Tennant is a lady and, for the moment under my protection. I will not have you getting, or giving, the wrong impression. There is nothing between us."

"It looked like something to me."

"Malcolm, I swear—"

"But then again, my upper story's never been well furnished. Must have got it wrong, eh? Often do. But I say, what was all that business about you being to blame for her niece's elopement?"

"Oh, that." Simon had hoped his brother had forgotten about that little slip. He ought to have known better. Malcolm took as much pleasure in a bit of scandal as a meddlesome old spinster. "It's rather complicated. A bit of a misunderstanding. I . . . er . . . gave the girl the impression that I approved of her attachment to Barkwith, and she seemed to think that meant I advised her to elope with the fellow."

"But I thought you didn't know Barkwith?"

"I don't. It was more in the nature of general advice."

Malcolm's brow furrowed up in confusion.

"I told you it was complicated," Simon said. He needed to steer his brother in another direction, and fast, before he revealed more than he should. "Would you and your friends like to stay at Tandy Hill tonight?"

His brother's eyes lit up. "Tandy Hill? Do you mean it?"

"Yes, of course. It's only a few miles from here

and you could leave early enough in the morning to catch your mill. It would certainly be more comfortable for you than curling up on a bench in the taproom."

"By Jove, it would. Ha! What a capital fellow you are, old boy. Wait till I tell Arbuthnot and Gates. I never even mentioned my brother had a house nearby. You always seem rather protective of your activities and friends up here in the Peak, so I hadn't wanted to impose. But Simon, wouldn't you prefer to use it yourself?"

"I will not leave Eleanor alone here, and I certainly will not take her unchaperoned to my home. Besides, the Runners will expect to find us here. No, you and your friends may take advantage of the house, so long as you promise not leave it in a shambles. I can send a message to the caretaker to expect you after dinner. What do you say?"

"I say you are a most excellent brother. A prince among men." He was pounding Simon on the back again.

"That's settled then. Now, let's see if we can find someplace to clean up before supper. We both look a little the worse for wear."

Malcolm poured himself another glass of wine and his brother discreetly moved the decanter out of his reach. The young man was slowly, and merrily, getting foxed. Eleanor passed the platter of roast beef and was pleased to see Malcolm carve several more slices to add to his plate. Perhaps if he ate more it would counteract the effects of the wine, though all evidence indicated otherwise.

She had never seen anyone, even her brother Benjamin, put away quite so much food in one sitting. Besides the roast beef, there had been ham, trout, eel, roasted game birds, potatoes, asparagus, peas, and jellies. Of course, Malcolm was a very large young man and no doubt required more sustenance than most. Unfortunately, his capacity for wine did not appear to equal his capacity for food.

"But I tell you," he said between bites, "it ain't at all like old Simon to use his fists the way he did tonight, Mrs. Tennant. Not like him at all. Never saw him do such a thing in my life." He leaned toward Eleanor and lowered his voice to a stage whisper. "To tell the truth, I never thought he had it in him. Bit on the scrawny side, don't you know." He hiccupped, covered his mouth, and laughed.

Eleanor was becoming rather embarrassed for Simon. His brother had done nothing but tease him since they had joined her for dinner. Malcolm found a great deal of amusement in the fact that his bookish brother had resorted to fisticuffs in public. He seemed to think the rare and unusual display a joke, at his brother's expense.

For once, however, Eleanor was feeling quite in charity with Simon, and not only for rescuing her in the taproom in yet another surprising display of physical strength. Or for the comfort of his arms afterward. It was also his doing, she knew, that her portmanteau had been sent up, along with soap and water and fresh towels.

She appreciated his thoughtfulness. And his unfailing generosity. She had no idea how much this was costing him, but he never complained and never failed to ensure her comfort.

It had been a relief to change out of clothes that reeked of ale from crawling along the taproom floor. She hoped a night's airing would help rid them of the rank odor else she would be thought a drunkard next time she wore them. She had not the luxury of an extensive wardrobe in the best of times, and on this journey she had brought along very little.

Eleanor wondered how the two brothers had managed to make themselves presentable without a bedchamber of their own. But each had changed his linen—no bloodstains—and coat. The cut above Simon's eye had been cleaned and did not look nearly as bad as the amount of blood had suggested. Just along the eyebrow, it was barely noticeable. The bruise on his jaw, however, could not be disguised.

"Father made us learn all the usual manly pursuits early on," Malcolm continued while carving up a small game hen. "Hunting, fishing, boxing, swordsmanship, all that sort of thing. Father's a tough old bird, but he was a game 'un in his time, they say. Wouldn't allow namby-pambyism in his sons, to be sure. But the sporting life has always suited me best. Sparring, racing, shooting—that's me. But Simon never enjoyed it by half, did you, old boy?"

"Not particularly." Simon eyed his brother warily while he addressed his own heaping plate of food. Eleanor could have fed herself and Belinda for a week on what these two packed away in a single meal.

"Never could understand it," Malcolm said. "Don't know what could possibly be more satisfying than a good mill or a horse race."

"I suspect your bother has other sources of amusement," Eleanor said.

Malcolm looked up from his plate, wiped his mouth, and laughed. "Don't he, though. Ain't much in the petticoat line myself, but old Simon here is a pistol where women are concerned."

"Is he indeed?" She cast a speculative glance in Simon's direction and saw the familiar blush. She ought to have known the arms that had felt so right around her had had a lot of practice.

"I should say so," Malcolm said. "Adores women. Can't look at a pretty woman that he don't fall top over tail in love with her. Old Simon's been in and out of love more times than I can count, making calf's eyes and spewing out poetry the like of which you never heard."

"Oh?" Her eyes never left Simon, whose blush had deepened to bright scarlet while he pretended to busy himself with a roasted guinea hen.

"Pages of pages of the flowery stuff," Malcolm

said, gesturing wildly with his fork. "Likes to pen sonnets on the delicate arch of an eyebrow or the shell-like curve of an ear. You wouldn't credit how long he can expound on a single insignificant body part."

"Malcolm—"

"And the ladies . . . well, I'm told his poetic offerings can make a woman melt into a puddle at his feet. Don't know how he does it. Never could string words together like that myself. But Simon's been scribbling that stuff since we was boys."

"Malcolm—"

"Ha! I recollect Squire Elliot's daughter—what was her name? Pretty little blond thing. Must've been about ten years old. Simon used to write little love poems and hide them for her to find. Only once, the squire found one of 'em and—"

"That's enough, Malcolm. Mrs. Tennant does not wish to hear of all my youthful follies."

"She don't mind, do you, Mrs. Tennant?"

"Not at all." Malcolm could yammer on as long as he wanted, as far as Eleanor was concerned. She needed to learn what sort of man his brother was. A libertine, apparently, though she would never have guessed it at first. Who would ever imagine such a man as a rake? A foolish question, when she had herself already become susceptible to his charm. She must strengthen her resolve to maintain her guard around him. What irony if she were to fall into the same trap she had been warning Belinda against.

"Well, I do mind," Simon said.

"Oh, don't be such an old poop," Malcolm said and turned to address Eleanor. "Just trying to make the point that Simon's been spouting verse practically since he could talk."

"I am not surprised to hear it," Eleanor said.

"No? Oh, I say, has he presented one to you already? Simon, you devil. I thought you said—"

"Malcolm!"

"No, I'm happy to say I have not received a poem from your brother," Eleanor said. "Nor have I had the . . . the pleasure of reading one." And frankly never hoped to be so honored. Judging from the florid prose of the Busybody, she imagined his poems would be as awful as those often printed in *The Ladies' Fashionable Cabinet*. Treacly things penned by poets with names like Crescenza and Alonzo and Zenobia and Fortunatus.

She did recollect that odd little speech when he was about to kiss her, something about a plump, ripe confection. Good Lord, was that his attempt to wax poetic? And if so, what body part—to use Malcolm's unpoetic turn of phrase—was he describing? Eleanor wanted to groan aloud.

"Oh, don't you worry, Mrs. Tennant," Malcolm said. "You'll get your poem. He's probably composing one about you this very minute."

"Malcolm!"

"Sorry, old chap," Malcolm said. He seemed finally to comprehend that his brother had gone beyond mortification to anger. "Never could keep my mouth shut after a few glasses of claret."

"I think you've had quite enough for tonight," Simon said, a bit stiff-lipped. He stood and put his hands on the back of his brother's chair. "Let us go round up your cronies and send you off to Tandy Hill before I am forced to exercise my fists again."

"But I ain't finished my dinner yet."

"Yes, you have. Come along, Malcolm. Thank you for your hospitality, Eleanor. I am sorry to have introduced such a boor into your company."

"I am not at all sorry. It has been a very enlightening evening. I thank you both for your company."

"I'll send someone up to clear away the plates," Simon said. "And I will look for you downstairs early tomorrow. We should have heard from the Runners by then." With that, he bundled up his large brother and ushered him out the door without a backward glance.

When they had gone, Eleanor poured herself a glass of wine and took it with her into the adjacent bedchamber. She checked the clothes airing before the fire and found the beery smell less strong, thank goodness. She quickly changed out of her dinner dress into a nightgown, curled up on the plump mattress, and sipped the wine while she pondered what she had learned about her traveling companion from his loose-lipped brother.

She was beginning to understand how Simon

came to be the Busybody. It made a foolish kind of sense that a man who adored women, who fell in love easily, and wrote flowery poetry to the objects of his affection would be just the sort who would advise a young girl to follow her heart. Apparently, he had been doing so himself for years, though he could not have been terribly successful since he was still unmarried. If he had fallen in love as many times as his brother implied, then he must surely have suffered a broken heart or two. Or three. Any ordinary man who'd experienced multiple failures in love would be more sanguine about the pitfalls of romance, and would not be so quick to advise an impressionable young girl to risk all for love.

But Simon was not an ordinary man. He was a true Romantic. Eleanor suspected he would never give up searching for that one perfect love, regardless of the number of times his heart was broken. In some ways, she admired such resiliency. But for the most part she still found the whole notion impractical and illogical, and his Busybody advice reckless and ill-considered.

She must keep that thought uppermost in her mind as far as Simon Westover was concerned: he was a dispenser of irresponsible advice to innocent young girls. If she concentrated on his foolhardy role as the Busybody, it would be easier not to think of him as a man of considerable strength of body and character, as a generous man willing to fund a madcap chase with a perfect stranger, as an attractive man with a romantic nature whose arms had felt decidedly warm and comfortable, and whose kiss had singed her to the tips of her toes. If she kept in mind Simon's contribution to Belinda's current situation and future unhappiness, perhaps she would not be bothered so much by the idea of him involved with countless women.

Yes, anger was the best solution. Anger and contempt. She must not allow other emotions to confuse the situation. Until Belinda's fate was settled, Eleanor would keep her thoughts on the red ribbon talisman that symbolized her duty to her niece. She would think of nothing else.

At least she would try.

A message from Hackett had arrived during the night reporting that the runaways had been seen in Manchester. Simon and Eleanor got an early start, before any of the sporting set had risen, so there was nothing to slow them in leaving Buxton.

Simon had not slept well due to the raucous reveling into the wee hours of dawn. He suspected Eleanor was equally exhausted. She barely spoke, and her jaw was set in a tense angle, the full lips thinned in a tight line.

Simon had spent his waking hours reliving those brief moments when he'd held her in his arms and kissed her. Lord, what a kiss it had been. The need of the moment had stripped away all his control. It had been a ruthless plundering of her mouth, a blistering moment of pure animal lust. But it was the kiss that had almost happened he regretted the most. By then, he had regained his wits and was ready to do a proper job of it, with tenderness and finesse. The look in her eyes told him she knew this time would be different.

Even after that pregnant moment had been interrupted by Malcolm, Simon had felt a change in her. Before, when he had sensed her admiration after pulling the carriage from the mud, she had regained her composure, her damnable control, rather quickly. She had not allowed admiration or attraction to discomfit her. This time, she had not been so quick to throw out her hedgehog spines. She had sent him admiring glances all evening. He had even sensed something more. Interest? Desire?

His poet's heart soared at the very idea. Or was he simply so smitten that he only imagined it?

In frustration, and despite the memory of his brother's teasing voice, Simon had worked during the night on his ode to Eleanor's upper lip.

Like a ruby set in the ivory face
The crimson treasure finds its place.
Then a purse, a pout, the two lips part
Sending blood hot signals to my heart.

Because of Malcolm's jibes, he would probably never have the courage now ever to present it to Eleanor. It would not be his first undelivered tribute, to be sure. As he had once told Eleanor, he had often worshipped from afar.

But this time the object of his affection sat close at his side, their legs and arms frequently touching with the bouncing and jostling of the carriage.

Eleanor kept her thoughts to herself during most of the day, offering only the occasional comment or brief response to a question as they followed the trail of messages from Hackett and Mumby. She did not mention their kiss. It seemed she was going to pretend it had not happened. Simon wasn't quite sure how to broach the subject, or even if it would be wise to do so, and so he, too, kept his thoughts to himself.

Eleanor remained mostly silent as they passed through the hilly countryside with its sinuous network of drystone enclosure walls, shining brilliant white in the morning sun; through craggy dales and rolling pastures dotted with herds of black-faced sheep; over Whaley Bridge, through to Disley, Hoo Lane, Bullock Smithy, and Stockport; and into the large manufacturing town of Manchester.

It was a sprawling, noisy, ugly town. Like the most crowded sections of London, it was a labyrinth of tiny lanes, alleys, and courts, here packed with squalid row houses alongside warehouses and factories of every kind. It reminded Simon of Spital-fields and was equally offensive to his aesthetic sensibilities—gloomy, smelly, and dirty. It pained him to watch the changes in his beloved countryside: land deforested and enclosed, country air fouled by the smoke of factories, villages pulled down to build towns, and towns swollen to unnatural numbers. It was enough to make an Englishman weep.

As they wound their way through Manchester, an astonishing amount of new construction was in progress at every turn. It was a wonder the Runners had been able to track anyone in such a busy, populous town.

The dour Francis Mumby met them at the Saracen's Head. "They know we're onto 'em," he said. " 'Stead of stickin' to the main road, they been crisscrossin' it since Ashbourne, tryin' to throw us off the scent. They came though Manchester to try and lose us. But we're keepin' on 'em, and they're still heading due north."

"Do we have any chance of running them to ground?" Simon asked.

"Depends on what they do. If they zigzag all the way to Scotland," the Runner said as he stroked the air with his long, thin fingers, "we just might catch 'em by goin' straight. But we won't waste your time reportin' every byway they take. Hackett and me'll try to keep you on the main road. From here, go on to Bolton. We'll leave word at the George."

When Mumby had taken his abrupt leave, Simon suggested they take time for a meal, but Eleanor was not hungry. The kitchen offered meat pies, however, and she suggested he buy one to take along.

"Capital idea," he said. "By God, I'm ravenous."

"Of course you are," she said. There seemed to be a hint of sarcasm in her remark, though Simon could not think why. A man had to eat, did he not?

The pies were not quite ready and so there would be a short wait. Eleanor paced about the inn yard restlessly, and Simon felt a bit guilty about making her wait. But he happened to glimpse through the taproom window something that might amuse her, that would help to pass the time. He popped inside to make sure he had correctly judged what he'd seen, made an arrangement with the gentleman at the corner table, and went back outside to fetch Eleanor.

"Come inside a moment," he said. "There is someone I'd like you to meet."

She looked wary, but followed him inside.

"This is Mr. Jackson," Simon said when they reached the corner table. "He is a profile painter. And this is Mrs. Tennant."

Eleanor lifted a brow. "How do you do, sir?"

"Can't complain," the man said. "Forgive me for not rising, but as you see, I'm short a leg. Left it in New York some years back. Make my living now as a profilist. Exact likenesses in miniature profile. This gentleman says he'd like me to make one of you."

Eleanor darted a look at Simon, then turned her attention to the artist. "That's a lovely idea, Mr. Jackson, but I'm afraid we haven't the time to spare. We are only waiting for Mr. Westover's meat pie, and then we must be back on the road. I'm terribly sorry."

Mr. Jackson cackled like an old hen. "Don't take but a minute. Well, it takes about three minutes, to be precise. And you can have it done on card or on plaster with a frame, or on ivory to be set in a locket or ring. If you don't believe it, here are some samples."

He opened a case from which an assortment of profile portraits spilled out onto the table. They were set in square papier-mâché frames, gilt oval frames, small red leather cases, lockets, bracelets, rings, snuffboxes, and toothpick holders. The profiles were delicately painted in black, with fine detail of hair and clothing.

"Oh, but these are lovely," Eleanor said, and picked up a locket to admire. "I used to cut them out as a child, but have always preferred the painted ones. These are exquisite, Mr. Jackson."

"Sit down, Mrs. Tennant, and I'll have you done in about two minutes."

Before Eleanor could object, Simon said, "Yes, please do, Mr. Jackson. Give her whatever she likes."

Eleanor still looked a bit leery. "What is fastest?"

"Don't matter. It's all the same. I can pop one in a frame in no time."

"All right," Eleanor said. "What do I do?"

Jackson had her sit down in a chair to which was

attached a special screen of thin paper. He set in place a bar across the front of the chair and told Eleanor to keep hold of it in order to remain steady. A candlestand was attached to the chair arm and the candlelight produced a stark shadow against the paper. Jackson sat on the opposite side of the screen and began to trace the outline of Eleanor's profile with a strange mechanical contraption he called a pantograph. It was made of folded wooden arms with a pencil fitted into each end. As Jackson traced the life-sized profile, the pantograph created an exact duplicate in miniature. It was a fascinating process and Simon wanted to stay and watch, but the landlord came to tell him the meat pies were ready.

By the time he came back from the kitchen, two pies in hand, Jackson had completed the profile. He was mounting it in an oval fame of hammered brass. He held it up for Simon to see.

"Remarkable. He has captured you, Eleanor. It is beautiful." And it was. Her soft curls, the tilt of her nose, the elegant curve of her jaw, the full upper lip were rendered perfectly. Even the lace at her throat was beautifully painted.

Eleanor looked pleased as well. He wondered if she would allow him to keep it?

He paid Jackson, then led Eleanor to their carriage to resume their journey.

"Thank you, Simon," she said. "That was very kind of you."

"Not at all. A beautiful woman deserves to be painted, even if only in miniature profile."

He took a bite of the second meat pie, and brushed away the crumbs from his waistcoat. He looked over to find Eleanor smiling at him. He was so pleased to see even a hint of cheerfulness from her that he could not hold back a broad smile. The profile had been a perfect diversion.

"What have I done that amuses you?"

"It is nothing," she said and shook her head.

"Eleanor?"

"Oh, all right. I was just thinking if you kept it up you might one day be as big as your brother."

He almost spewed out a mouthful of pie, but choked it down instead, setting off a fit of coughing and laughing. "I'll have you know," he said when he could speak, "that I can pack away more than Malcolm on any day. We're just built differently, that's all."

"In more ways than one, I should say."

"Yes, indeed. As I warned you."

"Malcolm may not be as well read as you, or as sentimental, but he has his charms."

"I fail to see them, but I bow to your feminine judgment on such matters. I hope you took most of what he said with a grain of salt."

"About your love affairs?"

"There, you see? He's given you the wrong impression, as I suspected. Just because I am sometimes moved to pen a verse about a woman does not necessarily mean I have had a love affair with her."

"So you have not left a trail of broken hearts?" she asked.

"I am afraid not. Though my own has been bruised a time or two. But never seriously. As I believe I once told you, I have not yet found my heart's desire. I am still in search of it."

"And you are quite sure you know what it is you seek?"

"Quite sure." He caught her gaze and held it, and the deeper he looked into those green eyes the closer he thought he'd come to finding his heart's desire.

"Are you certain you are not simply in love with the idea of love?" she asked.

He shrugged, but did not take his eyes from hers. "I suppose there is a bit of that in every Romantic. But I tell you this: when I find my one true love, I will never let her go, and I will love her until the day I die."

"Optimist."

He smiled. "Cynic."

And she could not hold back her own smile.

She allowed him to finish his second meat pie before pursuing the conversation.

"I hate to continue to impose my own cynicism on such a cockeyed optimist," she said, "but I feel obliged to point out the difficulties that optimism has wrought through the offices of the Busybody."

"I shall never live down my one mistake, shall I? I'll have you know I have been penning that column for years with many happy, satisfied readers."

"And I have been living for twenty-nine years and my wisdom and experience show me a world less perfect than yours."

"Twenty-nine years? As many as that? Well, my dear old crone, I have reached the crusty age of four-and-thirty and still find much to be optimistic about. Hence my always hopeful advice."

"And you are not ashamed to publish that advice under a pseudonym in a ladies' magazine?"

"No, of course not."

"Then why are you so afraid for your family to know about it?"

If Simon ignored or evaded her question again, as he had so often done in the past, Eleanor would no doubt continue thinking him a milksop who was afraid of his own father. How could he ever expect her to care for him, truly care for him, if she thought him so weak? But could he trust her with the truth?

Yes, he could. In fact, he had to trust her. He had been trying for days to win her trust. How could he expect to do so if he did not trust *her*?

He hoped his friends would forgive him for what he was about to do.

Chapter 11

It is a popular fallacy that gentlemen are disgusted by women of learning. In truth, any man would be delighted to discover those outward beauties which first attracted his admiration are accompanied by an enlightened mind.

The Busybody

"**W**hat I am about to tell you," Simon said haltingly, "must be kept in the strictest confidence."

Intrigued, Eleanor nodded and said only, "Of course."

"It is rather complicated," he said. "I am not sure where to begin." His head was bowed as he studied the hands fidgeting in his lap. A lock of red hair, unregarded, fell across his brow. "I believe I mentioned my friends and neighbors in the Peak district. They are more than friends. We are colleagues at the *Cabinet*. We share similar goals of a . . . a political nature."

"Political?"

"We were in France together in the early '90s, at the beginning of the Revolution. We were each of us exhilarated by the fires of Republicanism and re-

203

form, but were ultimately disappointed when the Revolution disintegrated into violence and chaos. When we returned to England, we hoped to foster more successful reform by concentrating not so much on political events as on the larger concerns of society itself. By then, however, a fierce reactionary spirit had taken hold in the wake of the Terror, and it was not safe to espouse Republican ideals in any sort of public forum."

Eleanor was not entirely surprised by the revelation of Simon's politics. "I believe many so-called Romantics or Sentimentalists are Republicans at heart, are they not? Those who are passionate about all things natural are very often reformers, I think. A sort of Whiggish optimism seems perfectly in keeping with the Romantic philosophy, as I understand it. However, I'm afraid I do not understand the connection between your political activities and *The Ladies' Fashionable Cabinet*."

He gazed at her with open admiration, as though pleased that she had even an inkling of what the Romantic movement was all about. "I will get to the *Cabinet* in a moment. At first, after we had settled in the Peak, we wrote and anonymously published several pamphlets supporting such things as the repeal of anti-sedition laws, general criticisms against strictures on speech, printing, assembly, the Combination Acts, and so on. Also a few pamphlets on the rights of women, liberally borrowing from Miss Wollstonecraft. But we were not reaching enough people, and were constantly alert to discovery. Any one of us could be jailed under the laws against 'seditious' activities."

Eleanor was more than a little astonished to discover Simon's politics to be more serious than she would have imagined. But perhaps politics was in his blood. Sir Harold Westover was a very prominent member of Parliament. On the Tory side of the aisle. "Your father is one of the more vocal opponents to the repeal of those laws, is he not?"

"He is. That is only one of the reasons I keep my activities secret." He rubbed his bruised jaw absently. "Not, mind you, because I am afraid for him to know, though it would surely give him no pleasure. But it would also jeopardize his standing in the House and, despite our different positions, I have no right and no wish to interfere in a career he has spent his life building."

Eleanor's brows lifted in surprise. The man she had thought so fearful of his formidable parent's wrath was instead simply a son who honored and respected his father. She felt a twinge of shame for ever thinking otherwise. "But I still do not see what all this has to do with a ladies' magazine."

"I'm getting to that. *The Ladies' Fashionable Cabinet*, as you may know, has been in existence for many years. It had always been written by a group of ladies under the editorship of its founder, a woman who happened to be great aunt to one of our group. Miss Edwina Parrish, one of my colleagues in the Peak, was a favorite of her great aunt. When the old woman died a few years back, she requested that the editorial reins be turned over to Edwina, though the magazine itself is still owned by her son, Edwina's uncle. He collects the profits, and because he believes it to be a silly female rag sheet, he ignores it. He has no idea what Edwina has done."

"I don't understand. What has she done?"

Simon smiled. "The fact that you don't know shows how successful the scheme has been."

"What scheme?"

"Do you also read the *Lady's Monthly Museum*?"

Eleanor gave him a quizzical look and wondered if he would ever get to the point. "Yes, I read it, along with every other woman in the country, I'm sure. But what has that to do with anything?"

"Quite a lot, actually. The *Museum* affects to be written by 'A Society of Ladies' but is in fact written by a group of exceedingly conservative men. One of the hidden goals of the publication is to defeat the advocates of Rationalism, Radicalism, and Republicanism. They use cunningly calculated indirection in their essays and stories to promote their conservative philosophies and manipulate their unsuspecting readers."

Eleanor was somewhat surprised to hear that such a fashionable publication had political motives, though she could not quite understand what purpose it served. "What good does it do them to promote their politics in a magazine directed at women?"

Simon shifted his position so that he almost

faced her. "Among the philosophies they fear," he said, "are those aimed at the rights of women, those of Mary Wollstonecraft, Mary Hays, Catherine Macauley, Thomas Paine, and others. The editors of the *Lady's Monthly Museum* ally themselves with arch conservatives like Hannah More and George Canning, promoting established hierarchical structures and a disposition of power purposefully unequal: woman's inherent weakness of body and mind oblige her to defer to man."

"Good heavens! I think you must exaggerate. The *Museum* is no more than an entertaining little magazine with bits of fashion and poetry and stories and other business thought to appeal to women. How is it you find such high-blown and sinister motives in descriptions of the latest fashions?"

"All the elements expected in a ladies' magazine are there," he said, "including the latest fashions. It is what draws female readers, after all. But if you look closely you will find subtle manipulation throughout. Just as an example, they frequently attack the very notion of education for females. More than once they have printed essays in which education for girls of no fortune is considered to be a bad thing because it unnaturally raises their views beyond the reach of their station and character. The fact is, they regard the broadening of education to females and the lower classes as presenting a threat to the conventions of civilized society, that the dissemination of knowledge might inspire a Reign of

Terror on British soil. And so they send subtle messages, and some not so subtle, to their readers that education for females is a foolish endeavor. Can you imagine anything more contemptible? Not to mention wrong-headed. Education does not breed anarchy. Neglect and despair do."

His free hand had become as animated as his voice, punctuating his words in the air. Eleanor could not reconcile this passionate reformer with the spineless fool she had once thought him. The dreamer was more grounded than she had imagined. She was humbled to think how completely and thoroughly she had misjudged him, in every possible way. He was a man of strong principles, and though she might not always agree with him, she could not help but admire him.

"The *Museum* editors attempt to offer 'guidance' to their readers," he went on, "but their moral doctrines guide their female readers into carefully constructed, narrowly defined subservient roles. When Edwina inherited the helm of the *Cabinet*, it seemed the perfect vehicle to combat such patriarchal attitudes. But her uncle, the formidable Victor Croyden, would close down the magazine if he knew that the sweet old ladies who once ran it were now totally out of the picture, and that men and radical women were controlling it."

"And that is why it is so important to keep your identities secret?"

"Yes. If Croyden found out a man was involved, he might become curious and be tempted to take a closer look. There are things in the account books, for example, that he must never see. It would be a shame to have the *Cabinet* shut down. We've made great progress. Our circulation has doubled and we actually turn a profit. We are able to provide regular stipends to some of our staff writers, and to request contributions from established essayists and poets who are in sympathy with our principles. Mr. Coleridge has recently submitted poems, and a few members of the Whig Club have provided articles."

"Coleridge? Does he perchance use a pseudonym? Something like Rodolfo?"

Simon colored and shook his head. "No, he always signs his initials."

Eleanor was glad to hear it. She rather liked what little she had read of Mr. Coleridge's works. She would hate to think of him as penning some of the poetic drivel she had read in the magazine. "I must say you have intrigued me, Simon. I had no notion there was such serious intent behind a seemingly frivolous publication like the *Cabinet*. Or such ferocious competition of principle with the *Lady's Monthly Museum*."

He nodded and his eyes blazed with fervor. He seemed remarkably pleased that she understood what he had been trying, in his very long-winded fashion, to explain. "My own personal grievance against the *Museum*," he said, "is the way in which they twist stories and historical essays to show how a woman should glory in giving up her own wishes to those of her husband, how a woman who thinks herself equal to her husband will necessarily find herself in an unhappy marriage. And they are forever espousing the notion that marriage to a complete stranger, so long as the match was arranged by her parents, is preferable to a young woman entering into a love match. You may call me a Romantic, but I believe women should not be forced into marriages that are little more than business contracts. I believe a woman should be allowed to love."

"And so the Busybody was born."

He grinned and the dimples twinkled. "Actually, she had already existed in the original publication. When Edwina took over the magazine, we maintained most of the original columns and pseudonyms. I became the Busybody. Nicholas Parrish, Edwina's brother, became the essayist Augusta Historica. All of us took on various roles. It has been our intention to beat the *Lady's Monthly Museum* at its own game."

"How so?"

"By filling our pages with veiled messages of female potential and strength and fortitude rather than female subjugation."

"I would not have thought a Romantic would appreciate strong and powerful women. I would have guessed he would prefer his women frail and weak, in constant need of a man's protection and reassurance."

He grinned. "Not this Romantic. I prefer a strong,

self-possessed woman of parts. One who would delight in arguing a point with me rather than one who would quietly submit to my authority. Someone like you. Have I not often compared you to an avenging angel? To Boadicea? There is much more to admire in a woman like you, Eleanor, who takes matters into her own hands, than in a wilting violet languishing on her chaise waiting for things to be done *for* her."

"That is very kind of you, I'm sure," she said, and hoped she was doing a good job of disguising the unexpected and unwelcome wave of pleasure that had swept over her at his very obvious regard. It both thrilled and frightened her to know that he truly admired her and didn't simply lust after her. "But I always associated Romantics with knights in shining armor rescuing damsels in distress. Have you not been my heroic rescuer more than once on this journey?"

At that moment, the carriage hit a deep rut that sent them both bouncing off the seat. Simon used the bumpy ride as an excuse to take her hand in his. His thumb stroked the skin above her glove where she still wore the red ribbon at her wrist. His touch sent a tremor up her arm that was almost too much to bear.

"My dear Eleanor, I can think of nothing more romantic than being your knight in shining armor, if you would allow it. A woman with the strength of character to accept help when it is needed is much more romantic to me than a helpless damsel in middling distress. There was nothing heroic in my actions last night in the taproom. You were putting up an admirable fight of your own. My reaction was one of pure animal rage at the sight of that brute with his hands on you."

The look in his eyes had become more intense than was comfortable. She would like to have explained it away as nothing more than a reflection of the passion of those political and social convictions he had revealed, but she rather suspected it was a different kind of passion altogether. As tempting as it was to cast all her prudent considerations to the winds and give in to the invitation in those bright blue eyes, she must remember to guard against such foolishness. She must remember Belinda and her plight.

Eleanor gently removed her hand from his. "Tell me more about these veiled messages in the magazines."

He sensed her discomfort and gave a rueful little smile. "It's quite simple," he said. "The *Museum*, as an example, relishes stories about young girls who fall in love, run away with their heart's desire, and end up miserably unhappy, socially ruined, hopelessly mad, or quite often dead—all because they went against the wishes of a parent or of society. You will notice the stories in the *Cabinet* always have a more uplifting ending. Young girls are shown to have character, to be fully capable of making their own decisions, and ultimately finding happiness. Unlike the *Museum*, we send messages that promote education of women, including the poor. We try to foster strength of mind, heart, and body for all females, for all people. Not to put too fine a point on it, we believe in women. We trust women."

He smiled, a bit roguishly, and Eleanor was reminded of his brother's words. *He adores women.*

"The *Lady's Monthly Museum*," he said, "though written for women, has nothing but contempt for them."

Blast it all, she believed him. Worse than that, she admired him for what he was doing. She would never again be able to read the *Lady's Monthly Museum* without being aware that some beastly man was attempting to manipulate her with his maudlin tales and moralistic essays.

Why, oh why did Simon have to be so damned admirable? Why couldn't he have turned out to be the fatuous fool she had expected him to be? Despite all her best intentions, she was already halfway smitten with him. His twinkling blue eyes, his infectious grin, his dimples, his lean muscular frame, his strong arms, his sense of honor and integrity, his kindness, even his wretched idealism all worked to break down her defenses. The fact that he was so clearly interested in her made it even more tempting to give in.

But Eleanor knew too well the dangers of such folly. She had once trusted a man and it had ruined her life. She could not allow it to happen again.

A bit of argument always helped to keep her

wits about her. She was determined to pursue a debate whether she agreed with Simon or not. It was safer. Or was it? He had said he preferred a woman who argued. Heavens, what was she to do?

"Are you certain the *Museum* is as nefarious as that?" she asked, unable in the end to resist an argument. "Perhaps they are simply trying to protect women from making reckless decisions."

"They are trying to protect women against the influence of new ideas that might interfere with the established order. I cannot tell you how much I deplore their consistent attitude of female weakness in need of protection, their moronic position on female education which blatantly admits to women's inferior minds. You are a strong woman with a mind of your own, Eleanor. Do you not feel your intellect the equal of most men?"

"Most assuredly."

"Then do you not object to a wholesale assumption of feminine weakness?"

"My dear sir, there is hardly a woman alive who has not used that assumption to her advantage. Believe me, it requires a great deal of cunning intellect to ensure that we receive the most protection and security for the least effort."

"Then like the *Museum*, you value fortune and security above love?"

"Absolutely."

His brows knit together in a perplexed frown. "How sad it is to hear you say that, my dear. Love is the great equalizer, and the most important thing in all the world. In my opinion, marriageable young girls should be taught the value of love over rank and fortune."

"Spoken just like a man who has never wanted for anything in his life. A man who can never imagine the tenuous situation of women—all women at all levels of society—who must rely on men for every aspect of their existence."

"Then you agree with the *Museum*'s position on settling for contentment with one's lot, on the importance of convenience over love, of security over affection? You agree with how they actively discourage reaching higher, going after one's true desires?"

"I only suggest that such a philosophy is more realistic and is potentially less hurtful to impressionable young minds. Fewer hearts would be broken if girls were not convinced by publications such as yours that true love and eternal bliss actually exist."

He gazed at her thoughtfully for a moment, then asked, "Who broke your heart, Eleanor?"

He had watched her closely during their conversation, initially to reaffirm his decision to trust her, which he did, but then simply to gauge her reaction. She had a very expressive face, due in great part to the way she used her mouth—her lips puckered and pursed and pouted and twisted and thinned and smiled; she pushed the delicious upper lip out; she caught the lower lip between her teeth; her tongue darted out to lick her lips. It was a dizzying display, but also revealed every emotion. A great number of them had played across her face: surprise, disbelief, admiration, pleasure, confusion, apprehension.

But all that had been wiped away with a single question. She had closed up once again. What the devil had possessed him? The truth was, the words had spilled out before he knew what he was doing.

She did not respond.

"I'm sorry, Eleanor. I should not have—"

"No, you should not have." She would not look at him. "My private life is none of your business and I resent your arrogant insinuations."

"You are quite right. It is none of my business. I am dreadfully sorry."

She turned away from him, not just her head but her entire body, so that she almost had her back to him. She had cut him off completely, and his heart sank. Dammit all, why couldn't he have kept his mouth shut? Any further words from him would simply make matters worse. It was probably best to keep his tongue between his teeth and leave her to her thoughts for a while.

And so Simon set his own muddled brain to untangling all that had been said and done. He reviewed her reactions to his explanation about the magazine and was satisfied that she understood the need for continued secrecy. He could trust her. She had not laughed or called him a fool. Despite her usual challenges, he thought she had been impressed with the work of the *Cabinet*. Once again, he had sensed that tiny spark of admiration that caused his heart to swell up in his throat with pride. Dammit, if only she weren't afraid of that spark, afraid to let herself feel something for him. Assuming she was inclined to do so, and he liked to think she was. There had been that kiss, after all.

But he kept coming back to that unfortunate question. Who had broken her heart?

Clearly, someone had. She would not have closed up like a fist otherwise. He guessed it had not been the late Mr. Tennant. Eleanor said theirs had not been a love match. Was it a youthful attachment before her marriage? A love affair during her marriage?

It was no use guessing, for unless she told him he would never know the truth. And she was right, it was none of his business. He did not really need to know the particulars. It was enough to know it had happened, and had hurt her deeply. It certainly added a level of difficulty to his goal of winning her trust, and perhaps even her affection. He was determined to achieve that goal, however, despite this damnable setback.

Simon kept his own counsel as they followed the messages of the Runners into Lancashire. The hilly countryside meant a sometimes rough ride, and they were continually jostled about inside the carriage, but Eleanor curled up against the window and clung tightly to the strap so there was almost no physical contact between them. Simon did not break the strained silence as they traversed the bleak moorland surrounding Bolton and the picturesque ravines beyond; nor as they crossed stone bridges over busy canals; nor as they drove past wild and windswept hillsides and wide open valleys; nor as they drove through Heaton, Horwich, and Chorley, skirting the fringes of the West Pennine Moors on the road to Preston.

Twilight had set in, dark clouds hung upon the hills, and a soft rain had begun to fall. The wind had kicked up, and the air was heavy with the threat of a storm. Simon was just about to suggest they stop in Preston for the night when Eleanor quite startled him by breaking her long silence.

"Why must you assume that everyone thinks and believes and acts as you do?" She seemed to be continuing their earlier conversation, as though several silent hours had not passed. "Just because I happen to have a more practical approach to life does not mean I am unhappy or have suffered a broken heart. It simply makes me a realist. Not a cynic, as you always claim. A realist."

He smiled to let her know how pleased he was to have her back, even in a peevish mood. He opened his mouth to agree with her, for the sake of establishing some sort of peace between them, but stopped short. Would she believe him if he agreed with her? Or would she think him merely patronizing? He was inclined to believe she would think less of him if he tried to placate her with disingenuous platitudes.

Eleanor was a woman who enjoyed a good argument. Perhaps that was what she needed just now. He would give her one, then. He would *not*, however, bring up the subject of her broken heart.

"There is a fine line between a realist and a pessimist, my dear."

"Oh, so now I am a pessimist? Just because I don't think it such a bad thing for a woman to seek security for her future?"

Simon grinned. "That, and other things."

She met his gaze squarely, but did not smile. "No, I won't accept that label. I still say I am a realist. Where the Romantic sees endless years of connubial bliss for two star-crossed lovers, the realist sees a short time of passion dwindling into years of disappointment and contempt when there is no money and the trials of daily life sap all the bliss from the marriage. Where the Romantic drives through the countryside bemoaning the number trees lost to the axe, the realist sees the practical use made of the timber."

"I prefer my hopeful Romanticism, if you please. Where the Romantic sees a runaway couple and believes a Scottish marriage is in store, the pessimist sees only dishonorable motives and ruin. You see, Eleanor, I will always hope for the best for Belinda."

"But you are wrong."

"It is simply my starry-eyed opinion, my dear. I will hang on to that hope until we find them."

"But you are wrong."

"You will pardon me for believing otherwise."

"But you are wrong."

"Your argument has become decidedly repetitive." He offered a smile, but got none in return. "Allow me respectfully to disagree with you. They are still heading north, straight toward Gretna. They may already be married."

"No. Barkwith will never marry her. He will seduce her and make her love him and use her and toss her out when he is through." She had curled up within herself, her shoulders hunched inward, her arms crossed tightly over her chest.

"How can you be so sure?" he asked.

She hesitated a long moment, and he thought she was not going to answer, that she would retreat back into silence. But then, in a small voice, she said, "Because I know."

"How do you know?"

She did not respond, and with sudden blinding clarity, Simon knew the answer. A cold, sickening sensation gripped his insides. "Eleanor? How do you know?"

"Because it happened to me."

Chapter 12

How fortunate is she who cultivates the heart and fills every vessel of it with affection. And how fortunate is he who wins that heart.

The Busybody

Dear God, what had she done?

"Eleanor. I am so sorry."

She could not look at Simon, could not bear to see in his eyes the distress and sorrow she heard in his voice. She kept her gaze out the window instead, where the approach to Preston was obscured by heavy rain, a pelting, pitiless downpour that echoed the storm of emotion in her breast.

She had not meant to tell him. It was humiliating and painful and private. She did not want him to know. She did not want anyone to know. Only a very few knew the whole sordid tale, and now this sweet man, this guileless Romantic who was practically a stranger, would hear it all.

She had put all memory of that horrible time behind her. Years ago, she had very consciously consigned the episode to some dark oubliette in her mind and thrown the bolt. It was not until Belinda had become infatuated with Barkwith that the memories had been unlocked and thrown into the open again. And because they were fresh in her mind, she had been careless enough to blurt out the truth to Simon.

"Eleanor."

She felt him take her hand, and though she was too mortified to relish his reassurance, she was also too tired to fight. She let him hold it. He covered it with his other hand and kept it gently captive, like a wounded bird. Somehow it made her want to cry.

"I am sorry I harassed you into that confession," he said. "It was unspeakably intrusive, and I regret it with all my heart." His voice was soft and velvety and wrapped itself around her, tender and soothing, like his hands around hers. It made her want to turn around, curl up against him, and let him hold her. It would be so easy.

She wanted to say something, to tell him it was not his fault, but she did not believe she could control her voice and so merely nodded.

"We will not speak of it again," he said. "It will be as if you never told me."

"No." The word burst from her lips, thin and small. Still, she could not look at him. He did not speak, only continued to softly caress her hand. "No, it cannot be as if I never told you." Her voice shook a little, and she made an effort to control it. "Now you know the truth. Now you know why I have been so anxious for Belinda."

"Yes. I understand now."

"I do not want Belinda to suffer as I did."

"Of course not. Lord, how wretched this must be for you, to watch your own history repeated with your niece. But perhaps knowing what happened to you, Belinda will ensure a better outcome for herself."

"She does not know what happened to me."

"Oh."

"And neither do you." Eleanor turned to face him at last, and immediately wished she had not. She had no defense against that benevolent blue gaze, and if he had pulled her into his arms then and there, she would have gone willingly. But he made no such move. Instead, he removed one of his hands from hers but kept hold with the other, entwining their fingers and giving a little squeeze. It was a gesture of support, of comfort, of kindness with no hint of the sensuality that had been so powerful at other times between them. After such a confession from her, he would be careful not to offer anything more than friendship. Bless the man for his good sense, for she had very little at the moment.

"I suppose I should tell you the whole story," she said. "Then you will understand why I feel the way I do, why I am such a cynic about so many things."

"That is not necessary, Eleanor. It is a private matter and you have no need to explain it to me."

"But I think I would like to." It was true. Though

she could not have explained why, she wanted Simon to know all of it. He had trusted her with his secrets. Now she wanted to share hers with him.

"I do not know what makes me worthy of your confidence, my dear, but if you wish to tell me, I promise to honor that confidence."

A flash of lightning was followed by a tremendous crack of thunder, rattling the windows of the carriage.

"I believe your tale will have to wait," Simon said. He gave her hand one more squeeze, then released it. "We are going to have to stop or the poor postboys will be swept away."

They had crossed a broad stone bridge over the Ribble into Preston. The drenched postillions hurried them to the center of town where they found the Rose and Crown, the coaching inn where the Runners had told them to await their next report. They would get no farther tonight in such weather, so Eleanor was glad to see it was a large, modern three-storied brick building with elegant sash-windowed shop fronts on either side of the coach entrance.

Simon bustled them into the main entry and, with his usual efficiency, arranged all that was needed for the evening and for their departure in the morning.

Eleanor made her way upstairs to her bedchamber. Still a bit rattled, she was glad to be alone for a while, and dismissed the efficient chambermaid who had brought lavender-scented soap and hot water and had offered to help her undress. The room was well furnished and had even been supplied with wax candles, a true luxury at a coaching inn.

Eleanor experienced another pang of guilt over what all this was costing Simon. At first, she had been so angry over the Busybody that she had been happy to let him fund the journey. But she realized now—had done for some time, in fact—that the Busybody had been no more than a convenient scapegoat. Belinda was as incorrigible as Eleanor had been at her age. She would have fled with Barkwith in the end regardless of what the Busybody had advised.

And so Eleanor had selfishly used poor Simon, had manipulated his kindhearted nature as artfully as Barkwith had Belinda. It pained her to consider how much he had spent so far. This inn, especially, must be dreadfully expensive.

A coal fire had been laid in a small grate. Sweet-smelling dried herbs had been scattered in the corners of the drawers and placed in bowls on the windowsill. The curtained bed looked clean and comfortable, and for once Eleanor did not entirely regret leaving her own sheets at home. She hoped Belinda had enough sense to insist on fresh, dry sheets, wherever she was. Or would she be so lost to passion she failed to notice damp, spotty bed linen?

In Belinda's place, Eleanor had not paid much attention to such details. It had been almost a dozen years, but she could still remember it as though it were yesterday. And she was about to dredge up those memories and serve them on a platter to Simon.

Was she making a huge mistake? Was it enough that he knew *something* had happened without laying bare all the tawdry details?

No, she was determined to tell him all. She wanted to tell him. It seemed somehow important that he know everything. Was she simply curious to see if he would still be interested in her if he knew her tainted history? Or in the deepest, most private corner of her heart, did she perhaps secretly hope there might be a chance for something between them, after this ramshackle business with Belinda was settled?

She could not bring herself to admit to that possibility. She had no right even to consider it. It was true that she had been fighting her attraction to Simon for most of their brief acquaintance. Wouldn't Constance laugh to know that Eleanor had decided he was indeed quite adorable, reddish hair and all. At least she was finally honest enough to admit it to herself. Besides being dangerously attracted to him— the touch of his hand could throw her heart into a wild disorder—she found him to be so thoroughly sweet. Even discounting his Romantic tendencies, so contrary to her own nature, she liked him. Simon was a good man. A kind, honorable, gentle man, and she had grown inordinately fond of him.

But he was still a man, and fundamentally no

different from the rest. Eleanor had been exposed from an early age to the often treacherous and insidious nature of men. She had been cruelly deceived once. She had no desire to suffer such heartache again.

She shook out her pelisse and draped it over a chair before the fire. She had worn it on each day of this journey, and it showed in the deep creases and dark, mud-colored blotches at the hem. The smell of ale from the brawl at Buxton was only barely noticeable. She retrieved the second of her two carriage dresses from the portmanteau, shook it out, and spread it over the top of a small chest of drawers in readiness for tomorrow.

Tomorrow. Another day on the road. Would they find Belinda at last? It would be five days she had been with Geoffrey Barkwith. Had he tired of her yet?

Eleanor steeled herself for the discussion she would have with Simon over dinner. It was a difficult and shameful story for her to tell, but he would surely understand her fears for Belinda once he'd heard it.

As she shook out and brushed off the dress she would wear for dinner, she hoped her story would be so engrossing that Simon would not notice he'd already seen the dress twice before. Men hardly ever noticed such things, though, thank heaven.

The meal might be a strained one, Simon thought as he waited for Eleanor to join him, but at least the surroundings were pleasant. He paced back and forth before the hearth in the small but nicely appointed parlor he'd hired for their supper. He supposed he had the prosperity of Preston's industry to thank for this excellent inn. If only the factories and housing for the workers were built with such care, perhaps he would not be so scornful of growth.

He was not looking forward to the conversation ahead. He had a rough idea of what had happened and had no burning desire to hear the details. But it pleased him enormously that she wanted to tell him. It was a small victory in his campaign to win her trust. And if she trusted him enough to share a painful secret, then how hard could it be to convince her to open herself to his . . . what? His admiration? His affection? His love?

Did he love her?

He was certainly a little bit *in* love with her—a common enough thing for him, as Malcolm had been so damned quick to point out. He couldn't help it. Beautiful women, especially beautiful intelligent women, affected him that way. And he'd certainly been smitten with Eleanor almost since their first meeting, when she'd slapped him hard across the face. But did he love her?

Though he'd been *in* love countless times—all right, it wasn't countless, it was seventeen times; he had notebooks of poetry to prove it—he'd never really loved. Truly loved. As he had told Eleanor, he was still searching for his heart's desire. He'd been infatuated and moonstruck and in serious lust, but he'd never felt the sort of bone-deep caring, the blending of souls, the all-consuming need he had always defined as love. He had come close once, but that was a long time ago.

In the short time he'd known Eleanor—could it really be only days?—he had come closer than ever before to those feelings he defined as love. He felt as though he were on a precipice, uncertain whether to jump. The merest sign from her that she would welcome or even, God help him, return his regard, and he would surely fall over the edge.

He sighed with a sudden rush of intense longing when the door opened and Eleanor entered, followed closely by three waiters with trays of food.

"I'm sorry, Simon. I have kept you waiting."

She had misinterpreted his sigh, and he thanked heaven for it. Even so, he felt his blasted face flush like a fever, just as though she knew what he'd been thinking before she walked in. He wondered if he would still be blushing when he was seventy. It was dashed embarrassing.

"Not at all," he said, willing the blush to fade. "As you see, our supper has only just arrived."

"Poor Simon. I'm sure you are starving, after only that insignificant meal in Manchester this afternoon."

Ha! She thought he was blushing over his eating habits. But why on earth should that embarrass him? He supposed anyone who ate like such a bird would naturally think his appetite excessive. Could he help it if he was always hungry? His mother had often remarked that her two sons had hollow legs, for she could not imagine where else they put all that food. And now that he thought about it, he was feeling a bit peckish.

Simon pulled out the chair for Eleanor, and basked in the view of her bare back and all its attendant glories: the long curve of neck, the delicate nape where a few wisps of coffee-dark hair refused to be pinned, the fine white skin unmarred by so much as a freckle and smelling sweetly of lavender. The low-backed Indian muslin gown again. Thank God her travel wardrobe was limited. This particular gown, though sadly out of date, was a delight. If he had the dressing of her, he would always put her in garments that revealed her soft, white, perfect back. Of course, if he had the dressing of her, he would likely keep her undressed.

When she was seated he tore his eyes away and took the chair opposite. One of the waiters ladled out bowls of mock turtle soup, which he placed before them. The others laid out a sideboard with poached sole, veal pie, sirloin of beef, Yorkshire puddings, stuffed moor hens, artichokes, stewed onions, French beans, and spring peas. There were also custards, fruit tarts, and cheeses. Simon eyed the spread hungrily and saw that Eleanor was trying not to smile.

He sent the waiters away, assuring them they would wait upon themselves, and gave his full attention to the soup. The mock turtle was a favorite, and this one was especially good. He looked up to find those splendid green eyes smiling at him over the rim of a wineglass.

"Please do not mention wolves, parsons, tapeworms, or wooden legs," he said. "I've heard them all, I assure you, mostly from my own mother."

"It must have cost a quarter's allowance and a kitchen staff of twenty to feed you two for a week," she said.

"We three. Malcolm and I inherited our healthy appetites from my father."

"Your cook must have been worked to death in such a household."

"She doted on us boys, I assure you. She felt appreciated. Your puny little appetite, my dear, would have put Cook into the sulks for a week."

She smiled, mostly with her eyes, and Simon thought she'd never looked more lovely. A pang of pure desire coiled low in his belly. Lord, but he was smitten.

"My brother Benjamin is the great eater in my family," she said. "But then he has been a sailor most of his life, and I think they do not often get good food at sea."

"He is Belinda's father?"

"Yes."

A heavy silence fell between them. Mention of her family brought the infamous untold story into the room, looming like a dark, unwelcome specter who would not be ignored. Simon would not be the first to broach the subject. It was her story, and if she had decided not to tell him, that was fine with him. Disappointing, but fine.

He rose and went to the sideboard. "Shall I fill a plate for you?"

She gave a soft chuckle and rose to join him. "Please don't. I would not be able to see you over such a mountain. I will do it myself."

They each filled their plates—his heaping, hers scarcely sufficient to feed a cat. When Simon returned to the table, she had put off all cheerfulness and donned a serious expression.

"I suppose you are wanting to hear my sorry tale," she said.

"Only if you want to tell me. You don't have to, you know."

"I know. But I do want to. It will be a relief to get it out in the open."

She seemed a little reluctant to begin, however, and took a bite of veal pie instead. She licked her lips, flicking her tongue into the very corner of her mouth to remove a crumb of pastry. Simon had to force himself to look away, else he would never be able to get up from the table again. God, he adored her mouth.

Her heard her take another bite and then a sip of wine before she finally spoke.

"I was just turned eighteen," she began, without preamble, "and had come to London for my first Season. My mother had hoped for a great match for me, and pulled every string she had to get me into all the best balls and parties. I'm afraid I was a green rustic with no polish, a true wide-eyed innocent.

"It was at a very elegant *ton* ball that I first met Henry. I won't tell you his full name. It does not matter. I am sure he is unknown to you. He was older—well, he was thirty, which seemed very old at the time—and he was devastatingly handsome. When he began to pay attention to me, I was beside myself, giddy with excitement that he should single me out. My parents didn't like him and discouraged an attachment. I did not know then that they were aware of his past notorious behavior, that he had ruined several young girls' reputations and was generally considered a scoundrel. My mother hinted as much to me, but I was too naïve to understand what she meant. And I was determined that she should not destroy my hopes for a match with Henry."

Simon could just imagine Eleanor as a young, headstrong girl with stars in her eyes. He wished he'd known her then.

"He was a seductive charmer," she said, "and I was susceptible to his every move. He knew it, and played on my gullibility to sweep me off my feet. I thought him the most glorious creature I'd ever known, and I was madly in love with him. When he suggested we run away together, I had never heard anything so romantic in my life. Without a second thought I agreed to travel with him to Scotland.

"At least I thought we were going to Scotland. He kept mentioning the Great North Road, and so I assumed we would go to Gretna or some other town and be married. Of course, I submitted to him on the very first night. Since we were to be married, what difference did it make?"

She looked down at her plate and pushed her food around with a fork. She had not looked at him once since she began her story. Simon, however, could not keep his eyes off her. His dinner sat forgotten on his plate. "But he did not take you to Scotland, did he?"

She shook her head but did not look up. "No. We got as far as Derbyshire when Henry said we were going to drop by the house of a friend. I was a bit anxious about getting to Scotland but he convinced me that we were in no particular hurry. I was so blinded with love for the man that he could have taken me anywhere. Since I had already given myself to him, I felt we were practically married anyway, that we had a special bond forged by a physical relationship. The minor detail of a marriage ceremony could wait a few days."

Her voice had grown flat, without expression or timbre. It was as though she recited a well-memorized story about someone else. Simon felt hot anger in the back of throat and his hands, resting on the tabletop, curled into fists.

"He took me to a small manor house in Derbyshire," Eleanor continued, "but his friend was away from home, as Henry had, of course, known he would be. It had all been arranged. I daresay I was not the first girl he'd brought there. He convinced me to stay a few days and enjoy the countryside. But, quite frankly, we didn't often leave the house."

Her voice had dropped to barely a whisper, and her chin had dropped almost to her chest. Shame had wrapped itself around her like a cloak. Simon wanted desperately to reach out and touch her, to pull her onto his lap and hold her tight, but he did not. It was not the right time.

"When I finally told him I thought we should leave and continue on to Scotland, he pretended not to know what I was talking about. He said he had never mentioned Scotland or marriage, and that I had presumed what he never intended. He laughed and said he would not be taken in by my pretense of innocence, he would not be manipulated into an unwanted marriage by a cunning little schemer. He would publicly ruin me first. He even implied"—her voice faltered, almost broke—"that he was not my first lover."

"Bloody hell!" Simon slammed his fist on the table before he realized what he was doing. Eleanor gave a startled little gasp. The dishes and cutlery rattled and his wineglass fell over, sending a blood red stain of claret spreading across the white cloth.

"I beg your pardon," he said. "It just makes me so angry." His voice rose with each word until he was almost shouting.

She offered a wan smile. "Please don't be. It was

my fault for being such a fool. Needless to say, I was devastated. Heartbroken. Angry. Scared. That night, when he was sleeping, I stole money from his purse and ran away. I took the stage back to London."

"Good God. Alone? In the middle of the night?"

"Yes. I didn't know what else to do. My parents were furious and packed me off to Surrey in disgrace. Shortly afterward, I realized there was to be a child."

She looked up at him then, for the first time. He could not imagine what she saw in his face. He felt sick.

"My father found a man who agreed to marry me," she said, "a business acquaintance about his own age. Maurice Tennant. I was so heartsore and ill that I agreed to the marriage without argument. Nothing mattered anymore. I didn't care what happened to me. Maurice apparently asked for a larger settlement than my father could afford—I was used goods, after all, and carrying another man's child. They came to some sort of arrangement, but I never knew the details."

Good Lord. No wonder she was a cynic. It all sounded like one of those wretched stories in the *Lady's Monthly Museum*. Simon wondered if his own idealism could have withstood such a blow. He reached for the fallen wineglass, refilled it, and drained it in a single swallow.

"So I became Mrs. Tennant," she said, "and

moved with my husband to Bristol. I lost the baby shortly afterward, and I was condemned to a distasteful marriage to a man who never let me forget my past."

Worse and worse. He did not believe he could stand much more.

"Maurice was capricious in his business dealings, always investing in some scheme or other, and always losing his money." Her voice had regained some of its color, and was now tinged with bitterness. "We'd been married six years when he died, and he left me nothing. I didn't have two shillings to rub together."

Simon reached over and refilled her wineglass, and with a tilt of his head indicated she should drink it. Lord knew, she must need it after such an exhausting tale. He certainly did. Eleanor thanked him with a nod and took a sip, then closed her eyes and took another. She expelled a long breath before continuing.

"You can see now why I am so anxious about Belinda. It is as if I am watching my own pathetic melodrama played out again on the stage, with a different set of actors. And Geoffrey Barkwith is *so* much like Henry. A charming seducer. He even has the same dark good looks."

"Poor Eleanor. This must be exceedingly distressing for you."

"And not only because of Belinda," she said. "Quite selfishly, I am also concerned about my own situation. When Maurice died and left me destitute, I had no place to go. Even had they offered, I would not have returned to my parents. We've been estranged since they sold me to Maurice. There is no affection between us, far from it, and I could not have lived with them again. But my brother Benjamin had lost his wife some years before Maurice died. Since he was so often away from home, he suggested I become a companion to his daughter. And so I've been living in his London house with Belinda these past five years. I am entirely dependent upon my brother's goodwill, Simon. He will throw me out on my ear if I allow his daughter's life to be ruined as mine was."

He fully comprehended her concern, though the Romantic in him still believed Belinda would be Mrs. Barkwith when they found her. Surely two such blackguards would not strike the same family.

"It is a delicate situation, to be sure," Simon said, "but I cannot believe your brother will cast you out. It would be a hateful thing to do when none of this is your fault. And your life is far from ruined, my dear. You made a mistake and paid dearly for it with an unhappy marriage. But you are a free woman now with a lifetime ahead of you."

She glared at him as though he were mad. "A lifetime of what? Being passed around from family to family as the poor relation? Or should I perhaps strike out on my own and try to find employment as a governess, or a lady's companion? It is a pretty bleak future, in any case. But I daresay I should be grateful. My father might just as well have tossed me in the gutter to fend for myself."

"Allow the optimist to suggest another alternative. You are a beautiful woman, Eleanor. You might marry again."

She smiled—a full, genuine smile. "Dear Simon, ever the Romantic."

"Ever hopeful, anyway." More than she could possibly know. "Whatever became of that damnable Henry fellow?"

"Living in Bristol kept me away from London society. It was, of course, one of the reasons my father approached Maurice in the first place. He and Mother would have done anything to avoid a scandal in London. Anyway, I never saw Henry again. A few years after my marriage, I heard he'd been killed in a duel."

"Thank God. I wish I'd fired the shot that killed him."

"So do I," she said. "That is, I wish *I'd* fired it, not you."

"Well, I am glad someone fired it, else I would have to hunt the cur down and do it myself. What a black-hearted scoundrel."

And then the most amazing thing happened. Eleanor reached over and laid her hand over his. Simon had been so careful not to touch her, so afraid she would not welcome it, that she might misinterpret and believe he only meant to seduce her like that scapegrace Henry. Yet now *she* touched *him*. His heart soared.

"I am glad I told you, Simon."

He covered her hand with his. "So am I."

She smiled and said, "Now you had better eat something before you become faint with hunger."

Chapter 13

A young woman of sensibility should never repine a lack of suitors. True love and affection will not long be withheld from a heart deserving and a tenderness refined.

The Busybody

Eleanor had slept like the dead. It had been an emotionally exhausting day, and she had been thoroughly drained by the time she'd gone to bed. This morning, however, she had awakened with a new resolve. Relating the events of her past had renewed her anger with Geoffrey Barkwith, and her determination to find Belinda, shake some sense into her, and take her back home. She would *not* allow her niece's life to be ruined as hers had been. One way or another, she was going to make things right for Belinda.

Simon, bless his idealistic heart, still believed Barkwith would marry the girl. Now that he knew about Eleanor's past, though, he was willing to concede that he might be wrong.

They had talked, and eaten, late into the night. Once the principal secrets had been laid bare—his politics and her shame—it had been easy to reveal more. They grew almost giddy with new insight and discovery as each of them sought to learn more about the other. She learned that he collected Italian landscape paintings and thought Mrs. Siddons highly overrated. He learned that she played the harp and liked to garden. But they never forgot the primary issue at hand, and spoke at length about Belinda, using the lessons of Eleanor's history to determine how best to handle the girl's situation.

On one point, however, Eleanor was unyielding: the need to get Belinda away from Barkwith, against her will if necessary. They could sort out matters afterward, but it was essential to remove her from Barkwith's influence. Even Simon acceded to that plan, in the event there had been no marriage, which, of course, there would not have been. Steadfast Romantic that he was, he promised to ride up on his white horse, sweep Belinda away, and deliver her into the arms of her doting aunt.

It was a lovely, chivalrous image straight out of a fairy tale, and he would probably do it if he could. Silly man. White horses were scarce and Belinda would probably scratch his eyes out. But it was a charming offer.

She and Simon breakfasted early in the large dining room that catered to stagecoach passengers who generally had little more than twenty minutes to spare before the stage departed. A long buffet was laid out to provide a fast meal. One group was just finishing when they entered the room, and waiters lined up to assist each passenger with hats, shawls, coats, and umbrellas so no time would be wasted. The sound of the guard blowing his yard of tin could be heard outside.

Even after such a large supper the night before, Simon had been ravenous and took full advantage of the groaning board. How he managed to remain so thin was a mystery. They spent little longer on breakfast than the stage passengers, however, and were soon back on the road through Lancashire toward Westmorland. The Runners had tracked the fugitives as far as Kendal.

The rain had stopped during the night, leaving the morning air fresh and clear. The road to Lancaster was straight and broad, and despite mud and rutting from the rains, they made good time. The wild, windswept northern landscape was fascinating to Eleanor, who'd never been farther north than Derbyshire.

Beyond Preston, there were limestone dales to the east with cliffs and gorges and craggy outcroppings bright in the morning sun. They passed broad sweeps of rough grassland and heathered moors. They crossed several rivers descending from the fells in the east, cutting into deep, lush river valleys. To the west was only flat pastureland supporting vast herds of sheep and the occasional windmill.

Simon watched the scenery with a keen eye,

now and then pointing out some especially beautiful or remarkable feature. "I love the fells," he said. "I suppose I am partial to hills and mountains.

"The verdant meads, the river's flow,
The wooded valleys, lush and low,
The windswept summit, wild and high,
Its gnarled fist reaching to the sky."

Eleanor smiled and said, "Wordsworth again?"
"Westover."

They spoke less often as they took in miles and miles of rolling moorland hills and long vistas across wide valleys. He made one or two disparaging remarks on the new enclosures, but most of the time they enjoyed long stretches of comfortable silence. A new bond had been forged between them the night before—friendship? amity? understanding?—and it seemed to have changed the very air they breathed.

As they sat side by side in the carriage that had been their tiny, confined world for five days, there was no longer any hint of awkwardness or tension or unease. They were perfectly relaxed together, as if they'd known each other all their lives. If there hadn't been the uncertainty about Belinda weighing heavy upon her, Eleanor would have said she was perfectly happy for the first time in years.

It was almost frightening.

There was room enough for three on the carriage seat, so there was more than enough space to accommodate the two of them. But when the swaying and bouncing and jostling of the carriage bumped them up against each other, neither of them moved. They sat close together in the center of the bench, their shoulders and thighs touching, and sometimes their hips, their arms, their hands, their feet.

There were moments when Eleanor was so aware of Simon's physical presence, points of contact sparked shimmers of heat that danced through her body and gathered in a single spot pulsing low in her belly. Once she had to let the window down partway to cool off. For the most part, however, it was a comfortable closeness, and that, too, was frightening. She did not want to become too accustomed to Simon's presence, though it would be the easiest thing in the world to do.

His interest in her was obvious. He did not even try to hide his regard. And though she knew very well that he was nothing at all like Henry, she was not quite ready to let down her guard. After all, he adored women, according to his brother, and apparently had been involved with several. But he was not married and claimed still to be seeking his true love. That could only mean that he dallied and flirted and trifled without purpose. Eleanor had no intention of being the object of his or any other man's dalliance ever again.

If only he didn't feel so good beside her.

Simon was prepared to spend the rest of his life in the carriage. Though it was normally cramped for a man of his height, he could not recall when he'd felt so cozy and comfortable.

She felt so good beside him.

The more he learned of Eleanor Tennant, the more infatuated he became. He'd learned a great deal last night, and had come closer to tumbling off that ledge into something deeper. In fact, he was fairly certain he had already tumbled and was falling. There was a strange light-headedness about him, as though he were floating.

It was odd to think he might have found the woman of his dreams in someone so very different from himself. It wasn't so much her cynicism, which was justifiable given what she'd been through and could probably be mollified over time once a little joy entered her life. The differences were more basic.

Simon would most likely always be a Romantic at heart, whereas Eleanor's nature was practical. He did not believe her youthful folly had been the result of any romantic disposition so much as simple naïveté. He could not imagine her ever succumbing to sentiment. Where he was sensitive, she was sensible. Where he was whimsical, she was level-headed. Where he preferred to lose himself in an epic poem, she preferred a history or biography.

Perhaps the old saying about how opposites attract was true, for he was definitely attracted to Eleanor. So much so that he had thought he might die if he didn't touch her, and had exaggerated the jostling movement of the carriage just to bump against her. When she hadn't moved away, he had closed his eyes and savored the sensation.

It was almost more than he could bear. He was so damned aware of her that his skin seemed to tingle all over. It was like having an itch he couldn't scratch. He *could* scratch it, he supposed, though he didn't believe that, once started, he'd be able to stop.

And there was the problem in a nutshell. He wanted her so badly, with so a fierce hunger, that he wanted to devour her. Bite by delicious bite. If he gave in to those urges, however, she would think him no better than old Henry Scapegrace.

So he took what pleasure he could—quite a lot, actually—from the simple closeness of her and the occasional chaste touch of an arm, a hand, a leg. But, Lord, how he would like to kiss her again.

They were to stop at Garstang for their first change of horses. The postboys slowed the team as they entered the town, and Eleanor said, "Oh, look at all the oak boughs. How lovely. I'd forgotten what day it is."

"By Jove, so had I." Most of the brick houses and whitewashed cottages had boughs of oak leaves tied in bunches over their doors or decorating their windows. "Oak Apple Day. And look where we're going."

The carriage was being led into the yard of a posting inn serendipitously called the Royal Oak. The galleried yard was festive green with boughs and garlands. Simon hopped out to pay for the new team—the postillions would stay with them until Lancaster—and was almost struck down by the thundering entrance of the Royal Mail. He dashed to safety beneath the overhanging gallery and watched the action.

The sleek black and maroon coach, with its distinctive red wheels and royal cipher on the door, rocked and swayed with the hurried, efficient action of the ostlers. The caped coachman kept his seat, but leaned down for a brief word with a pretty maid in white apron and cap who handed him a mug of ale. The dour red-coated guard, who had sat rigid and important upon the seat in the back, blunderbuss and horn at the ready, now jumped from his perch to receive the mail. A bag was handed to him, and he opened the boot beneath his seat, tossed it in, and hopped back on board. By the time the coachman had taken a long swallow of ale, the new team was in place and ready to go. He quickly handed down the mug, saluted the maid with his whip, and with a blast from the guard's horn, steered the team out of the yard and down the road at a cracking pace. It had all taken place in little more than two minutes.

Somewhat less important than the Mail, Simon had to wait his turn for his own change of team as there was one other post chaise ahead of him. He used the time to procure a tankard of ale for himself and a glass of lemonade for Eleanor. He handed it up to her through the carriage window. "Quite a sight, eh?" he said.

"Indeed. And all I can say is thank heavens Belinda and Barkwith didn't take the Mail. We'd never have caught up with them. They don't waste a moment, do they?"

"They have a very strict schedule, to be sure. As boys, Malcolm and I used to sneak down to Picadilly to watch the Mail coaches depart. It was the height of excitement, as I recall." Their new team was almost ready, so he took Eleanor's glass and handed it, along with his tankard, to a passing maid with a tray. He opened the door and took his seat once again, wondering if she would notice if he slid over a bit toward the center.

"Here's another thing I remember from my boyhood," he said. "Since you are not wearing an oak leaf, I believe you are going to have to be pinched, my dear. It's an Oak Apple Day tradition."

She smiled warily. "But you are not wearing one, either."

"Oh, but I am." He held open his coat to show a bright green leaf stuffed into the pocket of his waistcoat. "I took the liberty of filching one from the inn. But you, madam, are oakless, and you know what that means."

She laughed and scooted across the seat as far away from him as she could get. Damn. He'd bungled that one.

"If you dare to pinch me, sir, I shall be forced to defend myself. And you have already suffered one of my blows, so you should know I have no qualms about doing it again. Besides, I don't believe I know you well enough to allow a pinch."

"How can you say so?" He pressed a hand to his chest as though wounded. "I thought we were old friends?"

"Hardly old. We've only known each other five days."

"Oh, much longer than that. Only think. In these five days we have spent upward of sixteen hours a day together. If you break that down into minutes, and compare the total against all the minutes spent in the company of friends, I would say ours is the equivalent of an acquaintance of several months at least."

She smiled and said, "You have a point there. I think."

"Yes, and because that makes us old friends, I must act as one and protect you against any other threats of pinching you may encounter today." He reached into his waistcoat pocket and brought out two more oak leaves, crushed but green. "Here you are, my dear. Wear them in peace, in honor of that merry old monarch, King Charles."

She tucked the leaves into the buckle of her pelisse and hurriedly grabbed the strap just as the postillions gave the horses their heads, jerking them both hard against the seat back.

They continued to see signs of the day as they passed through tiny hamlets and villages on the road north, with festive boughs over doorways and hung from church towers. As they spoke of childhood memories of Oak Apple Day, Eleanor—

and this was his own fault, dammit—kept her place on the far side of the bench, with only the most pronounced jostling of the carriage bringing them into momentary contact.

They eventually came to the town of Lancaster, where they would make another change of horses. It was an old town situated on the looping River Lune, dominated by the castle on a rise overlooking the tangle of narrow streets and lanes below.

The yard at the posting inn was crowded with several yellow bounders, two other private chaises, and the great hulk of the Liverpool & Kendal *Expedition* preparing to depart. The coachman was already at his post, and the horses snorted and pawed the ground, anxious to be off. The cocky, officious guard was rounding up passengers as they left the coffee room, herding them like geese toward the big stagecoach, shouting out warnings that stragglers would be left behind.

Simon's stomach growled at the sight of the coffee room and suggested they stop for a quick meal.

"The next report from the Runners is due at Kendal," Eleanor said. "Do you not think you could wait until then to eat? I realize you are hungry, but Simon, you are *always* hungry. And I am anxious to get to Kendal to discover if the Runners are still on the trail. This is the first time I've felt we were really making good time, and I want to make every effort to catch up with them."

Simon reluctantly agreed to her wishes, being

more in sympathy with her sense of urgency since
their discussion the night before. Even so, he pur-
chased a sandwich while the horses were changed.
His stomach would not wait until Kendal.

The change of horses and postillions was
quickly done, and they were soon barreling down
the road once again. Eleanor seemed determined to
keep her distance and avoid the closeness of the
morning, and Simon wondered if he could ever
truly break down her defenses. She was a woman
of great courage, but would she ever have the
courage to accept the affection—the love?—he was
so keen to offer? He wanted to tread carefully and
not upset the new bond they'd developed last
night, but he did not know how long he could go
on without touching her.

The River Lune was crossed by a new stone
bridge, and they were afforded to the west a view of
Lancaster's long quay with its rows of warehouses,
and to the east a magnificent new aqueduct carrying
the canal over the river. The scenery was not as impressive as his beloved Peak, but Simon enjoyed the
vistas of undulating hills in a rich mosaic of wood-
land and pasture, in anticipation of the high fells of
the Lake District. Clipped hedgerows and stone
walls marked the new enclosures served by a myr-
iad of tiny villages with handsome church towers.

It was at one of those small villages, about an
hour out of Lancaster, that the carriage was slowed
and eventually stopped by a group of villagers
blocking the road.

"What's happening?" Eleanor asked.

Simon looked all about but did not see any apparent crisis that would cause the people to stop them, though other carriages had also pulled to the side of the road. The men and women who stopped them were laughing. Girls carrying huge baskets of greenery—oak boughs, of course—pulled the postboys off the leaders and began to decorate their hats with leaves. Others hung boughs all about the harnesses. A stocky, smiling man who looked to be a farmer opened the carriage door on Simon's side.

"C'mon down from there," he said in a loud, genial voice, ripe with northern vowels. "We don't allow no one to pass through our village on Oak Apple Day lest ye share a spot o' gooseberry wine wid us. Or a mug o' ale, if yer so inclined. Get yerselfs down here and raise a glass to old King Charles. Lest ye wanta be pinched."

Simon laughed and leaped down—for there was no other choice—and offered his hand to Eleanor. "I'm afraid you may not pinch us, sir, for we are armed with oak. As you see."

"Ah, good man. Now where are them trays? Tilly? Girl, we need drink for these fine folk."

A fresh-faced young girl, brimming with the exuberance of the day, ran up to him. "That last stage took all we had up here, Da," she said rather breathlessly. "Gotta get back to the Blue Boar and haul up a few more jugs." With that, she ran off down the slope toward the center of the tiny village, where there looked to be a full-fledged fete in progress.

There was even a great, tall oak tree decorated as a Maypole, with ribbon streamers and floral garlands. No doubt the village had made Oak Apple Day its traditional grand fete due to the huge, majestic tree in the center of the village green.

"Well, now. I 'spect there ain't nothing fer it but to wait for them jugs. Ye can't leave without a drink o' sumthin'. It's tradition. 'Course, if ye prefers, ye can go on down to the fete and partake o' the feast. Yer more'n welcome. And yer postboys can mind the cattle. What say ye?"

Eleanor could tell by the look in his eye that Simon was dying to go down to the little fete and get something substantial to eat. "All right," she said, and his dimpled smile told him she had been correct. "But only for a moment. We need to get to Kendal."

"Only a moment," Simon said. "I promise."

He grinned and took her by the hand to lead her to the tiny village green with the decorated oak tree. A fiddler played a jolly tune while girls and young men danced around the makeshift Maypole. Simple two-sided booths were set up here and there selling trinkets and offering games and competitions. Long trestle tables along the edges of the green were loaded with all sorts of food and drink. The smells were delicious: savory pies of meat and game bird, roasted lamb shanks, plum cakes, fruit tarts, gingerbread, steamed puddings, cheeses, and crusty brown bread. There were home-brewed ales, gooseberry wine, parsnip wine, cherry brandy, and cider. It was enticing enough even to tempt Eleanor.

Simon bought her a small pigeon pie, some gingerbread, and a mug of cider. For himself, he bought just about everything. They found room at a table where Simon was able to spread out his bounty.

"I suppose you arranged this ahead of time somehow," she said. "Probably bribed the postillions to take us in this direction, just so you wouldn't have to wait until Kendal to eat."

"You are uncommonly interested in my eating habits, madam. But I could not have planned it better, could I? And I daresay we would not have had such fare at Kendal. This lamb shank is outstanding. I trust that pitiful little repast is sufficient for your appetite?"

"Quite so. And you are right. This pie is rather tasty. And the celebration is lovely. I haven't seen an Oak Apple Day fete since I was a child. Oh, look over there. That woman is getting pinched!"

"Ha! Are you not grateful that I armed you against such an assault? Though it appears she is rather enjoying it."

"That be Cora Weathers," said a local woman seated down the table from them. "Bein' chased by her own husband, the silly ol' fool."

Simon looked at Eleanor and winked. "A happily married couple, I take it?" he said.

"I should say so," the woman said, and laughed. "Poor Cora's had fourteen children off that man, and he still chases her about like that every Oak Apple Day, jus' so's he can pinch her in public."

"Why doesn't she just wear a spring of oak leaves," Eleanor asked, "so she won't have to suffer his pinching?"

"Cuz she likes it, o' course. Crazy about the old fool. The day she wears oak leaves in May is the day you'll find old Weathers has cocked up his toes."

"Now, isn't that charming," Simon said. "A long and happy marriage. Who would ever think such a thing existed?"

"Mr. Weathers is not the only silly old fool here," Eleanor muttered, but she could not hold back a smile. Simon was determined to prove to her that affection could outlast the early throes of passion. Perhaps he was right. She had grown accustomed to thinking the marriages she'd seen up close—her parents' cold, contemptuous union; her brother's pedestrian, bloodless arrangement; her own un-wanted and unhappy match—were the common way of things. Suppose she was wrong? Suppose Constance's blissful marriage was not so unusual? It was a difficult notion to get her arms around.

Simon tore into his meal with the usual aban-don, all the while talking and laughing with the lo-cals. He did not dawdle, though, and she hoped they could return to the road soon. As lovely as the fete was, she wanted to be on the road. She had a feeling they were close to discovering Belinda's whereabouts, and was anxious to get on with it.

The music became louder, as other instruments

joined the lone fiddler. Cheers went up as the king and queen of the day made their appearance, pulled along in a garlanded cart: a fresh-faced young man and a girl with roses in her cheeks, each bedecked with ribbons about their clothes and crowns of oak leaves on their heads. They each held short staffs, their scepters, lavishly decorated with spring flowers, and sprigs of hawthorn and lilac, and they waved them about like wands, sending flower petals flying in every direction. A procession gathered behind them, with folks singing and cheering and dancing as they wound their way through the green.

The locals at their table got up to join in the merriment, and suddenly Eleanor's hand was grabbed from behind, and a young man pulled her to her feet. "Join the dance, mistress?" He did not wait for an answer, but tugged her along in a boisterous line that snaked all through the green and back again. The music became faster and the crowd began to clap in rhythm. Holding on to the young man in front of her, Eleanor followed as the line wove its way around tables and booths and trees and wagons and troughs in a long serpentine headed by the royal cart.

When her free hand was grabbed, she looked behind to find Simon dancing along behind her, laughing and beaming like a boy. He was thoroughly enjoying himself, and his delight was infectious. She found she was smiling almost as broadly.

The procession doubled back, and the young

king and queen passed beside them. The queen waved her scepter over their heads, covering them with flower petals. Simon stopped and bent to pick up something, then pulled Eleanor away from the procession now headed for the churchyard. Laughing, he leaned against the whitewashed wall of a cottage off the green. He held out a small spray of lilac, which must have fallen from the queen's scepter. He lifted it to his nose, breathed in its fragrance, and gave a satisfied sigh.

"Here you are, my dear," he said. "A memento of our impromptu fete.

> *"Behold the fairest bough of May:*
> *By Flora's hand each tiny bloom*
> *Is vernal dipped, and every spray*
> *Casts down on us its sweet perfume."*

"Westover again?" she asked, knowing the saccharine sentiment could be no one else's.

"Yes," he said, then pulled her close. Her breath caught. Dear God, he was going to kiss her. But no. Instead, he reached up and tucked the lilac into the ribbon of her bonnet. Its lush scent—a childhood favorite—wafted down to her, and she smiled.

Simon took her chin in his hand, tilted her head slightly, and surveyed his work. But only briefly, for his gaze soon dropped to meet hers. The look in his eyes intensified. It was a look she'd seen before, and combined with his touch on her face, it set up a fluttering in her stomach.

He didn't move and didn't speak. One hand held her elbow, the other cradled her face. His eyes flickered down to her mouth. His breathing became labored, and his brow knotted up as though he was in pain. When he finally spoke, his voice was low, with a throaty undercurrent of sensuality.

"I've tried so hard," he said. "I've wanted to be a gentleman. I haven't wanted to give you the wrong impression, after all you told me last night. But I do not believe I can bear it another moment, Eleanor. I have to kiss you."

She could not have spoken if she tried. She found she wanted him to kiss her again, wanted it badly, against all judgment and prudence and caution. She didn't care anymore about what it meant or what else might happen, and only wanted to yield to the powerful yearning that coursed through her blood. The fluttering in her belly had moved up into her breast and her throat, and if he didn't kiss her soon she thought she might go mad. *Just kiss me*, she wanted to scream.

He must have read the plea in her eyes, for he brought his mouth down and kissed her. Softly at first, tasting, testing, teasing. His lips were supple and dry and moved over hers in a gentle exploration that was as different from their last fiery kiss as night from day. Still cradling her face in one hand, he explored her lips with his own, slowly, tenderly, paying special tribute to her upper lip, which he grazed and nibbled and sucked with exquisite delicacy, as though it were a sweetmeat.

Eleanor was like an ascetic in the desert, parched and dry, who'd been given a flask of water. She hadn't realized how thirsty she'd been. She gave a little moan of pleasure, and he pulled her closer, taking the hand away from her face and wrapping it tight around her back. And before she even realized it, her own arms had snaked around his neck, pulling him down. Her fingers reached up to twine in his hair. He murmured her name against her lips, then deepened the kiss, coaxing her mouth open and gently caressing her tongue with his.

Eleanor had been ready to rush it, to drink great gulps of him, to get drunk on him, to give in mindlessly to all the passion she'd stifled for so long. But he kept it slow and easy and gentle, and it was wonderful. A thousand times more wonderful than the kiss at Buxton with all its blind passion. This time they were both aware of each other, of what they did. It was almost unbearably delicious. Her bones began to melt, and she felt as if she might collapse in a heap were Simon not holding her so tightly.

She had no idea how long they lingered against that wall, kissing and kissing, with the music and merriment of the fete wrapped around them. When Simon finally brought it to an end, he gave her one last soft kiss, pulled away slightly, then gave her another, as though he could not bring himself to end it.

Eleanor was breathless when it was over, her

mind a whirl of emotions, her body throbbing with sensation. Though it had been many years, it was a familiar, heady feeling, one she had never thought to experience again. She had almost believed she was no longer capable of such raw sensuality, that something inside her had shriveled up and died long ago. To discover it had not brought a sting of tears to the back of her eyes. She turned away so he would not see.

Simon would have none of her reticence, however, and took her chin in his hand and brought her face around to look at him. His eyes had grown heavy-lidded and darkened to the blue of twilight.

"Lord, Eleanor, I have wanted to do that for so long. Please don't look away. Don't be ashamed."

She wasn't, but did feel a twinge of embarrassment that she had given in so boldly. "I'm not ashamed, Simon. Just surprised. It was . . . lovely."

"More than lovely. It was perfect. Or something like that. God, for once I'm bereft of words."

She pulled away, still confused about how she felt. "I think we should go."

"Eleanor. Please don't close up on me again."

She adjusted her bonnet, which must be sadly askew, and retied the ribbon beneath her chin. "I am not closing up, whatever that means. I simply think we have spent too long here and need to get back on the road."

"You are uncomfortable. I am sorry about that, though I am not sorry about kissing you."

He smiled, and his eyes were back to their normal twinkle, the earlier sensual intensity now gone. Dear God, he really was adorable. What was she going to do about Simon Westover?

"I don't believe I'm sorry, either," she said, "but I also don't believe we should let it happen again. I have Belinda to think about. I cannot think of anything else just now. Please, let's go back to the coach. Let us be friends again and carry on as before."

"How long before? You're not going to slap me again, are you?"

She smiled, appreciating his attempt to put them back on familiar ground, bantering and arguing. "No, I'm not going to slap you. But I just might pinch you if you don't hurry up."

He pushed himself away from the wall and offered his arm. "Let us be off then. I'd hate to be subject to another one of your blows. I assure you, I'm too weak in the knees to withstand it."

Chapter 14

*Alas! at the shrine of Ambition we too often behold
the sacrifice of domestic bliss.*

The Busybody

The trip to Kendal was fraught with a new kind of tension. Their conversation was inconsequential and relaxed, but now and then, when their eyes met, it was like setting off a tiny electrical storm that shot through the interior of the carriage and charged the air. Awkward silences followed such moments, until one of them, usually Simon, shattered the disquiet with a comment about the roads or the weather or the distant fells and lush green pastures that dominated the view.

They never spoke of what had happened at the village fete, though the very fact of that kiss—those kisses—sat between them like a third passenger. They spoke around it, they tried to ignore it, but it was always there and always would be. Though they pretended otherwise, things between them had changed forever.

Simon maintained the pretense as best he could, but the kiss dominated his every thought. It had been a wondrous moment, blissful, dazzling—a conscious sharing that had not been a part of the kiss at Buxton. That one had simply been a result of his blood being up from the taproom brawl. It had been intense and almost feral, but not a joining of souls such as he'd experienced today. Those long minutes against the cottage wall were worthy of erotic Persian poetry in the way body and soul had pulsed with glorious sensation.

Eclipsing everything else, though, even the raw sexuality of it, were two things. First, Simon had not been able to get enough of her. He would never be able to get enough of her. That mouth, those lips—Lord, they were every bit as delectable as he had imagined, and he wanted to taste them again and again. She was like a drug, an opiate he could not live without. In thirty-four years he had never felt such a hunger, so powerful it outstripped all his other appetites.

For this alone, he had to have her.

Second, and more important, had been Eleanor's response. She had not pushed him away or fought him or submitted with passive resignation. He had given her every opportunity to object, but there had been clear invitation in those green eyes.

She had participated fully, had taken as much as she gave. Her hunger had been almost equal to his own, if possible. It was quite extraordinary to think she might want him as much as he wanted her. In fact, her mouth had been wild and eager at first. He had to coax her into a more succulent, unhurried, prolonged merging of lips and tongue, and she had followed his lead deliciously. She had, at last and with sweet abandon, relinquished her unwavering control and simply given herself over to the moment.

She was clearly embarrassed by what she'd done, and maybe even a little angry with herself for it. Simon still had much to teach her about trust, and he was more than willing to take his time. When she had said she could not think of anything but Belinda right now, Simon wanted to believe that *he* was the thing she wanted to think about but could not. Hope swelled in his breast.

By the time they reached Kendal, he and Eleanor had settled into a kind of quiet harmony. Simon did his best to keep the mood light, and to keep his hands to himself. Eleanor would have to come to terms with what had happened between them, but in her own way and in her own time. He would not rush her and would try his damnedest not to touch her.

They picked up the Runners' report in Kendal, which directed them to Penrith. They were getting closer to the border. Surely Eleanor must now accept the inevitability of a Scottish marriage for her niece. Simon would not, however, disturb the amity between them by mentioning it. When they had talked about it the night before, she did not seem ready to change her mind about Barkwith just because they might have gone to Scotland. There were places to take a girl in Scotland as well as England, she had said, and it might simply be a more elaborate ruse than the one that had lured her so many years ago. Eleanor's mind was fixed as far as Barkwith's villainy was concerned. Her own experience made it impossible for her to believe in any other outcome than Belinda's ruin, to keep the peace, Simon had given up trying to disabuse her of the notion.

She was right, however, about the time lost at the fete, and though he would not have missed that time and that kiss for anything on earth, they would have to hurry to make up for it. He promised the postillions a few extra coins if they made it to Penrith before nightfall. Anxious for the extra reward, they pushed the team to breakneck speeds, and drove them barreling down the road, weaving past coaches, post chaises, wagons, gigs, carts, mounted riders, sheep, and anything else on the road that got in their way.

Simon and Eleanor laughed at the pace, and each held on to the straps for safety. Once, overtaking a large private coach at a pace that set their own chaise at a dangerous angle, Simon had grabbed her hand, and—heaven be praised!—she let him keep hold of it. At the next change of horses, Simon promised the postillions an even higher reward if they got them to Penrith in one piece. They maintained good speed, but were less reckless in negotiating other vehicles.

It was a scenic land, and meant for more leisurely

travel, with rugged vistas of the wild Shap fells to the west and the Howgills and more distant Pennines to the east. It was neither lush nor dramatic, but the occasional sensual contour of overlapping, treeless ridges could take a man's breath away. Simon hated to rush through such raw beauty, but such was the price of a kiss.

As they neared Penrith, long stretches of open countryside were replaced by manmade scenery: charming villages, stone bridges, castle ruins, the imposing prospect of a large country seat.

They reached Penrith in record time. The majestic castle ruins overlooking the town were silhouetted black against the deep blue skies of late twilight. They were given no time to appreciate the red sandstone warmth of the town's principal buildings as the postboys hurried them into the inn yard of the King's Arms, an old timber-frame structure with upper stories nodding drunkenly over the road.

Simon paid off the tenacious postillions and took Eleanor's arm to lead her into the large inn. They were both somewhat giddy from the frantic pace, and were disheveled and laughing when they entered the reception area.

"My bones will be rattling for weeks," Eleanor said.

"And I am quite certain," Simon said, "that I have more than one goose egg on my head from hitting the ceiling. Lord, what a wild ride."

"My stars, Nickie, will you look at what the cat dragged in."

Simon started and turned at the familiar feminine voice.

"Lord, I'd know that laugh anywhere," another voice said, male and equally familiar. "Simon, old chap, what the devil brings you so far north."

"Nick! Edwina! How marvelous." Thrilled at their unexpected appearance, Simon lunged forward to greet his two closest friends in all the world. Amid laughter and clamorous greetings, he pounded Nicholas Parrish on the back and gave a great bear hug to Edwina Parrish. "I thought you were in Edinburgh."

"We were," Nicholas said. "But what about you? Don't tell me you are on your way to Scotland, too? Whatever—oomph!"

He was interrupted by a finger in the ribs from his sister. "Nickie, you will notice that Simon is not alone." Her eyes darted toward Eleanor, who had stepped back to allow the friends to greet one another, and returned to Simon, bright with inquiry. "I suspect there is a perfectly good explanation for a trip to the border."

"Oh!" Nicholas exclaimed, looking from Simon to Eleanor and back again with very wide eyes.

Simon laughed when he realized what they were thinking. "How very rag-mannered of me." He took Eleanor by the elbow and led her forward. "Allow me to introduce my friends to you. Mrs. Tennant, this is Miss Edwina Parrish and her brother Mr. Nicholas Parrish."

Edwina smiled warmly at Eleanor. "How very pleased I am to meet you, Mrs. Tennant."

"And I am equally honored, to be sure." Nicholas took Eleanor's outstretched hand and kissed the air above it. A fortunate move, for if he had presumed any more than that, Simon might have been obliged to exercise his right fist once again, despite the still bruised knuckles. Nicholas was a devilishly handsome fellow, and Simon did not at all relish the thought of him working his charms on Eleanor.

"But I say, Simon," Nicholas said, "this is a queer start, even for you. Aren't you a bit long in the tooth for this sort of adventure?"

"Nickie!" Edwina grabbed her brother rather tightly by the arm. "It is none of our business and I daresay we are horribly *de trop*. Now, let us leave them alone. We can talk with Simon another time."

Nicholas shrugged. "All right, then. Wish you the best, old boy." Guided by Edwina's tugging hand, he made as if to leave.

"Wait!" Simon could hardly speak from laughing. The looks on all three faces were too ridiculous: Nicholas, wary and incredulous; Edwina, motherly and indulgent; Eleanor, thoroughly confused. "Let me explain."

"There's no need, Simon." Edwina cast an appraising glance at Eleanor and broke into a warm smile. "It is quite clear to me."

"No, I do not think it is at all clear to you," Simon said, and burst into another fit of laughter.

Eleanor touched his sleeve. "Simon, what is going on here?"

"You will not credit it, Eleanor, but these two seem to think you and I are on the road to Gretna."

"But we are on the—Oh! You mean—"

"Yes, they think we are running off to be married."

"Oh, dear." Eleanor gave a smile that did not quite reach her eyes. "How amusing."

Nicholas looked goggle-eyed from one to the other. "You're *not* on the road to Gretna Green?"

"We are, in fact," Simon said, grinning, "but not for the reason you suppose."

"I think you had better explain," Edwina said, "before we make even bigger fools of ourselves."

And so Simon explained, in the broadest terms and leaving out several key details, the situation with Eleanor's niece. "The last report from the Runners tracked them this far. We are to wait here for the next message."

Edwina turned to Eleanor and briefly touched her arm. "Forgive us, Mrs. Tennant, for making such a rash presumption. How foolish you must think us. But you see, it just like Simon to do something so utterly romantic."

"Mrs. Tennant is not terribly impressed by my romantic nature, Edwina."

"No?" Edwina's dark eyes flashed with wry amusement. "Do not tell me you have found that rare creature: the unromantic woman?"

"Let us just say," Simon said, "that she holds my 'starry-eyed romanticism' as partly responsible for her niece's elopement."

"I don't understand," Edwina said.

Simon steeled himself for the reaction to what he was about to say. "I'm afraid her niece gave a great deal of credence to the advice of the Busybody."

His words hung in the air like stale smoke. Edwina's eyes blazed and Nicholas set his mouth in a grim, uncompromising line.

Simon held up a hand. "It's all right. She knows all about *The Ladies' Fashionable Cabinet*."

Brother and sister skewered him to the spot with identical dark gazes, rapier-sharp.

"Don't worry. We can trust Eleanor." He looked at her, smiled, and kept his eyes on her when he spoke again. "I trust her."

Eleanor smiled at him with her eyes, then turned to address Edwina. "Please do not blame Simon," she said. "I was furious about the Busybody's advice and went to great lengths to track him down. But I understand now about your motives, and about the need for secrecy. I will not compromise your efforts. You have nothing to fear from me, I promise you."

Edwina let out a pent-up breath, and her expression softened, though her eyes remained watchful. "Thank you, Mrs. Tennant. We bow to Simon's good judgment in trusting you with this information. My brother and I would be honored for you, and Simon, of course, to join us for dinner this evening. I would certainly enjoy hearing more about how you unmasked the Busybody."

"One step at a time, Ed," her brother said. "We have yet to secure rooms for the night. Where is that landlord?"

The man himself, stout and wheezing like a bellows, was standing not two steps away, all agog at having four new guests cluttering his entry parlor. He was thrilled to discover that these four would make him full up for the night. The ladies would have private bedchambers, but the gentlemen would have to double up. He was also able to provide a large private parlor where the four of them would be served a fine supper cooked by his wife and daughters.

Eleanor and Edwina followed a chambermaid upstairs to their rooms. Simon and Nicholas remained behind to attend to the details of luggage and horses and postillions.

"What brings you to Penrith?" Simon asked as they walked back from the busy stables laden with portmanteaux and bandboxes. "I presume you are on your way back to London."

"Yes, we are. We cannot leave poor Prudence to run everything for so long. We came down from Edinburgh to Carlisle so we could pay a visit to old Maggs. He's beside himself about Spence. Did you hear what happened?"

"No. I've been rather out of touch."

"Yes, well, he was found guilty of sedition two days ago and sentenced to a year in jail."

"Good God. All for the *Restorer of Society to Its Natural State*? The corresponding societies, the combinations, and now this. It's monstrous."

"Yes, and we shall all have to watch our steps more closely if we want to stay out of jail. And we can't leave Prudence alone now. What if something was discovered and she was threatened in our absence? We've got to get home. Poor old Maggs put us up last night, but he was so upset about Spence we stayed too long and got too late a start today to get any farther than this."

"Well, it is a pleasant coincidence indeed that finds us at the same inn."

They picked up their keys and trudged up two flights of stairs with their burdens. The two women had rooms on the top floor, at opposite ends of the labyrinthine corridor. Simon knocked on Eleanor's door and called out that her bag was just outside. He heard the door open just as he rounded the corner to meet Nicholas, and the two of them headed downstairs to the room they would share. It was large and comfortable with wood in the grate ready to be lit. The two of them began unpacking and laying out their clothes for supper.

"Tell me more about this Mrs. Tennant of yours," Nicholas said. "She's lovely. A man could drown in those big green eyes."

"Try not to, if you please."

Nicholas looked up, a flash of amusement in his eyes. "Aha. I knew something was in the wind. Are you writing poetry to those eyes?"

"No."

"What? No sonnet to her eyes? I am stunned. You must be off your feed, old boy." He returned his attention to the stack of carefully folded neck-cloths he'd removed from his bag.

"To her lip."

Nicholas looked up again. "What's that?"

"I've been working on an ode to her upper lip, if you must know." Simon had removed his coat and now hung it up on a peg, deliberately avoiding his friend's eye.

Nicholas gave a hoot of laughter. "The upper lip, eh? I am guessing it is not one of those stiff ones we English are supposed to have? I shall have to pay more attention to it when I next see her." He reached over and punched Simon playfully on the arm. "You devil. Would I be wrong in guessing you have done a close survey of that lip? A *very* close survey?"

"Shut up, Nick."

"A tender subject, apparently. Soft and moist and tender, I daresay."

"Nick, I swear—"

"All right, all right." He put both hands up as if to ward off blows. "Truce. No more teasing, I promise. It is difficult, to be sure, but I try very hard not to tease you about these little infatuations of yours. This one was no doubt inevitable. The two of you alone in a carriage for several days. She is distraught and beautiful and leaning on you in her hour of need."

Simon had to laugh at such a skewed impression of Eleanor. "In the first place, Eleanor—"

"Pretty free with her first name already. Simon, you dog, you've not wasted a moment, have you?"

"—is not distraught, nor is she leaning on me for support. Quite the opposite, in fact. She was angry as a baited bear at first, blaming me for her niece's folly. She slapped me hard across the face on the day we met."

Nicholas's eyebrows shot up. "She never did!"

"She did. And for most of the trip she has crossed swords with me on any number of topics, in both heated argument and polite debate. She has also endlessly teased and taunted me about my Romantic idealism."

"A match made in heaven, to be sure," Nicholas said as he continued unpacking. "And yet when you entered the inn, the two of you were laughing together like old friends."

"Yes, well, we have reached a sort of amity after all that time alone together. We are opposites in many ways, but she is a remarkable woman, Nick."

"Oh?"

"Yes, and that brings me to my second point. Eleanor is not one of my little infatuations. She is . . . special."

Nicholas rolled his eyes toward the ceiling. "Oh, Lord, you're in love again."

"No, no, this is different. Like nothing I've ever known. I tell you, I've never felt like this before, Nick. This is true and deep and very real."

"You will forgive me, old chap, but I have heard these romantic pronouncements of yours too many times in the past."

To his great mortification, Simon felt himself blush. He suddenly felt like the boy who cried "Wolf!" How could he convince his friend that this was not the same as all those other times? That Eleanor was not just another pretty face who inspired his pen?

"I have always had a weakness for pretty women, as you know too well. But I'm telling you, Nick, this really is different. It's as though all those other times were merely rehearsals, and this one is the real thing. It's hard to explain, but I've never felt like this. I believe Eleanor just may be the one I've been looking for all these years."

Nicholas stood very still and regarded him thoughtfully. "Well, well, well. I don't know what to say, except to wish you luck."

"I'm mad about her, Nick. Truly, I am."

"I thought as much when I saw the way you looked at her. That's one of the reasons we thought you were running away to Gretna. You had the mooncalf look of an impetuous bridegroom. Oh, I say. She *is* a widow, is she not? There is no Mr. Tennant likely to toss a glove in your face, I hope?"

"No, she is a widow."

"Thank God for that." He untied his neckcloth and tossed it on a chair. "I have no desire to be your second in some ramshackle business with a jealous husband. But tell me, Simon, is this going to be another one of those unrequited affairs, or does this one return your regard?"

"I'm not sure yet." Simon had removed his own neckcloth and now used it to try to put a bit more shine in his boots. His valet was going to have a stroke when he saw them. "It's only been five days, after all," he went on. "And she's had some unpleasantness in her life that makes her somewhat difficult to reach. A little skittish, if you know what I mean. I'm not sure if she's ready for something between us. But I am ever hopeful."

Nicholas grinned broadly. "Of course you are. I've never known you to be otherwise. I hope your dreams come true this time, my friend." He pulled his shirttails out of his pantaloons and tugged the garment over his head.

"So do I," Simon said. A thought struck him, and he stopped unbuttoning his waistcoat. "I do have rather a pitiful record with women, do I not?"

"Not so pitiful. As I recall, the poetic record is quite large, filling several notebooks."

Simon snorted. "That's not what I meant, dammit. It just occurred to me how many times I have fallen in love with someone unlikely ever to return my affection. I am wondering if I do it just so I can write brokenhearted, maudlin verse. Do you think I am that foolish a Romantic?"

"Seeking the unattainable ideal? The great Romantic agony? No, that's not you, Simon. Unless you have completely bamboozled me all these years, I'd say you are the perfect idealist. You don't wallow in failure. I think you simply pick the wrong women."

"Am I doing it again, with Eleanor? Setting myself up to fail?"

"I don't know, Simon. I would have to know more about the lady to assess her attainability." Nicholas grinned. "I shall make a study of her over supper."

Simon clucked his tongue and shook his head. Nicholas was an incorrigible flirt. He was a good friend, though, and always removed himself from the field when he knew someone else's interest was engaged.

Simon removed his waistcoat and shirt and surveyed his limited wardrobe. He had only one more clean shirt, but there was no sense in saving it. He shrugged into it, and had a momentary vision of Eleanor getting undressed upstairs. His body reacted, and he blew out a breath through puffed cheeks. "Lord, but I'm so damned crazy about her," he mused aloud, "it is almost unbearable. You cannot imagine how hard it is to sit inches from her, hours on end, and still remain a gentleman."

Nicholas clapped him on the back and laughed. "Poor old Simon. You must be exhausted from the effort. You will fall into a decline if you are not careful. I don't suppose you could cast your fine scruples to the winds and simply toss her on her back?"

Simon hunched a shoulder. "God knows I've wanted to. Perhaps if I did not care for her so much, I would. But she is not the sort of woman to welcome such an advance, and I want her to trust me. I've been trying to break down her defenses for five days now, but she's been hurt in the past and is being overly cautious, I think."

"You've gotten nowhere in five days? No progress at all?"

"Well, she did let me kiss her this afternoon," Simon said, and worked his hands through his short hair. "We came upon an Oak Apple Day fete, you see."

"Ah. A decorous salute in honor of randy old Charles, I presume."

"Hardly. I should rather say it was a fitting tribute to the Great Man. It was the sort of kiss that turns a man inside out and blisters his soul."

"Well, then." Nicholas could not keep the amusement from his voice. "Sounds like pretty good progress to me."

"Perhaps. But it is a delicate balance. It was effort enough just to get her to not think me a fool. I certainly don't want her now to think me a cad. It has been my greatest ambition these last days to get her to trust me. It would help if I could just find that troublesome niece of hers. Once that burden is lifted, I'm hoping she will be receptive to a serious courtship."

"Lord, Simon, she's a widow," Nicholas said as he tied his neckcloth. "She won't look for a courtship. She would no doubt prefer you to cast aside propriety and toss her on her back."

"I wouldn't want her to get the wrong idea."

"Then make her an offer, tell her you love her, and then toss her on her back. But don't waste a lot of time shilly-shallying with niceties. It ain't as though she's a green girl. You've been with a widow before. You know what they're like."

"This one is different, Nick. I'm not after a harmless bit of dalliance. She's worth much more than that."

Nicholas turned to face him and raised his eyebrows. "My God, you really have fallen hard, have you not?"

"Very hard."

Chapter 15

The gentleman who, in an attempt to be agreeable, degrades and renders insignificant his conversation in the presence of ladies, betrays not only arrogance, but a lack of sense and a lamentable abuse of the gifts of nature.

The Busybody

Eleanor looked down at her dress and sighed. She feared she was bound to appear dowdy next to the beautiful and dignified Miss Parrish. She had always been rather fond of this dress, with its short tunic of ikat muslin over a plain white muslin underdress. The beautiful ikat, woven in shades of blue and green against a white ground, had also been used to trim the hem of the underdress and to fashion a bandeau for her hair. The fabric had been a gift from her brother two years ago, and the dress had been made shortly afterward. It was, therefore, not remotely modish. And to make matters worse, it was badly creased.

She had brought along only two dinner dresses, though, and Simon had already seen the other one three times. It pained her to imagine what he would think to see her in such an unfashionable dress next to Miss Parrish, who was bound to look prettier no matter what she wore.

What on earth was wrong with her? Eleanor had never been envious of other women and their modish wardrobes—not much, anyway. She had become resigned to shabby gentility once she'd moved to Bristol with Maurice, and it had only become shabbier since his death. Why was she suddenly so prickly about how she looked?

She knew the answer, of course. She was simply embarrassed to admit it, even to herself.

Perhaps if he had not embraced Miss Parrish so fondly, smiled and laughed with her so easily, casually touched her arm or shoulder so often as he spoke—perhaps if he'd done none of those things Eleanor would not now be harboring a perfectly absurd jealousy.

Dear heaven, what had come over her? She had no claim on Simon. A kiss did not mean anything.

She reached up to touch her lips. If she closed her eyes she would swear she could still feel his imprint upon them. It might have meant nothing, but it had most definitely felt like something. God, it had felt wonderful. And it had been such a long time since she'd experienced anything like it. In truth, it had been so long, she could not even say for certain if she'd ever experienced anything like it.

But, no, that was not true. Henry had also known how to bring about that same sort of erotic thrumming in her body, and she had lost her head over it. At almost thirty years of age, was she about to lose her head again? Over a few kisses? How utterly nonsensical.

Had he kissed Miss Parrish in that same way? He had called her friend, but so had he called Eleanor. He was a man of strong romantic tendencies who adored women. According to his own brother, he fell in love with pretty women all the time, and Miss Parrish was more than just pretty. There was a slightly exotic look about her, with her nearly black hair and dark, penetrating eyes. She shared Simon's political passions as well. He had said he preferred a strong, self-possessed woman with a mind of her own. How could he fail to fall in love with a woman like Miss Parrish who managed and edited an entire magazine?

Stop it, she told herself. She was being horribly, embarrassingly stupid. Simon had kissed her and she had thoroughly enjoyed it. *Take it for what it was and move on. End of story.*

There was still Belinda's story to worry about, however, and Eleanor was increasingly concerned. They were less than forty miles from Scotland. The next report from the Runners, which had not been awaiting them at the inn as she'd expected, would be critical. If Belinda and Geoffrey Barkwith had not been tracked to Gretna Green, and if there was no record anywhere of a marriage, then there could be only one alternative: he was taking her to a house in Scotland. There would no longer be any question that she had been right about him. This was the only thing that mattered now, the only problem that must remain uppermost in her mind, not some petty jealousy over nothing.

Out of sheer contrariness, however, she took the tiny spray of lilac that was still tucked into her bonnet ribbon and attached it to the ikat bandeau in her hair. Perhaps it would remind Simon that *she* was the one he'd kissed that day. Besides, it looked rather nice, she thought as she admired her reflection in the small mirror above the chest of drawers. It might not be the latest stare of fashion, but it would do. The red ribbon, still tied on her wrist, stood out like a trumpet blast among the woodwinds, but she was resolved to wear it until Belinda was found.

A rapping on the bedchamber door interrupted the last-minute ministrations to her simple coiffure. It was Simon, neat as a pin and with barely a crease in his dark blue coat, figured silk waistcoat, and crisp linen. His eyes went straight to the flowers in her hair, and he smiled.

"The lilac suits you, my dear." He bent down slightly, and for one anxious moment she thought he meant to kiss her again, but he only put his nose close to her hair and took a whiff of the fragrant blossoms. He had to stand exceedingly close to do so, however, setting off that all-too-familiar warmth low in her belly.

"You smell delicious," he said in a husky voice, and lingered in the area of her hair for longer than was absolutely necessary, his breath tickling her brow. "Here, take my arm before I am overcome by the sweet perfume, and I shall take you in to dinner. The private parlor is down on the next floor, I'm afraid."

She closed the door, put the key in her reticule, and took his arm. He touched the red ribbon on her wrist briefly and smiled down at her. "You still wear the Gypsy's ribbon."

"Of course. It was your idea, you may recall. It will remain on my wrist until Belinda is found."

They came to the narrow stairway and made their careful way down its precarious twists and turns. "I hope you do not mind having dinner with my friends," Simon said, keeping a firm grip on her elbow.

"No, of course not." Had he read something otherwise in her face? "I am pleased to make their acquaintance."

"You realize, of course, they are the ones I mentioned, the ones who are neighbors of mine in the Peak?"

"Yes, I know. Miss Parrish is the editor of *The Ladies' Fashionable Cabinet*."

"Indeed. And Nick writes for it as well. They are my closest friends, Eleanor. I hope they can be your friends, too. You will like Edwina, I think. She is not quite the Romantic I am, but we do share political ideals."

"You were in France together, I believe." Was she too obviously probing?

"Yes, almost ten years ago. The three of us went together, along with a few others. Ah, here we are."

The Parrishes were already comfortably en-
sconced in the parlor. It was a beautiful old room
with a large tracery window of sixteen lights. The
fire was lit, and a sideboard was set out with
glasses and several decanters. Nicholas rose at
their entry.

"Come and join us," he said. "We have discovered the claret to be excellent."

He poured a glass and handed it to her. He had
the same dark good looks as his sister. His smile
was somewhat roguish and his eyes flirted, as
though it was a habit with him. He handed Simon a
glass as well, and raised his own. "To serendipity,"
he said, and they all raised their glasses with him.

"It is indeed serendipitous," Edwina said, "for
us all to have met in such a remote part of the country. Please come sit by the fire, Mrs. Tennant. It may
be practically June, but it is drafty in this old inn.
What a lovely dress you are wearing."

Pleased at the compliment, Eleanor took a seat in
a hard-backed armchair and tried not to stare. Edwina, minus the bulky pelisse and bag bonnet she'd
worn earlier, was quite simply stunning. Her glossy
black hair was twisted around the back of the head
in a complicated arrangement of braids held in place
by a single gold comb, with artfully disheveled curls
spilling forward in the front. Her eyes were large
and dark and highly expressive. Her round gown of
simple white muslin was not, as it happened, any
more fashionable than Eleanor's own. But with such

striking looks, who would ever notice what she wore?

More than merely beautiful, Edwina's was a face full of intelligence and vitality. Her smile was genuine, and Eleanor liked her at once. She felt a stab of anger at herself for having harbored even the tiniest pang of jealousy. Edwina was the sort of woman one would want as a friend, not a rival.

Of course, there was no reason for them to be in positions of rivalry. Eleanor glanced at Simon and reminded herself that it had been only a few kisses. There had been nothing proprietary in it.

"I daresay you are in no mood for talk of serendipity," Edwina said, "with your niece still at large. You must be beside yourself with worry."

"Yes," Eleanor said, "I am afraid I shall not feel at ease until her situation is resolved, one way or another. It is most distressing, to be sure."

"Perhaps we ought to toast the Royal Oak instead," Nicholas said, with a twinkle in his dark eyes that told her he knew about the fete, and most likely about the kiss. Could men never keep a secret?

"A smashing idea, Nickie," Edwina said. "We saw some of the loveliest oak boughs hung all about this morning. And when the Lancaster & Carlisle *Telegraph* bowled by, it was thoroughly bedecked and beribboned. So yes, let us toast merry old Charles and the Restoration."

They raised their glasses once again and drank to the monarchy. Eleanor found it odd that these three, who had apparently gone to France in search of Republicanism, would pay homage to any monarchy, but she kept her thoughts to herself.

"Simon tells me you came upon an Oak Apple fete today," Nicholas said, confirming Eleanor's fears. She shot a quelling look in Simon's direction.

"Did you?" Edwina said. "What fun."

"That is where Eleanor got her lilac," Simon said. "Directly from the queen's scepter."

"And it looks very fetching indeed, Mrs. Tennant," Nicholas said, "but I am not quite sure it serves the purpose. It is oak leaves, as I recall, that protect one against pinching."

"Pay no attention to my brother, Mrs. Tennant. He is an inveterate flirt and not to be trusted. If he so much as tries to pinch you, just fling that claret right in his face. Besides, I am inclined to believe a queen's lilac is protection enough."

The soup was brought in and the gentlemen helped the ladies to be seated at the table. Conversation was kept light at first, held to the trivialities of the weather and the roads. Simon remarked that the rains had made a mess of the roads in the Midlands. "Our carriage took a tumble in the Northamptonshire mud."

"That must be where you got the cut above your eye," Edwina said. She looked to be on the brink of a smile but kept her voice even. "And the bruise fading on your jaw."

Simon colored up and darted a glance at Eleanor

before returning his attention to the soup. "No, it's not from the carriage accident. There was a . . . um . . . a bit of a fight in Buxton."

Edwina covered her mouth to suppress a gurgle of laughter. Nicholas was busy choking on the soup.

"A fight?" he said when he could speak, his voice still a little raspy and trembling with restrained laughter.

"It was more in the nature of a brawl," Eleanor said. "And it was all my fault."

"Do tell, Mrs. Tennant," Edwina said, casting up her perfectly arched brows. "I am all agog."

Eleanor made brief work of the story, but did her best to stress the bravery, and skill, exhibited by Simon. She had no wish to sit through yet another meal during which he was berated for his lack of manly virtues.

"Well done, Simon," Edwina said.

"Lord, I wish I had been there," Nicholas said. "Lucky for you old Malcolm showed up, eh?"

"He did not need his brother's help, I assure you," Eleanor wondered why she felt so determined to stand up for him. These were his closest friends, after all, and surely would not need Eleanor to point out to them Simon's true nature. She felt a twinge of embarrassment for being so obvious. Hoping to recover some measure of dignity, she said, "Malcolm and his friends simply added to the melee."

"Quite so," Edwina said, her eyes darting between Eleanor and Simon with interest. "Simon can handle his own in just about any situation. Nickie, do you remember that night in Bruges . . ."

The conversation turned to reminiscences of their travels together. Both Edwina and her brother seemed determined to embarrass Simon with stories of his strength, courage, and cleverness, with the occasional tale of some youthful foolishness or other. Thoroughly rapt, Eleanor found that yesterday's revelations and the deep and varied conversation of last night had not been enough. She wanted to know everything about him.

Simon, however, looked miserably uncomfortable, and his color was still high. He changed the subject to the Parrishes' trip to Edinburgh. There was some business about political pamphlets that quite obviously was being couched in vague terms because of Eleanor's presence.

"Please feel free to speak openly," she said. "You need not fear that I will report you as engaging in seditious activities."

"You understand our motives, Mrs. Tennant?" Edwina asked, her gaze as forthright as her words.

"As far as *The Ladies' Fashionable Cabinet* is concerned, yes, I believe I understand."

"And do you support our efforts?"

"I understand your motives," Eleanor replied, "but I am not prepared to say that I support all you do without knowing more about it."

"Simon has told you about the *Lady's Monthly Museum*?"

"Yes, he has, though I remain somewhat skeptical."

Conversation ceased while the soup was removed and the next course set out. Clearly, there would be no discussion of the magazine or anything remotely political while strangers were in the room. With a few words from Simon, the waiters left all the dishes on a sideboard and departed. The two gentlemen wasted no time in leading the ladies to the food and heaping up plates of their own. It was the usual array of fish, meat, game, vegetables, and condiments, enough for a group of ten rather than four. Of course, one of those four was Simon.

Eleanor could not help but notice that his plate was piled twice as high as Nicholas's. Edwina caught her eye and grinned. She was no doubt accustomed to Simon's appetite. When they were seated once more, she continued the conversation as though there had been no interruption.

"My object at the *Cabinet*," she began, "is to provide a counterpoint to the rationalizations against progressive, Republican views that litter the pages of the *Museum*. We are all of us dedicated to the encouragement of education for girls, to the free and equal treatment of women in the laws of inheritance and custody, to the fostering of strength of mind and body for all females. To promote weakness in half of society is to effectively cripple that society. These principles inform everything we do at the *Cabinet*."

"The *Museum* is not the only publication that deliberately sets out to subvert its female readership," Nicholas said. "It is one of the most egregious, however, and the one already targeted as competition during my aunt's tenure."

"I still find it hard to believe that so much of what they do is based on politics," Eleanor said.

"It is subtly done," Nicholas said. "Did you read the recent article about the two wives of an Indian man who'd died? Only one of the wives threw herself on his funeral pyre, and she was held up as a model of feminine virtue and devotion. The other wife, who refused to kill herself, was scorned as unworthy."

"Or the essay on important women in history," Simon said, "that suggested many of them, including Queen Elizabeth, were not women at all, or were, at best, of the epicene gender. That one prompted Nick, writing as Augusta Historica, to develop the series on great heroines of British history."

"Or last month's *Museum* harangue about not discussing politics in mixed society," Edwina said, "in order to preserve the delicacy of the female mind. It so infuriated me that I began adding more political works to the books I review as Arbiter Literaria."

"I'm afraid I missed those articles," Eleanor said,

"though had I read them I assure you I would have been outraged. If you must know, I generally only skim that magazine, and yours, with a cursory look at the fashion plates with my niece, but little else. She reads every word, I assure you. From time to time I will read an essay, but in truth, not very often. It is not that I have anything against the attitudes and opinions expressed, it is just—"

"I believe Eleanor finds our prose a bit too florid for her taste," Simon said, smiling at her over a forkful of fricassee. "My prose, at least."

Edwina chuckled. "Simon is the purest Romantic of us all. A sentimentalist to his fingertips. That is why I assigned him to take over as the Busybody. And whenever we need a tale of requited love to counteract some horror in the *Museum* in which the heroine throws herself off a cliff, we have only to call upon Simon. There is also, of course, the poetry of Alonzo."

Oh, no. Not Alonzo. Not the worst, most sickeningly sentimental poet of the lot.

"His Alonzo poems are exceedingly popular," Edwina said.

Eleanor's stomach gave a little twitch, and she was not certain whether it was due to the mushrooms or the knowledge that Simon was indeed the odious Alonzo, he of the facile rhyme and the saccharine imagery.

"We receive letters about Alonzo, and poetic tributes, all the time," Edwina continued. "But even Simon's poetry, though its style may not appeal to everyone, is in keeping with our objectives. It extols the laws of Nature rather than the laws of Man, the individual over society. It is the essence of what we are all about."

"Thank you, Edwina," Simon said. "However, I do not think you will change Eleanor's opinion." Certainly not now that she knew him to be Alonzo as well as the Busybody. The rather qualmish look on her face told him what she thought of Alonzo's poetry. "She will have no truck with Romantics, especially one who has, quite unintentionally, encouraged her niece to run away."

"It is not only that, Simon," she said, "though I do hope what has happened with Belinda will encourage more responsible advice from the Busybody in the future." She looked across the table and caught Edwina's eye. "Though Simon prefers to label me a cynic, I have tried to convince him that I am a realist. To me, life is not a walk through the countryside feeling compassionate toward all God's creatures. Life is a struggle, at least mine has been—a sometimes bitter struggle against a world of temptation and danger."

"And our principles serve to strengthen women's character so they may more effectively face those dangers," Edwina retorted.

"I am not sure I agree with your methods, though," Eleanor said. "Just take Belinda, as a case in point. She hangs on every word of *The Ladies'*

Fashionable Cabinet. But for a young girl like her, willful and flighty, to consume your veiled messages of female independence simply gives her permission to thumb her nose at society. To disdain society only causes her ruin, and leads to a life of misery."

"I believe you exaggerate, Mrs. Tennant," Edwina said.

"Unfortunately, I do not," Eleanor said. "Such is the fate of many girls, I assure you." She looked to Simon briefly, and their gazes locked in the memory of her revelation the night before. "In many cases we are completely dependent upon the men in our lives for every morsel of food on our plates and the clothing on our backs. Society is not yet ready for us to be independent. Not all of us, anyway.

"And before you ask, yes, I have read *A Vindication of the Rights of Woman*, and I support much of what it says in regard to the subjugation of women." She gave a little smile. "I suppose, though, that I am more pragmatic about the application of those ideas. I am willing, for example, to accept the patriarchal hierarchies of our society because that is the world in which I live. I am less concerned with changing that world than living peacefully within it." She pulled a rueful face. "I cannot imagine someone harboring Miss Wollstonecraft's level of discontent will ever find any sort of peace."

Her words brought a somber quiet to the parlor.

Eleanor could not have said anything that more clearly evoked memories of a woman the other three had known well.

"She found a measure of peace at the end," Edwina said. "But you are right, Mrs. Tennant. Her life was not always a happy one. Mary's unhappiness, though, was of a personal and not a political nature. But I take your point."

Eleanor looked from one of them to the other, confusion and chagrin marking her brow. "I beg your pardon if I have said something to offend. I was speaking of the ideas, not their author. I had no idea she was someone known to you. And I do not disagree with her on a philosophical level. I simply choose not to fight those battles in my own life."

"No offense was taken, Mrs. Tennant, I assure you," Edwina said, and offered a genuine smile so there was no doubt of her sincerity. "And I hope you will take none when I say that I *do* choose to fight those battles."

"No, indeed," Eleanor said. "In fact, I admire you for putting action to your principles."

"But are you not doing the same, Eleanor?" Simon was unable to curb his open admiration for the way she had stood her ground in a room full of Republicans. Regardless of his own opinions, he was bursting with pride for her. "You are putting your own principles to work by chasing after your niece in hopes of saving her from . . . from an unhappy future."

"You believe she will be unhappy with this fellow she's run off with?" Nicholas asked.

Eleanor gave a little laugh, and there was a hint of self-mockery in it. "Let me say only that I do not trust the bloom would stay long on that connubial flower. I'd prefer she made a more thoughtful, logical choice."

"Ah, but Mrs. Tennant," Nicholas said, with a teasing glance at Simon, "love is not always logical, is it?"

"No, it is not." She returned Nicholas's smile. "That is precisely why I do not think it should rule our lives."

"Good Lord, Simon," Edwina said. "You have indeed found the rare unromantic woman. How provoking for you. But what a lovely challenge."

Damn Nicholas, for he had surely filled his sister's ear with Simon's romantic quandary over Eleanor. He was rather tired of being the focus, however indirectly, of tonight's conversation, and so lost no time in steering it toward other topics.

They had made good work of the sideboard, and the wine, when the waiter brought the final course of fruits and cheeses. The mood had become more languid and relaxed. Simon was pleased to think Eleanor liked his friends. And though she did not share the same passions or politics, Simon believed they liked her as well. She was quite obviously intelligent and strong-minded, and held her own in the more political discussions. She made him proud.

Eleanor was the first to call it an evening. She was sure there would be a message from the Runners by morning, she said, and wanted to make an early start. Simon should have taken the hint, but he was so enjoying the company of Nicholas and Edwina, he decided to stay awhile longer.

When she'd gone, Nicholas said, "Lord, Simon, you could barely tear your eyes from her."

"She's very pretty, Nickie."

"Yes, but I think our Simon is truly lost this time, Ed."

"I like her," Edwina said. "But she's not your usual type, is she, Simon?"

"No," he said, "she's more like you."

Edwina's dark eyes regarded him frankly, with curiosity and affection. "Simon."

"Don't worry, my dear," he said, "I have not been carrying that torch for ten years. But it has occurred to me this evening that I may have been deliberately falling for women who were *not* like you. Nick says I pick the wrong women, and it's true. I've been easily drawn to beautiful eyes or hair or cheeks or bosoms. But they had often belonged to fresh young girls without much more to offer. Remember what we talked about earlier, Nick? The unattainable ideal?"

"Yes," Nicholas said, "but I still don't see it."

"That's because you're too close to it," Simon said. "You see, my unattainable ideal has always been Edwina."

"Oh, Simon." Edwina's eyes grew soft and a little sad.

He smiled and reached across to touch her hand. "Don't get all weepy on me, Ed. I meant it when I said that torch was burned out, though you know how I will always feel about you. No, what I am trying to explain—and rather badly, I daresay—is that my true ideal has always been someone *like* you. A woman of strong character and principles, even if some of those principles differ from my own. A woman of dignity and confidence and self-assurance. And yet that is not the type of woman I have been routinely falling in love with for the last ten years. Why is that?"

"Because they were all unattainable and provided fodder for your poetry?" Nicholas said.

Simon laughed. "Yes, they were indeed unattainable, for all sorts of reasons. But I think I must have known all along that none of them was within my reach. My dismal luck has never been all that tragic to me, you know. My heart was never seriously broken, only a tad bruised."

"If I understand you, then," Nicholas said, "your intentions have never been serious."

"That's right."

"So rather than the tragic poet seeking his ideal," Nicholas said, "you have really only been dallying, trifling, flirting, philandering—"

"Lord, Nick, you make me sound like some sort of libertine. I was never that, I assure you." Simon laughed at the very notion of himself as a lecherous rake. "Until now, I do not think I have been playing out the grand Romantic theme of the unattainable ideal. Though I have lost my head over a woman more times than I care to count, I do not think I was ever seriously out to win any of them. Not truly. Not deep down in the most candid corner of my heart. But it is different this time. I want Eleanor. I want her badly. And Nick, you may wipe that leering grin off your face because you know damned well I am speaking not only of physical desire, though God knows it is there in spades. I want her heart and soul as well."

"So you believe Mrs. Tennant is the ideal you have been seeking?" Edwina asked.

"Yes, my dear, I do. I honestly believe she is the heart's desire that has so long eluded me. There is such strength in her, Ed, a level of courage you could never imagine. She's as hardheaded and obstinate as you can be. And almost as beautiful."

"So you're saying," Nicholas said, "that this time you really *are* faced with the unattainable ideal."

"Oh, Nickie, don't be such a pessimist," Edwina said. "Why should Mrs. Tennant be so unattainable? She seemed thoroughly smitten with Simon. Only think how nobly she defended him when you teased him about the fight at Buxton."

"Dammit, but I wish I'd been there," Nicholas said. "Both Westover brothers in action. What a sight that must have been."

A rapping on the parlor door saved Simon from

having to cut off Nicholas so he could ask Edwina more about Eleanor's perceived interest. The innkeeper bowed and stepped into the room.

"I beg your pardon," he said, "but there be a feller here what wants to have a word with Mr. Westover. Says his name's Hackett."

"He's one of our Runners," Simon said. He stood and stretched—Lord, how long had they been sitting?—and moved toward the door. "I'd better see what news he has."

"No need to come downstairs, sir," the innkeeper said. "He be standing right here."

Indeed, the stocky, bow-legged form of the Runner could be seen standing in the corridor. "Come on in, Hackett," Simon said.

The innkeeper stepped aside to allow the Runner in. Hackett gave the man a fish-eyed look, then shut the door behind him. "Evenin', guv'ner." He came into the parlor, removed his hat, and looked about the room. His gaze landed on Nicholas and Edwina, and he arched a skeptical brow.

"It's all right," Simon said. "You may speak freely here."

"The girl's aunt?" Hackett asked. "She still with you?"

"Yes, but she has retired for the evening," Simon said. "What news have you?"

Hackett rubbed the back of his neck and pulled a face. "Nothin' good, I fear. The whole business has me fair betwaddled. The long and the short of it is, we lost 'em."

Simon's heart flew up into his throat. "What? How? I thought they were heading straight to Gretna by the Carlisle road."

"Not straight, exactly. Such roundaboutation I've never seen. They zigged and they zagged like the stitches in a wound. What threw us, how-somever, is that the ostlers at one inn would say they was headed north, and at the next inn they was seen headed south. Me and Mumby've been chasing our tails for a full day, and now we've lost the trail completely. It's a perturbulatin' situation, but there you have it."

Oh, Lord, how was he going to tell Eleanor? "Mumby is still searching?"

" 'Course, he is. So will I be, soon's I leave here."

"Do what you can, Hackett. We can't give up now. You know, they may have gone off some-where else altogether. Not to Scotland at all."

"Not to worry, guv'ner, we ain't that green. Know a thing or two about gents what run off with young girls. And Mumby's got that keen, scientifi-cal brain o' his on the job. Couldn't ask fer better. We'll keep lookin'. We'll inquizify every inn and alehouse from border to border, if it be necessitary. And we'll find 'em, or my name ain't Obidiah Hackett. Best that you and the aunt stay here until you hear from us again."

He bowed to the room at large, and took his leave. Simon sank into a chair. "Oh, God."

He felt a hand on his shoulder and looked up

into Edwina's concerned eyes. "Try not to worry, Simon. It is likely just a temporary setback. The Runners will find them."

"Eventually. But now it looks as though Eleanor has been right all along. She never believed there would be a Scottish marriage."

"Oh, dear."

"Damn! I so wanted to make this one thing right for her, and now it's botched." Simon let out a great, noisy sigh. "I suppose I'd better let her know."

Chapter 16

Merit alone does not signify in the selection of a mate if one cannot feel that sentiment of affection so necessary in a lifelong commitment.

The Busybody

Eleanor sat on the side of the bed and brushed her hair. It was a nightly ritual—one hundred strokes—she had kept up since she was a young girl. It was often a time of reflection, when she considered the events of the day or plans for the morrow. Just as often, though, she sat with a book propped open on her knee.

There was no book tonight, however, and much to reflect upon. Belinda's situation was, as ever, of primary importance. Yet each time she pondered the poor girl's plight, thoughts of Simon drove everything else out of her head. The kisses. The laughter. The closeness. The conversations. The growing attraction.

How could she be so wrapped up in her own wants and needs at a time like this, when her niece was still missing? How could she be so selfish?

Her body would not be ignored, however. It reacted to thoughts of Simon almost as strongly as it did to his actual touch. She had only to close her eyes and relive today's kiss to cause her nipples to harden and that most intimate part of her to throb with desire.

Still, she did not know what to think about him. He was certainly interested, attracted to her, but it was likely no more than that. She should be wiser now, eleven years after her first encounter with a man who made her body tingle all over. But what wisdom had she gained? Had she learned to avoid such pitfalls altogether, or approach them with a mature pragmatism? Should she hold out for a serious, formal courtship or nothing at all? Or allow herself a bit of pleasure without strings attached?

What was she to do about Simon Westover?

And when would they find poor Belinda?

Both problems that plagued her were so fraught with emotion she was liable to suffer a nervous collapse. Once Belinda was restored to her, perhaps they could make a trip to Bath where Eleanor could be hauled about in a chair and take the waters.

She had made only seventy-two strokes of the brush when she was startled by a soft rapping at the door. It must be Edwina on her way to bed. Perhaps she had seen the light beneath the door and stopped by to wish her a good night.

Eleanor put down the brush and grabbed her wrapper. She slipped into it and held it closely about her without tying it while she opened the door.

Good God, it was Simon!

She hurriedly pulled the wrapper more tightly about her and tied it at the waist. For a brief instant, she regretted that it was such a dowdy, worn old thing and not something soft and feminine.

He looked troubled. "I am dreadfully sorry to wake you, Eleanor."

"I was not asleep. What has happened?"

He ran a hand through his hair. "Hackett was here. I am afraid the news is not good."

Eleanor gave a little gasp and brought her hand to cover her mouth. She stood paralyzed with fear.

"They've lost them, Eleanor. They came upon conflicting information, some saying they were headed north, some saying they were headed south. Hackett and Mumby have been running in circles trying to regain the trail. Hackett is confident they will be found in time, but for now, I am afraid they are lost."

Belinda! Dear heaven, where was she? Where had that monster taken her? Oh God oh God oh God. What was she to do? She could not think. She could not breathe. Her head swam. Her knees began to buckle.

"Oh, Eleanor."

Strong arms kept her from collapsing. She trembled with anguish and panic as Simon held her tight.

"My dear, I am so sorry."

He rocked her gently as he repeated over and over that he was sorry. Her hands flattened against his chest and she pressed her forehead to his shoulder.

"I had hoped . . . I thought perhaps . . . Oh, God, I suppose I . . . I held on to this thin little thread of hope that . . . that they were going to Gretna after all . . . I never wanted . . . I didn't think . . . Oh, God, it is just like . . . Where has he taken her? What if we can't find her? Oh, Simon, what . . . what am I g-going to d-do?"

A great sob rippled through her like a convulsion, and she wept. She wept for Belinda, for her lost innocence, for her wasted youth. She wept for fear, for frustration, for anger, for sorrow. She wept all the tears she'd held inside the past week. And all the while, Simon held her close, murmuring unintelligible sounds of comfort and support and affection.

He stroked her hair gently with one hand. The other rubbed up and down her back in a soothing motion.

She tried to talk, to thank him, to tell him how much better she felt with his arms around her. But she had lost control of her voice and words did not come out properly.

"Shh," he said. "Don't talk. Just let me hold you."

She obeyed him and simply stood there in his arms until the tears were spent and her breathing slowed to something close to normal. She sniffed and hiccupped and burrowed her head against his shoulder, unwilling just yet to move out of the cozy cocoon of his embrace. She nestled against his chest and gratefully absorbed the comfort he offered. It was some time before she was able to speak.

"I'm s-sorry, Simon." Her voice was muffled against his chest. His hand, moving idly in her hair, prevented her from lifting her head, though she had no real desire to do so. "It is not like m-me to break d-down like this. How m-mortifying."

"Shh," he said again. "It's all right."

She felt his lips in her hair, and it was at that instant when Eleanor recollected that she was in a shocking state of *déshabillé*. Very shocking. And very intimate. Her unconfined breasts were flattened against his chest. His hand on her back, so warm and gentle, had only the thin fabric of her wrapper and nightgown between it and her bare skin. His other hand caressed and combed through the hair hanging indecently loose over her shoulders.

She breathed in the scent of him, musky and male, and her traitorous body began to quiver like a bowstring.

He was only being kind. He offered comfort. She should not try to make it into something else, no matter how much she would have welcomed it.

Would she? Would she welcome something more than comfort from Simon?

Yes, God help her, she would. She must be a wanton, for she wanted it very badly. She really should pull herself out of his arms and send him back to his own bedchamber. But she did not have the will to do it. Eleanor felt so warm and safe right where she was, she did not want to move.

The tears had dried up, the hiccupping had ceased, the panic had eased, and her breathing had slowed. The storm of anguish had passed, and he need not hold her so closely anymore. But Eleanor did not move. Simon kept his arms about her. And somehow the door had closed behind them.

His lips were on her hair again, and she thought he murmured her name. He teased her head away from his chest, just enough to trail his gentle, comforting kisses along her temple and brow. Eleanor arched her neck to receive them, and he accepted her unspoken invitation by moving his lips to her cheek and her jaw and her eyes, kissing away the remnants of her tears.

When his mouth came, finally, inevitably, to her own, he stopped and poised only a breath away. "Eleanor." She could feel his lips, so close to hers, form the syllables of her name, and her eyes fluttered open. There was anxiety in that blue gaze, and a question. But she had ceased to struggle with her conscience over the desire this man had reawakened in her. She answered his question by pressing her lips upward to meet his.

The invitation sent a current of heat straight to his core. The hunger was upon Simon again, the insatiable hunger for Eleanor, his ideal, his heart's desire. He refused to think this wasn't meant to happen, that he was wrong to take advantage of the vulnerability of her distress. He refused to think of anything but how right she felt in his arms, how perfect her mouth, how silky her hair, how soft her body. And it could not be wrong because here was her mouth opening to his, here were her breasts pressing against him, here were her arms twining about his neck.

It was so very right, it was like two pieces of a Chinese puzzle locked ultimately, perfectly in place.

The kiss built and built with a new urgency. It was not the succulent, languorous exploration of the afternoon, but a wild torrent of seeking tongues and driving breath. She was as eager, as impatient, as hungry as he was, and the knowledge of her desire sent a wave of passion rolling through him. He clamped his arm around her waist and pulled her closer, tighter, every moment aware of the body only barely covered with her nightclothes. The reaction of his own body was intense, almost painful. He threaded his fingers in the heavy weight of her glorious hair, and savored the deep mingling of tongues in a greedy, desperate, sensual dance.

He could not get enough of her.

His mouth moved to her jaw and throat and neck—tasting, exploring, savoring. She arched herself to him, giving a little moan of pleasure. It was the sweetest poetry he'd ever heard. He brought his mouth back to hers and nibbled on the plump upper lip while his hand stroked the length of her hair, found her shoulder, and slid beneath the neck of her wrapper.

When he touched her breast, she gave a little gasp that brought him back to the moment. Good God, what was he doing? Alone with Eleanor in her bedchamber. She, in her nightclothes. He, taking advantage, giving in to his hunger. As right as it felt to him, he was very afraid it would be wrong for her.

He curved his hand around her waist and slowly brought the kiss to an end. They stood and stared at each other, panting, breathless, hot. Simon gazed hard into her eyes and searched for an answer to the question, unspoken yet thunderous, that hung in the air between them. He thought he read the answer clearly in those blazing green depths, glassy with desire. He reached up and brushed a lock of hair from her cheek, his fingers lingering on the fine, satiny skin.

"You had better send me away," he said, his voice rough and unsteady. "Right now. This minute."

She closed her eyes, sucked in a short breath, and exhaled with a little groan. When she opened them again, her eyes were plaintive, feverish.

"Eleanor? Send me away." *Before it is too late.*

She looked directly into his eyes and shook her head. Simon's breath caught.

"No," she said. "I want you to stay."

Oh, God. He took her face in both hands and

searched for any sign of uncertainty. "Eleanor. Ah, sweet Eleanor. Are you sure?"

She smiled, and his heart contracted in his chest so that he could barely breathe. "Yes. Please stay, Simon. I need you tonight."

"Need?" If that was all it was, it would not be right. She would hate him in the morning. "If you need only comforting, Eleanor, I cannot do it. I cannot hold you close just to keep you safe. Oh, I could hold you. But it would not be comfort. It would be more. I cannot stay for need only."

"Then stay because . . . must I say it, Simon?"

"Yes."

"You're a horrid man, do you know that? Why do you force me to say it?"

"Because it is not enough that I want you, though God knows I've never wanted anything more. But you must want me, too, my dear. I don't wish to hurt you. There's been enough hurt in your life. But if I stay, it must be because you want to make love with me, not because you feel wretched about Belinda. I'll stay if you want me to love you, but not if you only want me to comfort you."

"Stay. Stay because I want you. Stay because I want this for me, not for Belinda. Stay."

"Ah, Eleanor."

"I want you to love me tonight, Simon. Please."

He pulled her tight against him and buried his nose in her hair. "My dear Eleanor, nothing would give me more pleasure." He bent and kissed her

again, deeply, passionately, with a new understanding of what was to come. His heart soared
with pure joy. Eleanor, the unattainable ideal, suddenly attainable. He was going to love her and love
her until she cried out in pleasure. He was going to
devour her in small bites until he'd had his fill,
then start all over again. But he was going to ex-
plode if he didn't get her over to that bed soon.

Eleanor gave herself up to him completely and
their kiss became more ardent, his mouth demand-
ing, his tongue delving, his hands caressing. She
had not lied. She wanted him, she wanted this. It
had been so very long, and she had never thought
to feel like this again. But her body was on fire for
Simon, and she could think of nothing else but
making love with him.

She felt his fingers beneath her breasts as he
struggled to untie her wrapper. He held her
slightly away from him as he slid both hands over
her breasts and up over her shoulders, and pushed
the wrapper down her arms so that it fell to the
floor in a puddle at her feet. Eleanor looked down
at the ugly garment. What must he think of her, to
be wearing such a dowdy, spinsterish old thing?
She fussed with the neck of the muslin gown that
had grown thin from too many washings and was
patched at the sleeve. How mortifying, she
thought, and groaned aloud even as Simon began
to rain kisses on her neck and shoulder.

He pulled up sharply. "What is it? Have you changed your mind, Eleanor? You have only to say so, and I will leave."

"No, it is not that. I do not want you to leave." She could not bear it if he left now. "It is just . . . I just wish . . . Oh, Simon, how I wish you could have found me in silk and satin and lace instead of this horrid worn-out old thing. I want to look beautiful for you."

He reached out to stroke her face, then cupped her chin in his hand. "I have never seen anyone look more beautiful in all my life."

His words washed over her like a hot spring. The way his blue eyes darkened with desire made her feel beautiful. "You are very sweet, Simon, but even you cannot think this gown anything but ugly."

"You hate the gown?"

"Never so much as at this moment."

"Well, then, there is only one thing to do." He began to untie the ribbons at the neck. "If thy gown offend thee, take it off."

And suddenly it, too, was puddled at her feet and she stood in nothing but the cold night air and a single red ribbon, naked to his hungry gaze. It had been eleven years since she had stood thus with a man. She was no longer as firm, as slender as she had once been, and a sharp pang of embarrassment had her reaching to cover herself. But he took her hands away and held them out to her sides as he worshipped her with his eyes.

"Beautiful," he whispered, and drew her into his arms and kissed her. His tongue skimmed lightly over her lips while his hands roved up and down her bare spine, her hips, her buttocks. There was something strangely erotic about her nakedness pressed against his fully clothed person. But she wanted to feel his skin against hers, to run her hands over the chest she had glimpsed so briefly, to explore the hard muscles of the shoulders that had lifted the carriage out of the mud.

She ran her hands beneath the lapels of his coat and pushed them over his shoulders. He stood back a little, making room for her to help him shrug out of his coat. Its fit was so snug she did not know how he ever managed to get it off without help. He flung it across the floor, and she went to work on the buttons of his waistcoat. He explored the length of her neck with his lips and tongue, making concentration difficult, but she finally was able to slip the waistcoat over his arms.

Simon became more eager and unwound his neckcloth with impatience, flinging it aside to join the coat. Eleanor's trembling fingers pulled at his shirt buttons, stopping to stroke each new inch of chest revealed. He gave a groan and tugged at the shirttails, pulling them free, and tossing the shirt over his head.

Eleanor spread her hands across his firm chest, exploring the thick mat of auburn hair that covered it. When her lips took over the exploration, Simon threw his head back and breathed heavily. She kissed his neck and shoulders and pressed her breasts against him, rubbing her smooth skin against the coarse chest hair. Oh, yes. This was much more erotic than pressing her naked flesh against his waistcoat.

He sank his head over her shoulder and took hold of her hips. He rubbed against her in a counter movement so that they swayed and rocked, and her breasts tingled and peaked hard. His hands moved to cup her buttocks, and he began to move them against his own hips in a slow grind.

She could bear no more and reached a hand down between them to the buttons of his pantaloons. She managed one button and slid her hand inside to the smooth skin of his belly. He gave a kind of growl and suddenly scooped her up in his arms. He deposited her on the bed, tumbling down with her, and wrapped her in his arms for a blazing, torrid kiss.

She wanted more and plucked again at his pantaloons. He gave her one more quick kiss, then rolled off and pulled her to the edge of the bed, swinging her around so she was sitting up. He sat beside her and began to pull off his boots. "As impatient as I am," he said, "I refuse to make love with my boots on. Help me, Eleanor?"

And she did. She tugged and he pulled, and when the first one finally came free, she fell over from the effort. Laughing, they began on the second boot. After much yanking and straining and tumbling about and laughing, they got the boot off, and Eleanor flung it merrily across the room. Simon rose and stood before her as he slowly unbuttoned his pantaloons and peeled them off, along with the small clothes underneath. He stood before her in all his naked glory, fully aroused, large and beautiful.

The soft, flickering light of the single candle on the small table by the bed gilded the russet hair on his chest and legs and arms. He was lean and sinewy, well muscled but not bulky like his brother. He was thoroughly and splendidly masculine.

Eleanor, bold and wanton, ran a slow hand down his chest to the thick hair surrounding his erection, then lightly ran her fingers over the soft-hard heat of him. He sucked in his breath with a hoarse gasp, then gently pushed her back onto the bed and fell down beside her.

"Please, my dear, you will make me embarrass myself like a gauche schoolboy. Let us not rush our pleasure. Let me take a little time with you."

And he took his time, loving her slowly with his hands and mouth. He kissed her lightly, nibbling her upper lip, while he covered her small breast with his hand, caressing gently, squeezing, circling the erect nipple until she was lost in the magic of his touch. He skimmed his hands over hips and belly and shoulder and thigh, as though impatient to learn every inch of her.

He trailed kisses along her neck and throat and shoulder and collarbone. His head dipped low, and he ran his hot, wet tongue along the delicate underside of a breast. He slowly worked his way up to the puckered tip of her nipple and took it in his mouth, sending ripples of sensation all the way to the roots of her hair and making her gasp. She plunged her fingers in his soft hair and held him there. "Yes," she breathed, urging him never to stop.

After paying equal homage to the other breast, he rose up on his elbows to look at her. He smiled and ran a finger over her lip. The candle sputtered and his eyes darted briefly toward it, and then back again as though something had caught his eye. He reached over her, and she thought he meant to snuff the candle, but instead he picked up the lilac spray from the Oak Apple fete. He tickled her lips with it, making her giggle. "You shall be my May queen, Eleanor, covered in the heady scent of lilac."

He stroked the soft spray like a paintbrush over her neck and shoulders, tracing a meandering path to her breasts. He painted lilac circles around her nipples, the touch so light, so feather-soft, it was almost beyond bearing, and gooseflesh rose over all her body. He drew the flowers between her breasts and down over her stomach in ever widening circles. Down and down farther, until she arched off the bed and gave a whimpering moan. Her legs became limp and fell open to his caress. He drew the soft flowers down her inner thigh, behind her knee, and up again, gossamer light, hardly more than a breath. She shivered under the exquisite torment. He gave the same attention to the other leg, and by now she was writhing at the touch. When he finally, inexorably, stroked the spray against her sex, she cried out.

Simon seemed determined, though, to make it last, to keep full gratification at bay, and ever so slowly brought the lilac back up over her stomach and abdomen and breasts, leaving her breathless and wanting.

He then took the spray and began to remove its tiny blossoms, scattering them about her from head to toe. He placed some in her hair as well, which he fanned out on the pillows in a precise arrangement. He leaned above her to admire his handiwork.

"You are the vision of Flora herself. I'm afraid you cannot move, my dear. You look much too perfect. You make me want to pen an ode to spring."

"Dear God, not now, Simon. *Please*."

He tossed away the denuded lilac sprig and covered the strewn blossoms with his body. He took her in a powerful kiss, pressing hard against her from shoulder to thigh, moving in a sensuous undulation that filled the air with the raw musk of sex and sweat mixed with the thick fragrance of lilac released from the crushed blossoms.

Simon's tongue plunged deep in her mouth, then withdrew slowly, then plunged again, in a manner suggestive of what was to come. His hand reached down between them and touched her, his fingers as soft as the lilac had been. But she wanted more than a gentle touch and thrust up her pelvis to meet his hand.

Eleanor's sexuality had lain dormant for so long it took little to bring it to life. She moved against his hand and was almost instantly in the grip of a blazing climax that sent spasms of heat coursing through her body.

Simon took her mouth and swallowed her scream of ecstasy at the same moment the hot, hard length of him pushed inside her. *Oh, God!* She had forgotten how good it felt, to be so thoroughly, deliciously filled. He set up a rhythm of long, slow strokes, and she instinctively set a counter rhythm.

Simon raised up on his elbow to watch her. She felt self-conscious at his direct gaze and chewed on her lip. He smiled and said, "How plump, how ripe this sweet confection, with potent hint of sweet connection."

Good heavens, was he quoting erotic poetry to her? She giggled and he chuckled and they laughed joyously together at the wonder of what was happening. "Oh, God, Eleanor." His voice was gruff with passion and he increased the pace of his thrusts. He buried his face in her hair and drove her to a new crescendo as she writhed and bucked and shuddered beneath him. Her sigh of fulfillment had barely faded when his own sharp groan was muffled against her shoulder.

She lay beneath the full weight of him, spent, sated, exhausted. And happy.

Chapter 17

*He who recognizes true merit in a deserving
young lady without claims to beauty or fortune is
certain to be rewarded by affections roused to the
bliss of reciprocal delight.*

The Busybody

They lay together for some minutes, slick and
panting. Still buried inside her, Simon could
feel her inner muscles pulsing and contracting in
the way that always followed a powerful climax. It
pleased him that he had done that for her.

Finally, worried that he must surely be crushing
her, he lifted his head, kissed her, then rolled over
and gave a sigh of pure pleasure. He pulled
Eleanor, languid and limp, against his side and
looped an arm and a leg over her. She curled up
close, threw an arm across his chest, and entwined
her legs with his. He'd never been more content in
all his life. Or so thoroughly, crazily, wondrously in
love.

"Eleanor," he whispered against the top of her
head.

"Hmm."

She seemed on the brink of sleep, but there were words he had to say. This was not a night for rolling over and going to sleep. It had not been a simple coupling. It had been momentous. Earth-shaking. Soul-searing. At least it had been for him. He hoped it was true for her as well.

Perhaps he ought to wait. Perhaps it would not be wise to say anything in the afterglow of spectacular sex. But he did not want her to think him no better than old Henry Scapegrace. Simon had no intention of abandoning her, of using her and discarding her. Surely she knew that, but he wanted to tell her and didn't think he could stop the words anyway. They were ready to burst unbidden from his lips.

"Eleanor?"

"Hmm."

"Eleanor, I love you."

"Hmm"

Had she heard him? "Eleanor?" But there was only the heavy, regular breathing of deep sleep.

Damn. Should he shake her? Wake her up, make her open her eyes and look into his while he said it again?

But no, there was all the time in the world. For now, he would simply hold her close and think how happy, how lucky he was to have found her. He stroked her hair lightly, but she did not stir. Her breath was soft and warm on his chest.

He loved her. If there had ever been any doubt in his mind, there was none now. She was beautiful and passionate and fun—he could not recall ever laughing with a woman while they made love.

Her laughter was only one of the signs that he had finally won her trust. Once she had made the decision to ask him to stay, she seemed to have lost all her previous restraint and simply allowed herself to enjoy what was happening. Simon knew how big a step this must have been for her, and to think she made that step for him made him want to shout with joy.

He had reached his goal, and it was staggering to him. His world had been shaken to its roots. Eleanor had opened up to him, had trusted him, had loved him. Had it been as earth-shattering for her? Perhaps it had been, and that was why she fell into such an exhausted sleep.

But had she heard him? Did she know he loved her?

He would tell her again tomorrow when they were both awake and alert.

Simon must have fallen into his own exhausted sleep, for he awoke sometime later from a vivid dream. The candle had burned down and the room was pitch dark. He had been dreaming of Eleanor making love to him. He lay there on his back, in the misty edges of sleep, and could still feel the dream Eleanor touching him, running her hand along his hip and thigh.

"Nice," he murmured. "Very nice."

"Simon."

His eyes flew open. Eleanor was leaning on his

chest, trailing a finger along his breastbone. It was no dream. She was very real, and she was touching him. She wanted him. He would not make her say the words again. But clearly, she wanted him. And he wanted her. Again and always. He pulled her on top of him and found her mouth in the dark. They made slow, lazy, and finally frenzied love, and fell asleep again in each other's arms.

Simon awoke again when a thin shaft of daylight sliced through a chink in the shutters. Eleanor was on her side facing away from him, and his arm was draped loosely over her. He smiled when he noted the tiniest of snores. Not a loud, thundering masculine snore, but merely a soft, gentle, rusty breathing. Definitely a snore, however, and he would tease her about it later.

Dear God, though, it was daylight. He had to get out of her room before someone found him there. Simon rolled carefully and quietly off the bed and stood naked in the middle of the room. He was covered in tiny purple blossoms and brushed them to the floor. From this time forward, he would always associate lilac with Eleanor.

He looked at her in wonder. Her dark hair was spread across the pillow in abandoned disarray. The disheveled bedclothes revealed a glimpse of her beautiful back, the elegant line of her spine, the soft curve of her hip. She was every bit as lovely as he'd imagined, and God knew he'd imagined her like this many a time.

She was slender, but not thin. Her breasts were small but perfectly shaped, and there was a slight rounding of the belly that he found irresistibly attractive. The memory of the softness of her stomach pressed up against his made him grow hard again.

He turned away—for if he gazed at her any longer he would have to wake her—and looked about the room to locate all the articles of his clothing. There were bits here and bits there, thrown about in wild abandon. Lord, what a night it had been.

He found Eleanor's gown and wrapper and picked them up. As he folded them neatly and laid them over the chair, he recollected her chagrin at their shabbiness. From now on, he would make sure that she always had lovely silk gowns to make her feel feminine and beautiful. And though he loved the sensuous feel of silk, he would nevertheless always take them off her.

Simon found all his own clothes, but only pulled on his pantaloons and shirt. He would sneak back to the room he shared with Nicholas before anyone saw him there. He must leave her a note. He did not want to wake her, but he could not leave without a word. He searched around for paper and pen and found nothing. Damn. He had plenty of paper in his own bag downstairs. He assumed everyone traveled with the means to jot down a quick verse whenever the mood struck.

There was nothing for it but to go back to his own room, write a note, and sneak back in here to leave it for her. He draped his clothes over his arm, picked up his boots, and tiptoed barefoot into the corridor.

Though he could hear activity below in the kitchens and outside in the stables, he saw no one on the stairs or in the hallways, and made it to his bedchamber unseen. He opened the door quietly. Nicholas was sound asleep on his stomach, one bare foot twisted up in the sheets. He would know where Simon had been all night. There would be questions, but Simon was not concerned. He was in love, after all.

He stepped into the room and tossed his clothes on a chair. He stripped off his shirt and added it to the pile. He was about to dispense with his pantaloons when something caught his eye on the floor just inside the doorway. It looked like a folded piece of parchment. The bill, perhaps, slipped under the door? He went to pick it up and found it was a note addressed to him. He read it, and had to clamp a hand over his mouth to keep from whooping aloud.

Belinda Chadwick and Geoffrey Barkwith had been found.

The note had been written in the wee predawn hours by Hackett. The runaways were traced to an inn at a village less than four miles south of Penrith, where they were staying the night. Hackett provided specific directions to the inn, just in case Simon and Mrs. Tennant wanted to make the short journey.

Simon had thought nothing could have made him feel more joyful that morning, but this news had special significance. This news meant that the problem of Belinda could be settled at last and there would be no more cloud over Eleanor. Nothing more to keep her own happiness at bay. Nothing more to keep her from Simon.

Simon punched the air in his excitement, wanting to shout but afraid to wake Nicholas. He reached for his shirt again, anxious to tell Eleanor the news, when an idea came to him.

It was crazy. It was romantic. But by God, he was going to do it.

He was going to go now, this very minute, and collect Belinda himself. He had told Eleanor once that he would like to be her knight in shining armor, to ride up on a white horse, sweep Belinda away from the villain Barkwith, and deliver her to the loving arms of her aunt. Eleanor had laughed, and Simon had really been speaking only figuratively, but now it looked as though he might actually be able to do it. To be Eleanor's knight in shining armor. To be her romantic hero. The very notion made him giddy.

Simon quickly and quietly got dressed in riding clothes, boots, and spurs, taking care to tuck the Runner's note in a pocket. He found a sheet of paper and his traveling inkwell, and sat down to write a note to Eleanor. He penned a few brief lines. There was no time for rhapsodic stanzas on their extraordinary night together, only time enough to tell her the good news so she would not be worried.

He finished the note, sanded it, and was ready to leave when Nicholas stirred.

"Simon? That you?"

"Yes, old boy, go back to sleep."

"You going somewhere?"

"I am indeed. Eleanor's niece has been found. I am going to collect her and bring her back here."

"Ah. Well done."

"Go back to sleep, Nick."

Simon heard his friend mutter something, then roll over in a billow of rustling sheets. His heavy, regular breathing suggested he was already asleep. Simon closed the door quietly and crept back up the stairs to Eleanor's room. He inched the door open so he would not startle her if she was awake. She was not. She was exactly as he'd left her, curled on her side away from the door, one hand beneath her cheek, the other stretched out and hanging limply over the side of the bed.

Simon folded the note and placed it on the pillow that still had the mark of his head upon it. He bent and lightly kissed her hair. She did not waken, but her outflung hand twitched a little, and it was then he noticed the ribbon. She still wore the red ribbon he'd bought from the Gypsy. She said she would wear it until Belinda was found, and then he could have it as a reminder of his role in this episode. Well, Belinda was found. He would take the ribbon so that her bare wrist would be another symbol of the end of her ordeal.

It was tied in a simple bow and was silky slick. The merest tug on the bow loosened it, and without even a twitch of the sleeping hand, it was removed. He tucked it in his waistcoat pocket, then pulled out a pencil, scribbled a few more words on the note, and replaced it on the pillow.

Simon took one more lingering look at Eleanor, beautiful and naked and relaxed in sleep. God, how he loved her. He could not wait to deliver her niece safely back to her. Surely she would love him a little bit, just for that.

He made his way down to the stables to see about hiring a horse. There was no white one. He supposed that would have been too much to ask. He had to settle for a chestnut gelding, but it would do. Once it had been saddled, he mounted and galloped down the road at top speed on his romantic quest to impress his lady fair.

Eleanor rolled over onto her back and stretched like a cat. She became aware of her nakedness, and a sudden full-blown recollection of the night's events burst upon her mind.

She opened her eyes to find the bed empty beside her. Groaning aloud, she turned her face into the pillow, only to inhale the musky masculine smell of Simon.

For an instant, a knot of anguish gripped her belly. Had she given herself to a man once again, only to be abandoned? But no, she knew Simon better than that. Or thought she did. He would not be so callous. She brushed a crushed flower petal from her nose. No man who sprinkled a woman with lilac blossoms would be cold enough to simply walk away. She smiled to think what a romantic he was, and moaned a little to think of what else he'd done with the lilac. She would never be able to smell its distinctive fragrance again without thinking of Simon.

No, such a man would not abandon her. Simon was a gentleman, however, and had no doubt left her room before he could be caught there with her. The sweet, wonderful man. He had always been so concerned with her reputation.

Eleanor closed her eyes and considered all that had happened. Had she really been so bold, so brazen, so wanton? She could hardly believe all the things she'd done, the things she'd let him do. She blushed to think how she had responded with such shameless abandon. Something about Simon had made it easy for her to let down all inhibitions.

She had awakened in the night to find herself snuggled up against his warm body, and before she knew what she was doing, her hand had begun to explore. Henry had been handsome of face, but his body had been rather soft, with little definition of the muscle beneath. Simon, though slimmer, was firmly muscled, and Eleanor was fascinated by the lean shape of him. She had also thought to be repelled by so much hair on his chest—Henry had been smooth as a baby—but instead found it tantalizing.

Simon had eventually stirred beneath her hands, giving a small moan of sleepy pleasure. He was soon wide awake, though, and loving her again. He pulled her on top of him and she had remained there, riding him to another explosive climax.

Had it ever been so good with Henry? Time and anger had faded many of the details of what had happened with him, but Eleanor could not imagine he could have outperformed Simon.

Thoughts of Henry reminded her to be cautious in her feelings for Simon. She must not make too much of what had happened last night. She had finally allowed herself to indulge in a mature, honest, physical relationship. It was the sort of thing widows did all the time. There was nothing more to it. She would certainly not allow it to be the precursor to another broken heart. It had been passionate and sensuous and wonderful, but it was nothing special. She did not want anything special.

Then why did it feel so important? So breathtaking?

Doubtless it was only because it had been so long. Five years since any man had touched her.

Eleven years since any man had touched her like Simon. After such a long time, what woman would not feel elated?

But there was something else. The words Simon had whispered after their first loving. She had pretended sleep so she would not have to respond, but the words clanged like hammer blows in her head.

Eleanor, I love you.

She refused to believe him, though heaven knew she would like to. It would be so easy to take those words and hold them close to her heart. Yet his brother had said Simon fell in love routinely, so they were no doubt facile words, often spoken. He had not repeated them during or after their second loving, so Eleanor was convinced he had merely murmured well-used words in the dizzy afterglow of lovemaking, thinking perhaps that was what every woman wanted to hear at such a time. She would not consider them. She would not fall victim again to a practiced seducer. She might allow her body to be seduced, but she would not let her heart be broken again. She was older and wiser this time. She would take what Simon had to offer, and she would enjoy it immensely, but she would expect and ask for no more.

Besides, there was still Belinda to consider.

Belinda!

Good Lord, she had become so involved in her own pleasure, she'd forgot that Belinda was now well and truly missing. She scrambled out of bed, scattering the blasted lilac everywhere, and heard something fall to the floor. It was a folded piece of parchment. She bent to pick it up and immediately saw the big sprawling S at the bottom. It was a letter from Simon. She sat back down on the bed to read it.

Dearest Eleanor,

I have the happiest of news. Belinda has been found! She and Barkwith are staying at an inn only a few miles south. I have gone to fetch her for you.

Eleanor gave a little shriek. She was found! Thank the heavens above, she was found at long last. She clasped the note to her breast and gave in to the emotion that threatened to overwhelm her. Tears fell unheeded down her cheeks. Bless Simon for riding off to collect her. Eleanor could not wait to fold the girl in her arms and hug her close. Afterward, she might be tempted to throttle her, but first, a hug. She took a deep, shuddery breath and resumed the note.

I have also taken the liberty of removing the talisman which I now believe I can claim as mine.

Eleanor looked to her naked wrist. Simon was welcome to the ribbon and she would remind him that it was meant to warn him against future frivolous advice. She hoped he had learned his lesson, that it is sometimes dangerous to chase after romantic fantasies.

I shall never forget our glorious night together, my beautiful Lilac Queen.

She smiled and reminded herself to follow her own advice where romantic fantasies were concerned. Dangerous, indeed.

While sweet golden slumbers kiss your eyes
May sweet dreams be yours till you arise.

Yours,
Simon

She ought to have expected a line or two of poetry from him. The silly, charming, adorable romantic. And here he was charging off to rescue Belinda, just as he'd promised. Probably found a white horse and a suit of shining armor, too. She was grateful to him, though, for taking the initiative. Simon Westover, starry-eyed dreamer, had turned out to be much more useful than she would have guessed a week ago.

Very useful, indeed, she thought as she retrieved the neatly folded gown and wrapper from the chair where he'd placed them. Useful in more wonderful ways than she could ever have imagined.

Simon followed the road south toward the village of Highthorpe where the Runner had located Belinda. He had been so excited at the news and so anxious to be the one to bring Belinda back to

Eleanor, he had not given much thought to what exactly he was going to do when he got there.

If the girl was still with Barkwith, as it sounded, what if she had no desire to be torn away from him? What would convince her to leave with Simon, a perfect stranger? It occurred to him that this might not be as easy as he'd hoped. He had better come up with a plan.

Yet each time he rehearsed the various possibilities in his mind, the vision would transform into one in which he rode up to the dragon's lair on his powerful white steed, snatched the girl from the teeth of the dragon, and rode away with her clasped safely in his arms.

It was an epic image, and Simon could not shake it from his mind. He could feel the power of the beast beneath him as he charged toward the craggy, forbidding retreat of the evil dragon. He could hear the clatter and clank of his armor, glistening in the morning sun. He could see the swooning, helpless young maiden silhouetted against the fiery breath of the dragon. He could feel her grateful arms clinging to him as they rode away from danger.

The heroic images still spun wildly in his head when the village of Highthorpe was suddenly upon him. He had spent the entire ride immersed in his romantic fantasy, and now here he was with no plan at all. He was going to have to make it up as he went.

It was easy enough to locate the Cat and Fiddle.

It was the only inn to be found in Highthorpe. Simon rode into the inn yard and found it surprisingly busy for an inn off the main coach road. There was a yellow bounder being hitched to a fresh team, and his eye was drawn to a young woman standing near the carriage. Even with her face half shaded by her bonnet, he recognized the likeness. Though the hair was a shade darker and the eyes a shade lighter, she was the very image of her aunt Eleanor.

He pulled up his horse next to where she stood. "Miss Chadwick?"

She furrowed her brows and gave him a wary look, but in a tentative voice said, "Yes?"

He would never know what came over him that morning, what possessed him to do what he did. It must have been those epic images he'd conjured up in his head, with villains and dragons and damsels in distress. The heroic vision must have overtaken him completely. There was no other explanation.

For no sooner had she spoken that single word when Simon reached down, grabbed her beneath the armpits, and hauled her up before him on the horse. He held her tightly about the waist and turned his mount back toward the road. Several voices were shouting behind them at the inn, but he paid them no heed. The girl was shrieking and kicking, and he held her tight against him so she would not fall from her precarious perch in front of the saddle.

"What are you doing?" she shouted. "Put me

down!" She kicked him hard on the shin. "Put me down, I tell you. Put me down!"

"Stay still, Belinda. I'll have you safe in no time."

"Safe? What are you talking about." She tried to wrench her arms free and jabbed him painfully in the ribs. "Where are you taking me? And how the devil do you know my name?" She pinched him hard on the arm. "Put me down!"

Damn. She was a fighter. "Please stay still. I'm not going to hurt you. You'll be safe soon."

"What are you talking about?" Each word was punctuated with a poke to the ribs or a whack to the shin. "Put me down at once! Oh. Oh, no. I know who you are! You're one of those wretched Bow Street Runners who've been chasing us across the country. Well, you can't just kidnap a person who hasn't committed a crime. Put me down! Put me down!" She bent over and bit him hard on the hand.

"Ow! Stay still, you little termagant." This was not turning out at all as he'd imagined. This spitfire of a girl was no damsel in distress. But he could hear her aunt's words clearly in his head, telling him they would abduct the girl against her will if necessary. If that was what Eleanor wanted, he would suffer the short ride to Penrith with this little vixen.

"Please stay still. You will only fall and hurt yourself."

"I won't." She bit him again. "I won't be carted off by some infuriating brute hired by my aunt."

And again. "Now, put me down or I'll make you sorry you didn't." And again.

At this rate, he'd be lucky to make it to Penrith without her drawing blood. But this was what Eleanor wanted. She'd said so over and over.

Drag her away kicking and screaming. Bind her and gag her if necessary.

One more bite from her sharp little teeth and it would be necessary.

"Put me down!" She bit him especially hard that time, and Simon had had enough.

Somehow managing to keep one arm around her like a vise, he began to pluck at his neckcloth. "I had not wanted to do this," he said as he struggled to unwind the length of cloth from his neck, "but you leave me no choice."

"How dare you! Don't you even try— mummppff."

Her shrill cries were cut off as he covered her mouth with the neckcloth and nudged her bonnet forward so he could loosely tie the gag behind her neck. She kicked harder and flailed more wildly, and it was a wonder the horse didn't come to a complete halt in all the confusion of directions. The ride going was obviously not going to be as quick and easy as the one coming.

"Try to stay calm, Belinda. I'm a friend and I'm taking you to your aunt. We'll get there a lot sooner if you'll just stay still."

"Ugghh iiii owww!" Even the gag didn't shut

her up, and for good measure she gave him another jab hard in the ribs.

He gave a groan of pain and wished he was
wearing that shining armor he'd been dreaming
about. He'd be black and blue before reaching
Penrith.

This hero business certainly wasn't all it was
cracked up to be. But Eleanor needed a hero, and
by God, he was going to be one for her.

If he survived the trip.

Chapter 18

If the gentleman who has strayed from the path of honor repents and perseveres, he may yet be blessed to win that modest but forgiving smile that pardons his wanderings and stimulates him to prove worthy of a virtuous unassuming affection.

The Busybody

"I wonder how much longer he will be?" Eleanor paced the coffee room as she waited impatiently for Simon to return with Belinda. Her gut was churning with a dozen conflicting emotions. Was Belinda all right? Would she be angry? Or rather, how angry would she be? What would Simon tell her? How would he get her to come back with him?

And now that this whole wretched affair was almost over what, if anything, would happen between her and Simon?

"I should think he will be back very soon," Edwina replied.

They had encountered each other in the corridor and when Edwina heard the news, she had decided to postpone her own departure to wait with Eleanor. Nicholas had joined them as well, and

Eleanor felt her cheeks color. He and Simon were to have shared a bedchamber. He would know, of course, where Simon had spent the night. He made no suggestive remarks, however, and sent no knowing glances her way. Perhaps it was not unusual for Simon to spend the night with a woman, and Nicholas thought nothing of it. One more reason for Eleanor to keep up her guard.

"I don't understand why he left the carriage behind," Nicholas said between mouthfuls of curried egg. "Why take a horse? It makes no sense. How's he going to get the girl back here?"

Eleanor thought she knew the answer, and it made her very uneasy to consider it. Surely he had been joking. Could he really be that foolish a romantic?

She wandered once more to the window overlooking the inn yard and gave a little squeal. "There he is!" Simon had just ridden into the yard with a female perched up in front of him. Eleanor hitched up her skirts and dashed outside to meet them.

Belinda, for it could be no one else, was squirming on the horse, and she had something that looked suspiciously like a gag around her mouth.

What on earth?

Belinda caught sight of her and gave a muffled shriek. Simon released his tight grip and Belinda reached up to push the cloth away from her mouth. "Aunt Ellie!"

Before an ostler could help her down, Belinda

gave Simon a hard punch in the stomach, then jumped off the horse and straight into the arms of Eleanor, almost knocking her to the ground. Eleanor regained her balance and enfolded the girl in her arms. "Belinda! Oh, Belinda, my love, I have been so worried." She held tight and rocked her niece in her arms, just as she'd done so many times in the past. "I am so happy to see you. But you have frightened me to death, you wretched girl. How could you have done such a wild and reckless thing?"

"Me?" Belinda pulled away. "How could *I* do such a thing? Aunt Ellie, how could *you* do this to *me*?" Belinda's voice was laced with tears. "How could you be so mean? Why did you send that horrid man after me like that?"

Eleanor looked over her niece's shoulder to see Simon dismount and turn the reins over to a stable boy. She caught his eye and saw an expression of perplexity and frustration. What in the world had happened here?

"What horrid man, my love?" she asked, just to be sure.

Belinda pulled away and pointed to Simon. "That one. That horrible Runner. He swooped on me like a highwayman and forced me onto his horse. He had no right to do that. You had no right to ask him to do that, Aunt Ellie. He gagged me!" She reached down and unwound the limp cloth that still hung around her neck and flung it to the ground.

Eleanor looked to Simon. He was not wearing a

neckcloth. Could this be the same man who'd made such sweet love to her last night? This man who'd terrified her niece? It didn't make any sense. "Simon? You *gagged* her?"

He gave a sheepish shrug. "She bit me."

Eleanor's confusion began to take on an edge of anger. "You forced her onto a horse," she said through tight lips, "abducted her in broad daylight, and gagged her?"

"Well . . . yes. I did it just as you wanted."

"Just as I . . ." She closed her eyes and took a deep breath. She tried to recall all their discussions about Belinda. What had she said to make him think *this* was what she had wanted? Yes, she had wanted Belinda removed from Barkwith's clutches, but not like this. "What the devil are you talking about? When have I ever wanted to frighten the poor girl to death? Whatever has got into you? You terrified her, Simon, snatching her away like that."

Simon's eyes darkened with an unreadable expression. "That one is not terrified. I'm the one who's shaking in my boots. She is little virago, and I'm lucky to have made it here alive. Besides, Eleanor, it was you who said she must be taken kicking and screaming, bound and gagged."

"Oh, Aunt Ellie! How could you!"

Eleanor held on to her temper with difficulty. She *had* said those words. But no sane person would fail to recognize a figure of speech. "Simon, you surely cannot have believed I meant it literally."

Simon looked somewhat abashed. "Well, actually, I did. I thought . . . I thought you'd be pleased."

Eleanor wanted to shriek in frustration. Was this all her fault? For allowing a sentimental fool to twist her figurative words into a romantic quest? "Pleased? Pleased that my poor niece has been frightened, possibly even harmed, by your foolishness? Simon, how could you be so . . ." *Stupid.*

Simon glared at her for a long moment and then his eyes softened as though willing her to remember their night together. But she did not want to think about that right now. It was too confusing. How could she reconcile giving herself to a man foolish enough to think she wanted her niece to be kidnapped by force?

"I beg your pardon," he said at last. "I must have misunderstood. I did tell you, though, what I meant to do. You never objected."

Her anger had increased from a simmer to a boil. She did not want the responsibility for this. It was not her fault. It couldn't be. "Good God, was I supposed to take you seriously when you talked about knights on white horses?"

"I was perfectly serious, though I had to settle for a chestnut gelding."

Belinda looked from Simon to Eleanor, a perplexed frown marking her brow.

"I ought to have known." Eleanor's voice rose

with righteous, fiery anger. "Leave it to the dreamy-eyed romantic to attempt something so unutterably stupid."

He looked as though she had slapped him, and she suddenly wanted to reach out to him and apologize, tell him she hadn't meant it, tell him it was really quite a sweet, if ill-advised, gesture. She could hardly bear the look in his eyes.

But something spurred her on. Niggling little wads of insecurity and doubt pressed against her heart, compelling her to put further distance between them, to push him away, and she could not seem to hold back the words.

"I was right about you from the very beginning," she said. "You are nothing but a trouble-making meddler, with your starry-eyed advice to the lovelorn. Your foolish romanticism started this whole mess, and look where it's ended. I should have known better than to trust a romantic."

"Aunt Ellie, what on earth are you talking about? I thought he was a Bow Street Runner. Who is he?"

"This, my love, is your precious Busybody, that renowned dispenser of sage advice, that paragon of romantic wisdom from the pages of *The Ladies' Fashionable Cabinet*. She is not the wise old woman you believed in, but this foolish, foolish man. *He* is the Busybody."

A chorus of gasps made Eleanor aware for the first time of the crowd that had gathered. A crowd to whom she had just announced the identity of the Busybody, loud and clear.

Simon's eyes closed briefly and his shoulders sank. She had revealed his secret. She had betrayed his trust. He turned his back, but did not walk away.

Belinda stared at Simon wide-eyed. "Him? The Busybody?"

Eleanor lowered her voice and spoke only to Belinda. "Yes, and when I discovered his identity, I dragged him along so he could talk some sense into you. I thought you might listen to the Busybody and realize you'd made a mistake, and then come back home with me."

"But Aunt Ellie—"

"That's the only reason he's here, but I see now it was a huge mistake to bring him along. He is the very last person I'd ask to give you sound advice. A man who abducts young girls like a pirate, for God's sake. How very romantic."

"But Aunt Ellie—"

"I can only hope you see what a fool he is and will ignore all the Busybody's advice in future. Now, let us get you home and see what we can do about—"

"Aunt Ellie! You don't understand."

Just then a horseman came pounding into the yard at full speed, kicking up a huge dust, and reining in his mount so sharply the horse reared up before coming to a stop.

"Geoffrey!" Belinda's eyes lit with excitement. "Oh, thank goodness."

Geoffrey Barkwith, dark eyes blazing with fury, swung down from the horse, and Belinda flew into his arms. Good God, this drama had yet to play itself out. He had not abandoned Belinda, at least, or cast her aside. In fact he had come after her. That was not what Eleanor expected of him. She had assumed once he'd been caught, he would slink away and leave Belinda to face the consequences. But here he was, running after her in the face of an apparent abduction. This was not at all what was supposed to happen. He was supposed to be a cad, a scoundrel, a blackguard who would abandon Belinda as easily as Henry had abandoned Eleanor. A scoundrel would not come running after her. Something was very wrong here.

Barkwith gently extricated himself from Belinda's grasp and put her to his side. "Is that the fellow?" he asked, pointing his crop at Simon.

Belinda nodded. Barkwith eyed Simon with intense hatred, all the while removing one of his gloves. He then marched up to Simon, and flung the glove in his face. "Name your seconds, sirrah."

Eleanor gasped. The blood drained from Simon's face causing ginger freckles to stand out against the pallor. "I beg your pardon?" he said.

"You have dared to lay hands on my wife," Barkwith said. "You will answer for it."

"Your wife?" Eleanor said, her voice rising in astonishment.

"Yes, Aunt Ellie. I've been trying and trying to tell you. I don't need rescuing from Geoffrey. We were married yesterday in Scotland."

"You're married?" Dear God, how could she have been so wrong about everything and everyone? "Oh, my dear girl." She took her niece in her arms and hugged her tight. Simon had been right. She was a cynic. But it had all turned out just as Simon had said it would. "I'm so glad."

"You are?" Belinda squeaked.

"Yes, yes, my love. I had thought . . . well, I did not know Mr. Barkwith's intentions, you see, and I expected the worst. I thought he had . . . other ideas. That's why I came after you."

"But I told you what his intentions were," Belinda said. "I left a note."

"Yes, but I . . . I had my doubts."

"Well, that was just silly. You know I was determined to marry him."

"Yes, I do know," Eleanor said. "I ought to have known if he asked you to run away, you would not hesitate. How foolish of me."

Eleanor's eyes darted to Simon, expecting to see a smug I-told-you-so expression. But he was still white-faced. Dear God, he had been challenged to a duel. But surely it will not happen now. It was all a misunderstanding. On her part. It was all her fault.

"Oh, but it wasn't Geoffrey's idea to run away," Belinda said. "It was mine."

Eleanor stared at her niece. "Yours?"

"Well, you didn't seem to approve of him. You were always pushing forward that old bore, Charles Pendleton. I didn't think you'd ever let me accept Geoffrey's offer, so I took the Busybody's advice"—she looked warily at Simon—"and convinced Geoffrey we should elope. You mustn't blame him, Aunt Ellie. He wanted to come to you nice and proper. I told him you would refuse, so he agreed to run away with me."

Eleanor ought to have known it. She ought to have known Belinda, headstrong and willful, would be the instigator of such a scrape. There was so much she ought to have known. When had she grown so stupid? She looked up at Barkwith, who walked over to her.

"I am sorry if we distressed you, ma'am," he said. "But I'm afraid your niece can wrap me around her little finger. I hope we may have your blessing?"

"Yes, of course," Eleanor said, and offered her hand. Barkwith took it and, always the rake, kissed it. Lord, he would lead Belinda a merry dance. Or would it perhaps be the other way around?

"In the meantime," he said, "I have to deal with this scoundrel." He turned toward Simon. "I have not heard you name your seconds, sirrah."

"Oh, but surely there is no need for such action,"

Eleanor said. "You see that it was all a misunderstanding."

"That does not excuse this fellow from manhandling my wife. He will answer for it. I ask you again, sir, name your seconds."

Nicholas Parrish stepped forward. Eleanor had completely forgotten about him. "I'll be his second," he said, looking thoroughly disgusted. "Name's Parrish. His, by the way, is Westover. Might be a good thing to know the name of the man you're trying to kill."

Eleanor's heart lurched up into her throat. *Kill?*

"Right. And I'll ask one of the ostlers to second me," Barkwith said.

"As Westover's second," Nicholas said, "I am compelled to ask if you will accept an apology and forgo the duel. As Mrs. Tennant has said, it was all a misunderstanding."

"That man grabbed my wife, spirited her away against her will, and apparently bound and gagged her. There is no apology for such behavior." Barkwith stood tall, glowing with righteous anger. "I will have satisfaction."

Dear God.

Nicholas shook his head in disgust. "It is still Westover's right to choose weapons. What will it be, Simon?"

Simon glared at Barkwith and straightened to his full, considerable height. "Pistols. I have a case in my carriage."

Dear God, were they really going to go through

with this? "Mr. Barkwith," Eleanor said, "Geoffrey, surely this is not necessary."

"I am sorry, Mrs. Tennant, but this is man's business. You would not understand. No one touches my wife like that. No one. Mr. Parrish, if you will be so kind as to locate the pistols, I will engage one of the ostlers as my second." He turned on his heel to do so, and Mr. Parrish grabbed Simon and headed toward the carriage.

"Oh, God," Belinda wailed, "he's going to be killed. Aunt Ellie, what am I going to do? Am I to be a widow after only one day of marriage? Can't we do something to stop this?" She broke into a torrent of tears and flung herself into Eleanor's arms.

"There, there, my love," Eleanor said. "Simon will not kill him, I promise you."

But her stomach had tied itself into knots thinking that Geoffrey just might kill Simon.

Edwina came up and put a hand on Eleanor's arm. "Try not to worry," she said. "Perhaps they will both fire into the air."

"But men are such idiots about these things," Eleanor said. "Will they feel honor has been upheld if they don't actually take aim at each other?"

"We can only hope," Edwina said.

Within mere minutes, the arrangements had been made for the duel to take place in a field behind the inn. Belinda would have it that she *must* be there, and though Eleanor did not think she could bear to watch, she and Edwina came along.

While Geoffrey was dealing with a sobbing, clinging Belinda, Simon walked over to Eleanor. His mouth was set in a grim line. There was so much Eleanor wanted to say to him, but her tongue was tied with knots of confusion and fear and anger. She didn't know what to think about anything anymore. Had it only been a few hours ago that she had lain naked in his arms? And now he might be killed.

"I honored our bargain," Simon said. "I did everything you asked. And yet you betrayed me, you betrayed my secret. You are unattainable after all. I am sorry. But there is something else I wanted to say to you. Last night—"

"No." Eleanor thought she knew what he wanted to say and she did not want to hear it. If this foolish man was about to get himself killed, she did not want to know that he loved her despite her betrayal. She could not bear it. "No, I don't think there is anything more to say."

"As you wish," he said, and sketched a bow. He walked away and began to remove his jacket.

Dear God, what had she done?

Belinda had come to join them, sobbing quietly. Eleanor put an arm around her. The seconds checked the guns and handed them to Simon and Geoffrey.

Eleanor inhaled a great shuddery breath, and a hint of sweet fragrance filled her nostrils. She looked up sharply. Standing tall and lush at the other side of the field was a lilac tree, adorned with the last flourish of its annual bloom.

Lilac.

The two men stood back to back, and at Nicholas's count, began to pace ten steps. They turned to face each other. Eleanor reached out and clutched Edwina's hand. She felt rather faint. Nicholas rose his voice and said, "Ready."

Edwina squeezed her hand. Eleanor squeezed back, hard, and shut her eyes. The heady scent of lilac wrapped itself around her.

"Aim."

No! Eleanor let go of Edwina's hand and took a step toward the field.

"Fi—"

"Hold on just a minute there, guv'ner." The familiar Cockney of Obidiah Hackett rang out like an organ with all the stops pulled.

Simon and Geoffrey dropped their arms. Eleanor almost swooned with relief. Out of the corner of her eye she noticed Edwina rubbing her hand.

The little bandy-legged Runner strutted to the center of the field with the gangly, dour Francis Mumby following close behind. He stood with his hands behind his back, like a politician about to give a speech. The posture served to thrust his bright red waistcoat into full view, and he looked for all the world like a plump little cock of the walk.

"It looks to me," he said, "that a criminal act is about to take place. 'Fraid I can't allow such an illicitous thing to happen, guv'ner. Not under Obidiah Hackett's watch. Now, if you gentlemen will drop yer guns and step back, Mumby and I will pretend we never seen a thing. I don't recommend any argumentation. You don't want to get old Mumby here angry. Got a prodigitous temper, he does. Mean as fire when he gets riled. So, set 'em down and move back."

Simon and Geoffrey did as he asked, and Hackett stepped forward and picked up the guns. He fired one in the air, and the report was so loud and unexpected that Eleanor nearly jumped out of her skin. He then fired the second one, and handed both guns to Nicholas. "Now put these barking irons away safe and sound, like. And don't let me see 'em again."

Simon stood in the middle of the field and felt like a hot air balloon with all the air squeezed out of it. He was empty. No heart. No soul. No hope. He'd never felt so drained in all his life.

Hackett was herding everyone toward the inn, but Simon didn't move. Nicholas came up to him and pulled him by the arm so that he was forced to put one foot in front of the other. "Thank God for that little Runner," Nicholas said. "I wasn't looking forward to planting flowers on your grave, my friend. That Barkwith fellow meant business. He would have blown a hole in you for sure."

"I know. I'd said my last prayers." He'd been ready to die.

"It was the great Romantic Agony after all, was it not?"

"She betrayed me, Nick. I had trusted her, and she betrayed me."

"I'm sorry, old man. Are you going to be all right?"

"My head aches," Simon said, "but that is only because my brain is still spinning. I feel like a man in a dream—no, a nightmare—who doesn't know what strange twist was coming next. I have certainly never spent such a day in all my life, full of ups and downs enough to make a man dizzy. And it is still morning."

Simon caught up with the others and pulled Barkwith aside. The young man was still furious. "You did not wish to hear it before," Simon said, "but I hope you will now accept my apology. I am sorry I kidnapped Belinda. Mrs. Barkwith, that is."

"It was a damned fool thing to do," Barkwith said. "You scared the life out of her."

Simon thought not, but would cut his tongue out before saying so to her hot-blooded husband. "Yes, well, I thought I was doing what her aunt wished. Made a prime mess of it, though. We didn't know you were married, you know."

"Well, what the devil did you think we went to Scotland for? The fishing?"

"As I say, we were wrong, and I made a terrible mistake. I hope you will accept my apology."

Barkwith nodded, grumbled an acceptance, and moved away to take his bride's arm.

One hurdle cleared. Now, what to do about Eleanor.

He could hardly believe the woman who had flung such hateful words at him earlier, who'd betrayed his secret, was the same woman who'd melted in his arms the night before.

And she had been so cold when he had wanted to speak to her before the duel. She had not expressed any regrets for her betrayal, and hadn't wanted him to say anything at all. He had been about to tell her he loved her. Despite everything, he was going to his death loving her. He had wanted her to know it, but she wouldn't let him say it. How had he been so wrong about her? Had she even cared that he might die?

Apparently not.

He had to speak to her. He had to know if the night before had been just another fantasy and not a momentous reality. As the group of them reached the coffee room, he took her arm and pulled her gently aside.

"Eleanor, could we speak privately for a moment?"

She nodded, but kept a frown on her face as he led her out of the inn yard and across the street where there was a small park with trees and gravel paths. He led her to a stone bench and sat down beside her. His stomach churned with apprehension.

"I'm very sorry, Simon. I had no wish for you to become embroiled in a duel. You might have been k-killed."

"Would you have been sorry?"

"How can you ask such a thing?"

"You betrayed my trust. You might as well have put a bullet through me."

She gave an exasperated sigh. "Oh, Simon, must you always be the great romantic? Knights on white horses and duels of honor, for God's sake."

"You're still angry with me."

Her brow was furrowed in a thunderous scowl, and Simon found himself a little shaken by the cold green gaze. "Yes, I am, but I'm more angry with myself. I should have trusted my instincts."

"And what did those instincts tell you?"

"That you were a romantic fool who believed in fairy tales and had no notion of the ordinary, everyday world in which the rest of us struggle to live peacefully."

Her anger fueled Simon's own wrath. "And you still think me a fool?"

"How could I not? Who but a fool would think that kidnapping a young girl would do anything but frighten her to death? Who but a fool would have justified it by blaming it on a few words metaphorically spoken?"

"You were quite adamant, Eleanor. More than once you mentioned getting her away from Barkwith at all costs."

"But I never meant for you to abduct her in such a ridiculous way. It was absurd."

"I daresay we all have an absurd notion now and then. Your own notion about Barkwith's intentions, for example."

"I was wrong, I admit it. Thank God I was wrong. But you know very well that I had good reason to believe in his villainy."

"I know that you can't get over your own hurt long enough to realize that not every man is a villain."

"And you can't get over the idea that not every ending is a happy one. You can't get the idea of romance out of your foolish head."

"You did not seem to mind a bit of romance last night."

And without warning, she hauled off and slapped him hard across the face. "You, sir, are no gentleman."

"I think you had better leave, Eleanor," he said, and rubbed his cheek. "I have no wish to speak to you anymore. I'm not sure I wish to know you anymore. You have betrayed my trust. You have humiliated me in public. You have made me feel a fool. Enough."

She rose to her feet. "I thank you for all you have done to help track down Belinda, but I think we can now bring an end to our association." She spun on her heels and stormed back across the street to the inn.

Simon dropped his head into his hands. Nothing was turning out as he'd expected. He had just sent out of his life the woman he loved. How had things gone so topsy-turvy in less than a day? How had he managed to make such a mull of everything? Perhaps he was every inch the fool she thought him.

He had sat there alone on the bench for a good quarter hour, nursing his anger. He was angry that Eleanor had trumpeted his secret for all the world to hear. He was angry that he'd ever trusted her. He was angry over the hateful words she'd thrown in his face. He was angry that her wishes, her often spoken, clearly articulated wishes, had led him to an action that had almost got him killed. He was angry that she didn't seem to care that he might have died. He was angry that last night had meant nothing to her. He was angry at Belinda for kicking and biting him like a wild cat. He was angry with himself for trying to do something romantic. He was angry at the world.

He had worked himself into a fine rage when he heard footsteps on the gravel path. He looked up to find Nicholas looming over him.

"What the hell happened between you two?" he asked.

"I do not wish to talk about it, Nick."

Nicholas sat down, and it was a moment before he spoke again. "She stormed into the inn a while ago and asked if she could return to London in our carriage."

"She doesn't want to see me again."

"So I gathered."

"Nor I her. Don't you see, Nick?" He gave a mirthless chuckle. "It's the ultimate unattainable ideal. She has made me not want her. I cannot have her because I will not have her. Isn't that a joke? I have no more desire to succumb to that romantic weakness. I am tired of being the incurable romantic. I'm through with all of it."

"What about last night?"

"What the devil do you mean by that?"

"No need to bite my head off. It is clear whose bed you slept in last night, that's all. I had thought, considering all you had said after dinner, that if such a thing were to happen, it would be a fairly significant step."

"It was. For me, anyway. But I was wrong about her."

"And so you let her walk away?"

"I sent her away. She thinks I am a fool, Nick, and felt no qualms about betraying my secret in public. I daresay she may be right about me being a fool. Look at what happened today. I was only doing what I thought she wanted. I did it for her. So what does she do but make a public spectacle of me just for attempting to please her. And believe me, it was not a pleasant ordeal. That Belinda is a little tigress with claws. And teeth."

"So what happens now?"

"I stop playing the fool. I am through with romantic fantasies. I will never again set myself up for another failure. No more unattainable ideals. I'm going to find myself an eminently attainable less-than-ideal woman and be done with it. To hell with romance. And to hell with Eleanor."

Chapter 19

*No young woman should accept the addresses of a
gentleman unless she favors him above all others
in existence, loves him with every fiber of her being, and believes it will be his life's study to promote her happiness and ensure her felicity by every
proof of affection.*

The Busybody

Eleanor sat beside Edwina in the hired post
chaise that was not nearly as comfortable as
Simon's carriage. They were bouncing along the
road south to Westmorland on the journey back to
London. Nicholas had given up his place to
Eleanor, while he took her place in Simon's chariot.
It was a fortuitous arrangement. She did not know
what she would have done if the Parrishes had not
been at hand. Belinda would not have appreciated
having her aunt squeezed into the carriage between her and her bridegroom.

Simon and Nicholas had left much earlier and,
of course, had the four-horse team. She and Ed-

wina had only two horses, and would be much slower. There would be several hours between them. That satisfied Eleanor, who was in no mood to meet up with Simon at an inn on the way.

"I am sorry that you and Simon have quarreled," Edwina said. "Is it a serious quarrel?"

"I'm afraid so." Eleanor had made certain it was. She could have apologized, she could have forgiven and begged forgiveness. Something inside her, though, seemed to require her to push this lovely man away. She was not sure why she had done it. She supposed it was for the best, since there was no possibility of her heart getting broken again.

Or was it possible to break one's own heart?

"I had thought . . . I had hoped . . . Well, let me just say I have known Simon for years and I have never seen him so besotted."

Eleanor's head jerked up. "What?"

"He seemed to be crazy about you. After you left the dining parlor last night, he spoke of nothing else. I had hoped that perhaps you returned his regard."

"Oh." Had she made a terrible mistake? "His brother said that Simon falls in love a lot. I daresay I was simply another infatuation for him. Nothing serious."

"Malcolm is right," Edwina said. "Simon is forever falling in love. He is always searching for the right woman, you see, and he is forever hopeful that each one is the right one. He even was a little bit in love with me for a time, many years ago."

"Oh?" Just as Eleanor had suspected.

"But I wasn't the right one, either. One thing I have long known about Simon that he only just discovered: he falls in love with women who have not the remotest interest in him. They never turn out to be the right one, of course. He shrugs it off and blames it on the unattainable ideal."

"He mentioned that term," Eleanor said, "but I didn't know what he meant."

"I believe Simon so wanted to *be* a Romantic that he made as if all these women were his ideals, and therefore unattainable. But it was never true. He was just playing at romance. And writing bad poetry in the attempt."

"Oh, dear. It *is* bad, is it not? It is not just me?"

Edwina laughed. "Most of it is positively horrid. But it is facile enough to appeal to many, so I go ahead and print some of it in the *Cabinet* from time to time."

"Alonzo." Eleanor shuddered.

"Just so. But Simon never even realized he was a false Romantic, until he met you."

"What do you mean?"

"I mean that you really are his ideal. He has discovered, or thought he had, that you are the right one. I suppose he is a true Romantic now, for obviously his ideal *is* unattainable. Lord, what poetry you will inspire."

Eleanor suddenly felt the sting of tears and choked back a sob. "But it was he who sent me away.

He didn't want to know me anymore, he said."

"Oh, dear. It is worse than I thought."

"I broke his trust," Eleanor said. "I betrayed his secret."

"Oh, I am very much aware of that. It is my secret, too, you know. But I suspect there is no real harm done. No one at the inn knows us."

"It was a shameful thing to do."

"Yes, it was. But I believe it was done impetuously in the heat of the moment, and without malice. Simon knows that. But he is punishing himself for loving you."

Eleanor could stand no more and burst into tears.

Edwina reached over and touched her hand. "My dear Mrs. Tennant! Whatever is the matter?"

"He told me he loved me and I d-didn't believe him!"

"Ah. Because of what Malcolm said?"

"Yes, that and . . . other things. I was . . . afraid."

"I understand, Mrs. Tennant. Believe me, I do. I often find it difficult to trust a man, too. Once one's heart is broken, it is not easy to put oneself in the position to have it broken again."

"Is that what h-happened to you?"

"Yes, many years ago. And I am guessing the same thing happened to you."

"Yes, and I never want to g-go through that again."

"No one does. But if I may play Simon's champion for a moment, if there was ever a man to trust,

Simon is that man. He is good and honorable and decent. Yes, he is a Romantic in the broadest sense, but his idealism is true and honest. He believes in people. He has hope for the future. If my heart had not been engaged at the time, I would have fallen in love with Simon. He is a dear man."

Eleanor was crying in earnest now. "He is. He is so d-dear. He is ad-d-dorable."

Edwina chuckled. "Ah yes, those dimples."

"And the w-way he blushes."

"Lord, but he hates that. Mrs. Tennant, are you saying that you do, in fact, return his regard?"

"I d-do." Tears were streaming down her cheeks. "I think he's w-wonderful. But I was hateful. I said s-such awful things to him. I told him he was a fool and I never w-wanted to see him again. But it was m-mostly because I was ashamed of br-breaking my promise to him."

Edwina patted her hand. "You must do as you wish, of course, but I suspect some of those hateful words can be unsaid. I do so want to see Simon happy, and I truly think you can make him so."

"Do you r-really?"

"Indeed. And if you are agreeable, I think I might have just the plan to get him back."

Simon had been back in London for a week and he was no less miserable today than the day before. He had hoped this melancholy would begin to fade. It had been almost two weeks since he'd seen her, after all. He should be forgetting her by now. It was a curious thing, though. He'd lost women before but had never been so down pin about it for so long. He couldn't even seem to write poetry.

Of course, he had not actually lost this woman. He'd thrown her away.

One thing was clear: none of those other women had meant anything to him compared to Eleanor. He'd never felt like this, where the pain in his chest was so tight and constricting he sometimes couldn't breathe.

He had trouble sleeping, and he even tried drinking himself into a stupor just so he could fall asleep. Strangest of all, he had no appetite. He couldn't seem to eat more than a bite of anything. Cook had become hysterical, and his mother had called a physician.

But there was nothing wrong with his body. It was his soul that was crushed.

Simon's days and nights—especially the nights—were filled with thoughts of Eleanor. He decided the best way to keep his mind off her was to put his mind to other things. He threw himself into work on a story for the *Cabinet*, but he found his tale sounding more like one of the tragic sagas in the *Lady's Monthly Museum*. All his heroines were coming to bad ends. He was in no frame of mind to write an uplifting, happy-ending romance.

There was a great deal of correspondence that had piled up during his absence. Perhaps some of it would take his mind off Eleanor. The publisher had sent several packets of letters to the Busybody. He really ought to write a few columns. The ones he had already queued up for future issues were quickly dwindling.

The first letter was from an unhappy young girl who could not attract the attention of the one man she most desired. Simon told her she was wasting her time and to move on to more promising prospects. The next letter was from a young woman with a surfeit of suitors. She described each one and asked which she should pick. Simon told her to keep looking.

The next letter was from a woman who'd driven away the man she most admired.

I have made a dreadful mistake. I feared he would break my heart, and have foolishly driven away the best of men, a man who showed a serious and honorable interest in me. He even told me he loved me once, but I refused to believe him. I should have trusted him, but I did not. Instead, I said horrible things I did not mean and in a moment of pique I broke a promise. I betrayed him quite shamefully. And so I have lost him and made myself miserable. I know now that he is truly my heart's desire and I love him dearly. Do you think if I told him so, he would come back to me?

The Lilac Queen

Simon stared at the page, unwilling to believe his eyes. Was it a trick? A joke? Could it truly be from Eleanor?

His heart began to pound like a thousand drums as he read it again. It was from her. It could be no one else. She was his Lilac Queen and she loved him. She loved him!

He wanted to climb up to the roof and shout for joy. He wanted to go to her. He wanted to pull her into his arms and kiss her breathless. He just wanted to see her again, just to look at her.

He wanted to do everything at once, and was instead immobilized with the enormity of it all. He thought he'd lost her forever, his one true love, and never understood why. He had never been able to reconcile the warm, passionate woman of one night with the cold, snappish woman of the next morning.

She had been afraid. He ought to have known that, ought to have expected it, even. After what had happened to her, naturally she was afraid to give her heart again.

She had overcome that fear somehow, though, and written to let him know. A letter to the Busybody had brought them together once before. He hoped it would do so again.

And so before doing all those things he wanted so much to do, he would answer her letter.

And then he would ring the kitchen. He was suddenly starving.

* * *

Eleanor had been back in London for over a
week. It had been a leisurely trip home, and she
and Edwina Parrish had become fast friends. Once
Eleanor had admitted her feelings for Simon, she
had spent much of the time probing for information. She wanted to know all about France and the
Revolution. She wanted to know about the various
reform movements with which he was involved.
She wanted to know everything about him.

Edwina must have been heartily sick of the subject by the time they reached London. Eleanor had
admitted to having been jealous, thinking Simon
must surely be in love with Edwina. They had
laughed over that, and over many other things.
Eleanor had even gone so far as to confide in Edwina about what had happened that one night between them. She had cried again to think how
stupid and fearful she had been. How instead of
telling him so, she had lashed out at him. She did
everything she could to ensure he could never love
her, angered him so much that he sent her away.
She hoped to God it was not too late to undo all
she'd done.

The house was quiet without Belinda. She had
gone to live with her new husband, of course. Geoffrey's father had been so pleased that his rakehell
son had settled down, he had presented them with
the lease on a small town house as a wedding gift.

So Eleanor was in the Charlotte Street house
with only the servants for company. Constance

came by frequently, and had teased Eleanor about her adorable Busybody. But Constance had been feeling a bit out of sorts the last few days and Eleanor was left to her own devices. Frankly, she was beginning to find her own company a trial. She couldn't concentrate on books or embroidery or anything else that had once occupied her mind. Her mind was full of Simon, and she could think of nothing else.

On the eighth day since her return from the north, she sat in the small drawing room and attempted a bit of sewing. She took up a hem and allowed her mind to wander to the ubiquitous subject of Simon. It had been almost a week since she'd sent the letter to the Busybody. Had he read it yet? Had he known it was from her? He must have. He would know at once, as she meant for him to do. Then why hadn't she heard from him? She had expected he would call on her.

But perhaps he had not yet read the letter. Edwina said he was sometimes overwhelmed with the number of letters received and had difficulty selecting the ones for publication. She would be patient. He would get to hers eventually. And if not, she would simply send another. And another and another, until he replied.

Eleanor looked up from her sewing when the housekeeper entered with the mail. She left it on the table and departed without a word. How odd. That was not like her at all. She usually stayed to see what letters came from whom, what invitations had arrived, and so on. She must not be feeling well, poor old dear, to have left in such a hurry.

Eleanor looked at the small stack of cards and letters. One was particularly bulky. It must be from Benjamin. It had been an age since they'd heard from him, and he always enclosed all sorts of interesting things from his travels. What would he think when he received her letter about Belinda's marriage?

Eleanor picked up the package, but there was no indication it had come from the Naval Office or from overseas or from anywhere else, for that matter. It had only her own name on the outside. It must have been hand delivered.

Her heart began to flutter in her breast.

She opened the package to find a bright new issue of *The Ladies' Fashionable Cabinet* . . . wrapped in a shiny red ribbon. She caught her breath. It was the Gypsy's ribbon.

She untied the ribbon and found it had been tucked inside like a bookmark. It marked the page for the Busybody. Her eyes fell at once to her own letter, signed "The Lilac Queen." She hungrily read the answer.

> *The Busybody's heart is overflowing with hope for the Lilac Queen. Should you tell your gallant that you love him? The Busybody believes that you have already managed to convey to him your sweet message, and that if you will but look, you will find your heart's desire no farther away than your doorstep.*

Eleanor gave a little squeal of delight and jumped from her seat. He was here! He was at the front door. She ran to the window to see if she could get a glimpse of him below, but the front steps were empty. He must be in the entry hall. That's why Mrs. Davies had acted so mysteriously.

Eleanor dashed to the drawing room door, flung it open, and ran smack against a familiar and very dear chest, covered with bunches and bunches of lilac. "Simon!"

"Hold on, my dear, or you'll crush my fine floral tribute."

But she didn't care. She threw her arms around his neck and buried her head against his shoulder. His arms came up to enfold her, and lilac cuttings spilled all about their feet.

"Simon." It was all she could manage to say before his mouth covered hers and took her in a powerful, passionate, hungry kiss.

Sometime later, after the lilac had been gathered up off the floor and arranged in a vase, and one tiny spray tucked in her bodice; after tears had been spent over regrets and joys; after apologies had been offered and accepted; after kisses had been bestowed one upon another and another; after pledges had been made and declarations of love repeated; after questions of the future had been asked and answered; after a miniature portrait profile had been requested and presented; Eleanor sat on the settee nestled in Simon's arms.

"Do you still think I'm a romantic fool?" he said.

"Who else would go to such lengths to find an armload of lilacs at the very end of its season?"

"A fool?"

"A romantic."

"Do you think it's possible that a realist could ever learn to live with a romantic?"

"It's possible. If he were to write a sonnet to her emerald eyes."

His face fell and she wondered what she had said to cause such distress. "What is it, Simon?"

"I'm afraid I do not have a sonnet to your eyes."

"Oh, my love, it doesn't matter."

"But I do have an ode to your upper lip."

She gave a gurgle of laughter. "My upper lip?"

"Shall I read it to you?" He reached in his pocket and pulled out several pages of parchment.

Eleanor eyed the endless stanzas with skepticism, and a twinge of horror. "Later, if you please. I'd rather explore *your* lips at the moment." And she reached up and kissed him.

He took her face in his hands and said, "I love you, my Lilac Queen."

"And I love you, my knight in shining armor."

He laughed and drew her into another kiss, succulent and soft, and full of promise for the future.

Author's Note

The magazine for which Simon writes, *The Ladies' Fashionable Cabinet*, is a fictional publication. However, its rival and political adversary, the *Lady's Monthly Museum*, was very real.

The *Museum* was a fashionable magazine that began publication in 1798 and continued until 1832. Between its covers each month were essays, serialized fiction, poetry, book reviews, and fashion plates. The full title was *Lady's Monthly Museum; or Polite Repository of Amusement and Instruction Being an Assemblage of Whatever Can Tend to Please the Fancy, Interest the Mind, or Exalt the Character of the British Fair, by a Society of Ladies.*

That Society of Ladies, however, was indeed a group of men, and only very occasionally a woman. Just as in this story, they were political reactionaries attempting to combat liberal Republican ideas through subtle manipulation of their readers. The politics of early feminists like Mary Wollstonecraft were anathema to the *LMM*. The specific anti-feminist articles mentioned in the story did actually appear in its pages, though truthfully some did not appear until slightly after the time of this book.

From the earliest issues of the *LMM* in 1798, there was a columnist called the Old Woman who offered social commentary and advice. In 1808, she was replaced by a new columnist called the Busy Body. It was a combination of these columnists that inspired the Busybody of this tale.

I shamelessly borrowed the pen name simply because I liked it. The flowery language of the Busybody's letters and excerpts was also inspired by the writings in the *LMM*. And Simon's poetry is just bad enough to have been appropriate for the "Apollonian Wreath," the poetry section of the *LMM*.

Look for more adventures involving *The Ladies' Fashionable Cabinet* in *Once a Gambler*, coming in Summer 2003.

Forget the chocolate this Valentine's Day ...
dally with sexy heroes from Avon Books!

♡ ♡

BORN IN SIN by Kinley MacGregor
An Avon Romantic Treasure

He is the infamous "Lord Sin," a mysterious stranger whom everyone fears. He despises his Scottish heritage, but now, to unmask the king's enemies, he will return to the Highlands and wed a bewitching lass whose flaming red hair matches the fire of her spirit . . . and whose beauty and grace awaken a perilous need he's never known.

STUCK ON YOU by Patti Berg
An Avon Contemporary Romance

Trouble bubbles over the day Logan Wolfe arrives in Plentiful, Wyoming. One look at this gorgeous hunk was enough to knock Scarlett O'Malley off her sky-high heels, but she is sure this stranger is up to something. Logan doesn't need a screwball sleuth dogging his footsteps, but when her wacky investigation takes a surprising turn, this ex-cop finds himself glued to her side, keeping her out of trouble—and falling in love.

INTO TEMPTATION by Kathryn Smith
An Avon Romance

Julian Rexley, Earl of Wolfram, knows Lady Sophia Aberley is the "anonymous" author of a tell-all about their scandalous past. Though she refuses to admit that *he* was the wronged party, Julian still aches for the exquisite lady. But he is determined to resist the intoxicating lure of her kiss, for they both know the kind of trouble *that* can lead to!

INNOCENT PASSIONS by Brenda Hiatt
An Avon Romance

Dashing Noel Paxton has taken on the guise of the legendary Saint of Seven Dials to expose a dangerous spy in London. Is country beauty Rowena Riverstone in league with his prime suspect? Noel longs to discover if her enchanting innocence is real . . . and release her passionate fire with a sensuous kiss.

♡ **Coming in February** ♡

Don't Miss Any of the Fun and Sexy Novels from Avon Trade Paperback

Ain't Nobody's Business If I Do
by Valerie Wilson Wesley
0-06-051592-9 • $13.95 US • $20.95 Can
"Outstanding . . .[a] warm, witty comedy of midlife manners."
Boston Herald

The Boy Next Door
by Meggin Cabot
0-06-009619-5 • $13.95 US • $20.95 Can

A Promising Man (and About Time, Too)
by Elizabeth Young
0-06-050784-5 • $13.95 US

A Pair Like No Otha'
by Hunter Hayes
0-380-81485-4 • $13.95 US • $20.95 Can

A Little Help From Above
by Saralee Rosenberg
0-06-009620-9 • $13.95 US • $21.95 Can

And Coming Soon

The Accidental Virgin
by Valerie Frankel
0-06-093841-2 • $13.95 US • $21.95 Can
There *are* no accidents . . .